KILLING GROUND

DOCTOR WHO – THE MISSING ADVENTURES

Also available:

KILLING GROUND

Steve Lyons

DOCTOR WHO

THE MISSING ADVENTURES

First published in Great Britain in 1996 by
Doctor Who Books
an imprint of Virgin Publishing Ltd
332 Ladbroke Grove
London W10 5AH

ISBN 0 426 20474 3

Cover illustration by Alister Pearson

Typeset by Galleon Typesetting, Ipswich
Printed and bound in Great Britain by
Mackays of Chatham PLC

Cyber Notes

In establishing a continuity framework for the Cybermen's exploits in *Killing Ground*, I have relied heavily on David Banks's excellent and definitive reference book, *Cybermen* (Who Dares/Silver Fist 1988, Virgin 1990, illustrated by Andrew Skilleter). My outline of Cyber chronology in Chapters 2 and 4 is all based on his work.

While I was at it, I borrowed ArcHivist Hegelia, David's first-person researcher character from *Cybermen*, who appears by his kind permission. Reference to the Arc Hives is by permission of David and of Andrew Skilleter, whose unique design for a Hive ship also crops up in my text.

Prologue

The unwieldy vessel strained and wrenched itself, with noticeable effort, from the planet's clutches. Cheers were raised and bands struck up across the globe as satellite cameras beamed its triumph to eight hundred million spectators. Space travel, they were saying, was no longer for the élite. The multinational conglomerates had made dreams affordable. The Century Program would establish outposts on a dozen worlds, alleviating Earth's overcrowding and providing its footholds amongst the stars.

They were saying that the Colonial Age had begun.

'It's a logical idea, I'll grant them.' The Doctor rubbed his chin and frowned at the scanner screen. 'The rich aren't interested in building new societies without the luxuries to which they're accustomed. If incentives exist for others to do it, then Earth's expansion can proceed. In a few decades, there should be enough comfortably settled worlds for relocation to be attractive.'

'Which is when the price goes back up,' surmised Grant. He was squinting through dusty spectacle lenses at the image of the *New Hope*: all reflective golds and chunky add-ons which ultimately served no function at all. Aesthetically, it was quite exciting. It was complex and important-looking and it pointed to the future.

They were in the TARDIS, ninety-one years into Grant's past, four hundred thousand miles above the surface of Mars. 'That ship,' said the Doctor, 'is destined for the Centraxis system. Its passengers will establish the most remote of the prototype colonies.'

Grant sighed. 'And they will name that planet Agora.'

1

He shrugged as the Doctor turned to glare at him. 'It was pretty obvious. My personal history.'

'You might know less about that than you think.'

Grant looked up sharply. The Doctor was regarding him through hooded eyes. 'What do you mean?'

'Have you ever opened a tin of dog food in front of an Alsatian?'

'I'm sorry?'

The Doctor began to work at the console. Grant was relieved to be freed from his scrutiny. He didn't like the way his new travelling partner was talking. He was reminded how little he knew about the man.

'The Great Intelligence,' said the Doctor suddenly. 'Autons, Axons, Zygons. You've never heard of any of them, have you?' He didn't wait for an answer. 'The governments of Earth have. They're covering up enough invasion attempts to make their official history read like a work of fiction. And where do you suppose all those defeated and embittered would-be conquerors are now? Just waiting for Mankind to come out of its "tin"!'

Grant's attention flickered back to the screen, across which the *New Hope* meandered. He suddenly felt afraid for the people it held, but he told himself that such fear was irrational. 'We know they get to Agora though, don't we?'

'Their security precautions amount to crossed fingers and a prayer that no one will have to explain their deaths. But yes, they're lucky.'

'But?'

The Doctor's gaze returned to him, an eyebrow raised. 'You seem pretty sure there's a "but".'

The *New Hope* left the TARDIS's scanning range. On board, its occupants were adjusting to the reality of their planned exodus. Mingled with a measure of homesickness was excitement at the adventure upon which they were embarking. The Administrative Council was discussing what Colony World #A7 should be like. There was strong support for a return to the basics; for leaving the blueprints and materials of technology firmly locked in their chambers.

Back on Earth, the parties were in full swing. They were saying that the launch had been a success; that, within the decade, a new world would be established, with all the commensurate opportunities for tourism and emigration. It would be a wonderful place, they said. The air would be breathable without the aid of filters. Birth restrictions and space allocations would no longer be necessary. Beneath a bright new star, humans could live in peace and happiness.

So they were saying.

The rain sliced down with stinging ferocity and the saturated ground slipped and churned at Taggart's feet. The rebels were trying their best to regroup; to fight back against the creatures which had herded them from the complex. They were following them still now, out into the open, and the rebels took fresh positions and fired. The renewed barrage was as ineffectual as the last. Taggart's sight was obscured by choking smoke, his hearing deadened by explosions of blaster fire.

The Cybermen kept coming.

Their weapons clattered in fatal response and the bodies of good friends fell and writhed in agony. Taggart didn't bother to aim. He just kept firing as if that might protect him. Blue sparks crackled across the attackers' metallic bodies, but they remained unscathed. Too soon, the charge in his gun was exhausted. He dropped it and tried to pull back away from the war zone. In the noise and the chaos, he collided with somebody. He thrashed about to keep his balance, but cold mud filled his mouth and nostrils. He was down and the home front was retreating past him. He closed his eyes and whimpered as metal boots tramped closer. And Ben Taggart cursed the fates for birthing him into the unceasing hellish war that had ripped Agora apart.

The expected killing blow never came. It was at least a

minute before he opened his eyes; another before he dared raise his head. The one-sided struggle had passed beyond him, its participants believing him dead. He could see the backs of four Cybermen through the haze, and the blasts and screams had diminished in volume. There was nothing he could do now to help his comrades. He could only try to cling on to his own life.

Taggart struggled to raise his aching body, his gaze fixed on the Cybermen by a terrible compulsion and the fear that they may turn and see him. He backed away slowly . . . and his shoulders touched metal. He screamed and whipped around to confront his destiny. His throat constricted and a second cry was stifled. An expressionless silver face loomed over him. He stared at its slit mouth and the teardrop shapes which pulled at blank eyes. It almost looked as if it might be sad to kill him. But not quite.

The Cyberman lunged and Taggart flinched, breath taken by panic. Suddenly, he was looking at the back of its head and registering the pitiful, rattling whine which rose from its chest unit. The Cyberman pitched face-down into the mud, its arms encircling Taggart's leg in a belated attempt to support itself. He shook it free with revulsion. It convulsed, then was still.

'So they can be killed. That's nice to know.'

Taggart started at the voice, relaxing as he saw that it was Lakesmith's. 'What's happened to it?' he asked numbly, staring down at the fallen monster.

'The guns must have had a cumulative effect. We've got a chance. We'd better take it.'

Arthur Lakesmith was the rebellion's instigator: a giant, bearded man with an overpowering presence. It was hard to imagine him falling in defeat, even before the Cybermen. They had followed him, all of them, with that thought in mind. But things had gone wrong. The resistance was being routed.

'What are you doing here?' asked Taggart.

'Going back into the complex.'

4

He was aghast. 'Population Control?'

'I need you.'

'You what?'

'Ray's dead. I need back-up. You're the only candidate.'

'I can't go in there!'

'It's our best chance. The Cybermen have deactivated the explosives, but they can't have expected me to get past their troops with more.'

For the first time, Taggart saw what Lakesmith was holding: a bulky agglomeration of machine spares, a flask of engine fuel at its heart. He had seen many similar in the past weeks. It was a crude and jury-rigged, but workable, bomb. 'If we can take out the control centre and maybe their ship, we can turn this battle our way,' Lakesmith said.

Taggart shook his head furiously. 'There's no chance, don't you see? There are probably more of those things still in there!'

'So we take them out too,' said Lakesmith, eyes afire. 'They've destroyed our planet. Now we're going to destroy them!'

'I can't do this. They'll kill us!'

'They'll do that anyway!'

'We could survive. They don't take everyone. Why don't we just let them put things back to normal?' Even to Taggart, his bleatings sounded hollow.

Lakesmith reached out with a swarthy hand and gripped the cotton front of Taggart's tunic. He swung him about and pinned him against the metal wall of Population Control. His granite jaw was set in determination. 'I'm sorry,' he snarled, 'but I can't indulge your cowardice. You're coming in, whether you like it or not.'

He held Taggart still for a moment longer, then released his grip and stepped away. The black clouds intensified their deluge and Taggart almost welcomed the cold, drenching punishment. Lakesmith had one hand on his gun. Taggart hated to think that he might actually use it. Against his stomach's wishes, he turned and made his way along the wall. He reached the jagged hole through which they had emerged. He took one last look at his old friend, who was following as resolute as ever. Then he pulled free of the grasping mud and entered the building, every nerve he had protesting.

'Take this,' said Lakesmith, when they were in the darkness of the vandalized complex. He pushed the bomb into Taggart's hands and hefted the Overseer-issue gun with his own.

'Don't you have any more of those?' Taggart asked. 'What about that Cyberman?'

'Doesn't have one. Doesn't need one. They can kill with their headpieces. The guns just give them range and power.' Lakesmith set off with unnerving confidence down a bare corridor. Taggart followed, clinging to the bomb as if it could offer him some protection.

They walked in silence, uncomfortable in sodden clothes. They passed through laboratories and by too many cramped cells, all serving to remind them why this was so important. Too many people had died here. With upsetting regularity, they encountered the corpses of luckless rebels, strewn in the corridors. The bodies seemed intact, but only from without. The internal organs had been boiled in their juices.

As Taggart was beginning to think he would be trapped in this labyrinth for ever, they reached a corner and Lakesmith pulled back. 'Cybermen!' he hissed. They flattened themselves against the wall and Taggart held his breath. He heard no sound, which was vaguely disconcerting. He was sure that the Cybermen could not approach without footfalls ringing out on the metal floor. But still, he wished for some clue to their location.

He got one. A fist punched through the wall between them and an arm clamped itself across Lakesmith's chest. Taggart screamed as a Cyberman rent the thin metal and forced its way into the passage. He ran, but his trembling

6

legs would not support him for long and he fell, the bomb's sharp edges impacting painfully with his ribs. The air above him fizzled and he smelt burnt ozone. He had tumbled beneath a fatal blast. He rolled onto his back and stared up miserably at the harbinger of his inevitable death.

The Cyberman still held Lakesmith, but the rebel leader was far stronger than it could have anticipated. He squirmed and thrashed, threw his captor off-balance and managed to discharge his gun into its chest. He squealed as, unharmed, it reasserted its dominance, propelling him into the wall and seizing his gun hand. Taggart watched, with fear and disgust, as the Cyberman tightened its grip and the bones in Lakesmith's lower arm began to pop.

'Get going, Ben!' Lakesmith yelled through pain-gritted teeth.

Taggart rose, his body working on adrenalin, his mind strangely disconnected. He faltered, eyes glued to Lakesmith.

'*Get out of here!*' the older man screamed, words gurgling and indistinct through the blood that rushed into his mouth.

Taggart ran, and as he pounded down the corridor, a rattling scream followed him, then the sickening crump of Lakesmith's body hitting the floor. He tried to forget the sounds, to press on without thinking. He hoped he could still find his way to the control centre.

He skidded into an Overseers' rest area (no point in sneaking around now) and made for the door at the opposite end. He was halfway there when a Cyberman stepped in to block it. He checked his momentum, reversed his path and saw, to his horror, that another was behind him. Taggart froze as the giants closed in from each side. In desperation, his hand moved to the bomb. They hesitated.

That's right, he wanted to say. You take another step and I'll blow you sky high. Just let me go free and we'll all survive this. But he was starting to hyperventilate and speech was beyond him.

'You will drop the explosive device or be destroyed.' The voice was deep and soulless, the threat sounding like immutable fact. Taggart had no reason to doubt that it was.

He could set off the bomb. He could take out at least these two, and a substantial section of the complex as well. He might even disable their ship if luck was with him. He might give the rebellion the boost it needed. His name would be legendary. He would die a hero. But that was the problem.

He might make a difference. He might well not. Only one thing was certain. He would die, without even knowing if he had helped.

He looked from one Cyberman to the other. Somehow, they were all the more intimidating for their stillness. They were statues, ready to reanimate if he made the wrong move. Could he trust them to spare his life if he obeyed?

Slowly, carefully, Ben Taggart stooped and placed the bomb on the floor in front of him. Then he straightened, raised his hands with fingers crossed and closed his eyes.

He listened to the steadying rhythm of his heart and awaited its cessation.

1

Blood and Wire

Chief Overseer Madrox slipped on the leather glove with studded knuckles and caressed his prisoner's face. He ran his hand across the Doctor's cheek and wiped away a stray fleck of blood. 'You will tell me what I wish to know,' he said, with as much menace as his nasal monotone could convey.

The Doctor looked at him, neck straining upwards in the restraints. His tear ducts brimmed as he fought to hold his swollen right eye open through a livid purple bruise. His fair hair was plastered down with sweat and a scab had formed over a cut on his forehead. His expression was defiant. 'I came here alone,' he answered evenly, with neither pain nor impatience.

Madrox hit him. The backhanded swipe drew blood and snapped his victim's head aside with a vicious whiplash. He showed no signs of discomfort. 'I know that isn't true!'

The Doctor mocked him with a sardonic grin. 'How do you know? Because the Cybermen said so?'

'They told me everything about you, Doctor.'

'Well, you can't believe all you hear.'

Madrox dropped to his haunches and took the Doctor's chin in his gloved hand, resisting the temptation to crush the impudent alien's windpipe. He brought his face closer to the Doctor's own and glared at him as if he could will him to crack beneath his scorn. 'It would be easier for you if you co-operated.'

'I'll be killed more quickly, is that the deal?' The Doctor returned the glare with equal force and Madrox's frustration boiled over.

'I'll rip you apart myself!'

'You can't. I don't think your masters would like that much. And what they don't like, you die for. Right?' Madrox jerked back, stung by the incisive truth. He raised his hand to strike again. 'I wouldn't do too much of that either,' said the Doctor. 'I might just expire on you.'

'I don't think so.' Madrox stayed his hand anyway. His ire had settled and he knew that a calculated, psychological attack was the best way to penetrate his foe's defences. He stood and flexed his fingers, regarding him coldly. It was time for the *coup de grâce*. 'The Cybermen know of your regenerative powers. You lose one body and you only grow another.' The Doctor was silent and Madrox drove his point home with glee. 'I can do whatever I like to you and you'll remain intact. And that's all they care about. I suggest you remember that.' He made a smart turn and marched to the far end of the cell, enjoying the sound of his boots on metal. He halted, nose against the wall. He measured the pause and imagined his prisoner's suspense. It tasted delicious.

'Now, Doctor,' he purred, 'I wish to know who your companions are and where I might find them. Are you going to tell me?' He turned to subject his vanquished enemy to a precisely timed intimidating stare. The Doctor was ignoring him. He had managed to twist so that he could lick one finger and use it to clean his fresh cuts.

Madrox crossed the room in a second and slapped him with his bare hand, four times, so that each of his cheeks was red and the skin broken. He stepped back, breathing heavily from the spurt of activity. Still, the Doctor didn't complain. 'How do you know,' he said mildly, 'that, when this body dies, I won't be reborn light-years away? There could be a laboratory full of spare Doctors on a distant planet. If you kill me, you might only help me to escape.'

Madrox turned to hide his face. He didn't want the Doctor to see how effective his passive resistance was proving; far more so than had the indignant rantings which accompanied the Time Lord's first days in custody. At least he had known how to handle them.

'The Cybermen gave you strict instructions, didn't they? They told you what to do if I arrived. They said I'd be with friends and that you'd have to find them. What happens to you, Madrox, if you can't do that?'

'I am asking the questions, Doctor!' But still, Madrox didn't dare turn and face him.

'And I'm not going to answer them, so let's drop the charade. Why don't you set me free? It might be better to pretend I was never here than to show me to your masters and admit failure.'

Madrox refused to listen to any more. He gave a snort of derision before marching stiffly from the cell. He paused on the threshold to send back a parting shot. 'We will get your companions, be sure of that – and they will suffer for your insolence!' He slammed the door with a clang which made the thin but strong walls tremble. Then he clenched his fists so tightly that his palms hurt as he tried to steady a tide of anger.

The Doctor was, irritatingly, right. The Cybermen had left Madrox with very specific orders. Their automated mechanisms had detected the arrival of the Time Lord's ship three weeks ago now; he had been arrested immediately and locked into the prepared restraints. The pockets of his multi-coloured coat had been emptied (a process which had taken an hour) and Overseers checked his cell every fifteen minutes. But the Cybermen had warned Madrox about the Doctor's companions. They were chosen, so they said, for their courage and resourcefulness. Until they were dealt with, the Doctor was not completely defeated. He had escaped from inescapable traps before.

The problem was that, no matter how they searched, Madrox's Overseers could find no more aliens. He could not do what the Cybermen wanted. And, as the Doctor had also said, what displeased them would certainly prove fatal to him.

11

With their next visit due in a mere two days' time, the Chief Overseer had every reason to be worried.

When the Doctor estimated that his captor was out of earshot, he released a sigh of controlled frustration. It was against his volatile nature to accept such treatment from a sadist like Madrox. However, his early outbursts had only served to prolong the interrogations. Getting under his skin was a better plan; one which had its own satisfactions.

He adjusted his position to make himself more comfortable. It wasn't easy. His knees and feet hurt from kneeling on hard metal. His hands were numb from the shackles which encircled his wrists and attached them via short chains to the wall. His neck was clamped by a set of stocks, electronically locked and bolted to the floor. His head was sore and sweating in the close environment and Madrox's blows had left the salted-iron taste of blood on his tongue and lips.

The Doctor allowed his eyelids to fall and he drifted into a semi-trance. Even at night, being in Population Control was like listening to somebody playing drums on a row of filing cabinets whilst being trapped in the top drawer of the middle one. The unceasing clatters and muted clangs of movement around the complex merged into a distant lullaby as the Doctor's heart rate slowed and his breathing became more shallow. Without this Time Lord gift, his situation would have been unbearable. He had rarely spent so long in captivity, but the Cybermen had made their plans too well. They had told the Overseers to take no chances.

His consciousness resurfaced an indeterminate time later; most likely, the Doctor thought, but a few minutes. The distant noises regained their volume and, at first, he didn't know what might have woken him. Then a more regular sound detached itself from the clamour: a rhythm of knuckles upon metal. Two knocks, then a pause. Two more. Nearby.

12

'Hello?' came a voice, somewhere over to his right, muffled by the intervening wall. 'Are you in there?'

Maxine Carter woke to the same sounds each night. The splintering crunch of boots through wood. The identifying shout: 'Overseer Patrol, do not resist!' Most times, she lay there, thin cotton sheets clinging to wet skin, pulse racing as the dreadful echoes receded into her subconscious. Tonight, there were footsteps on the stairs, Martin was yelling his throat raw and Max knew that the nightmare had been real.

She was out of her bedroom in seconds and fighting to prevent the four-man patrol from entering his. Its Leader tried to push her aside and she clung to his tunic and dug her long nails into his shoulder. He grimaced and she shoved hard, hoping to knock him down the stairs. For a moment, he was teetering. She saw that the lobby below was filling as spectators spilled out of the downstairs rooms. They wouldn't help. Too many were young men, as eligible as Martin. It wasn't worth throwing away their lives for. The Leader's colleagues caught him and he was swept to safety as they surged up the final steps and past her. She stopped one, but the first had already barged his way through the door and into Martin's room.

'You scum, that's my brother!' She pursued him and jumped onto his back, but another Overseer wrenched her away and held her as she clawed and spat. Martin had stopped shouting. He was shellshocked and made no move to resist as the Leader chained his wrist to a deputy's. The fourth invader held back in the doorway. He was middle-aged, short and a little stout. His wiry black hair sprouted around a circular bald patch. He had a thick moustache and a naturally doleful face. Max knew him, and knew what he was. She scowled and he shrugged his shoulders slightly before dropping his gaze to the floor.

The sight of her brother being hauled away gave Max the strength to break free from her captor. She twisted

13

about and got hold of his blaster. The Patrol Leader saw and moved in quickly. He cracked his gun butt across her forehead and Max fell painfully, one leg turned beneath her. The Leader lashed out with wild ferocity. The brutal blows were aimed at her stomach, but she managed to fend most off with her arms.

The beating stopped and, through tears, Max saw that the fourth man had finally interceded. The Patrol Leader glared at his mutinous subordinate. The junior Overseer whispered urgently, 'Don't you know whose that is?' He pointed and they all turned to look. Max felt like a patient surrounded by trainee doctors. She rested a hand on the hated lump and sensed the baby within her stirring. She didn't know if that was good or bad.

The Patrol Leader nodded, clapped the other man on the back and signalled to his group that it was time to move out. They sent Martin first, staring over his shoulder, too scared to speak.

'Why are you taking him?' Now Max was pleading. 'He's obeyed you, he's done nothing wrong.'

'I know,' said the Patrol Leader. 'This is to teach *you* a lesson.'

'No!' she screamed: a pointless outburst. The Leader had gone and his cruel, forced laugh was drifting back to her through the open door. The fourth man hesitated, just for a moment, and regarded the fallen woman apologetically, as if to say *What could I have done?*

'You traitor!' she hissed, voice dripping with hatred. His face fell and Max thought he might actually cry.

But then, Ben Taggart could hardly deny the truth of her damning accusation.

'It sounded like Madrox was rough on you,' said the boy in the cell behind the Doctor's own.

'No more so than I can handle,' he called back, as brightly as he could.

'What did he want?'

The Doctor hesitated. It occurred to him that this could

14

be some trick on the Overseers' part to gain information. He doubted if Madrox had the wit, but it might still pay to be circumspect. 'He's looking for someone. I think he's getting quite tired of not finding them.'

'They treat you differently from the rest of us, don't they?'

'In what way?'

'The interrogations. And sometimes I hear them talking about you in the corridors. I've been here a week now and all they've done to me is lock me in a cubicle and feed me.'

'How long has all this been going on then?' As well as diverting the conversation from the subject of himself, the Doctor genuinely wanted to learn more. At least he could confirm some unpleasant theories. The boy, however, didn't answer. 'When did the Cybermen first come here?' he prompted.

'You're not from the colony, are you?'

'Quite evidently not. When did they arrive?'

His fellow prisoner was silent for a moment. When he spoke again, his voice sounded hollow and subdued. The Doctor suspected that he had reminded him of the awful fate which had doubtless been ordained for him. 'They came to Agora before I was born. Back in the fifties. It was a simple world then. Our people were farmers and they had no weapons. They didn't think they were likely to need any.'

'But into every Paradise comes a serpent.' The Doctor fumed at the injustice of it all. 'And the Cybermen, having gained one easy victory, decided to make their visits regular.'

'They come back every three years, by Earth's calendar.'

'Or by the Mondasian one.'

'They take five hundred healthy young males to be converted into their own kind.'

'And Madrox and his cronies select the candidates?'

'Their job is to fill Population Control. They decide who's to be taken and they make sure the breeding rate stays high. For future intakes, you see.'

'I feared as much.'

'If you don't meet the conception quotas, you end up here, to be given to the Cybermen. Along with anyone who looks cross-eyed at an Overseer.' The boy's voice took on a note of bitterness. 'And then there are those of us who make up the numbers.'

'So the Cybermen have turned this planet into a breeding colony! I knew they were heartless, quite literally, but this is . . . this . . .' For once, the Doctor lacked the words. He was angry, disgusted and even affronted. How many times did he have to confront them before they learned? How long before humankind could be safe from their amoral schemes?

'You make it sound like you already know them.'

'Oh, yes. Of old. I've defeated them many times.' With a measure of pride, he added, 'I'm their arch-foe.'

'That's why you're getting the special treatment?'

'No doubt.'

'What will they do to you?'

The Doctor considered. 'I'm afraid I don't know. If they wanted me dead, they could have let their human puppets do it. There's no logic in keeping me here just for the pleasure of killing me themselves. At least, they would claim not.'

'They're due back soon.'

'I thought they must be. The Chief Overseer has been getting quite agitated. When?'

'Two days.'

'That doesn't leave much time.'

'For what?'

'To escape. And to work out how to defeat them.'

'Can you do that?' asked the boy with fresh hope.

The Doctor gave a melancholy sigh. 'Not this time, unfortunately. Not alone.'

The patrol marched smartly through the streets of Sector Four – the village which had once been known as Equality.

The day had been hot, but the night sky was cloudy and the afternoon warmth was held beneath its veil.

Ben Taggart hated being on the night shift. He hated the activities which took place after dark. At least, after this one, it would be over. The Cybermen would collect their tariff and Agora would rest more easily. Until the next time. He only wished they hadn't taken the Carter boy. He could add Max to the growing list of people whom he daren't look straight in the eye any more.

The Leader halted and inspected their surroundings. 'No more malcontents to round up,' he said. 'Looks like number five hundred's going to be random. Let's see who's closest.' He unfolded the tech-unit from his bulky chest armour. Taggart knew that he was checking the census records. 'Over here,' he ordered, seconds later. They followed obediently to a single-storey wooden hut. The Overseer who held Martin Carter watched as the Patrol Leader beckoned the others forward. 'Go on then, Taggart, this one can be yours.'

He hesitated only fractionally. Any qualms could make him a prisoner himself. If he didn't do this job, then someone else would take it, and do it to him.

The first kick sent shock waves juddering up his leg, but he felt the door give. On the second, it broke. 'Overseer Patrol, do not resist!' The Patrol Leader pushed into the nearest room, where a youngster, roused and panicked, was leaping from his bed. Time moved with a strobe effect, each frame imprinting itself on Taggart's mind for ever. Or until the next face superseded this one.

As his wrist was locked to that of the boy, the heavily pregnant mother appeared in the connecting doorway, wailing: 'He's only sixteen, you can't do this. Please!' The Patrol Leader turned his back, as always. Taggart cringed as he saw the young girl hiding behind the woman's legs, four or five years old, her eyes like saucers.

The prisoner tried to stand his ground, which was the last thing Taggart needed. He didn't want to have to get physical. The Patrol Leader spared him that necessity by punching the boy across the face. He whimpered and gave up resistance. The chain between them went slack and he stumbled along after Taggart, who kept his head down and left with all speed. The mother followed them into the hallway and grabbed the Patrol Leader's arm in desperation. He reminded her that that was an offence, but still she clung. He made to strike her and she blurted out, 'Don't take him, I can give you information!'

The Patrol Leader waited. She had her chance. Taggart hoped that she had nothing to say. It was unfair and he hated himself for it. But if she gained a reprieve for her son, he would only have to go through this again. Someone else's little boy would die.

'He's gone. He's planning another rebellion. I don't know where he is, but he's left the house. Check with the people there, you'll see. They're pretending he's still in that room, but he hasn't been seen for weeks.'

That evidently exhausted her knowledge. She looked imploringly into the Patrol Leader's eyes and Taggart could almost hear her prayers. His stomach turned. If she was saying what he thought she was, his night was about to get far worse.

'For the avoidance of doubt,' said the Patrol Leader steadily, 'can you tell me please who we're talking about here?'

She swallowed. 'Lakesmith. Arthur Lakesmith.'

Taggart sweated as the Leader turned to stare at him.

Madrox's office was simple and bare. He had considered the opulent look – deep carpets, attractive wall hangings, expensive trinkets – but decided against it. He didn't need to present himself as one who lived luxuriously. Rather, his confining walls and stark lighting accentuated the sinister, hard-edged aspects of his persona – and he knew that it met with the Cybermen's approval. He sat deliberately so that shadows hid his face. Across a basic table, Overseer 4/3 squirmed on a metal chair.

'You don't like the Cybermen much, do you?' He let

his voice come out as a drawl, retaining a relaxed posture. Taggart tried to shrug in a non-committal way, but didn't quite achieve the movement. Half-formed words came out as mewlings. 'It's all right,' said Madrox, 'you have that in common with most of the Overseers. And it's no secret that you fought them, back in the rebellion.'

'No, sir.'

'The failed rebellion.' He paused for effect. 'They maimed your best friend, didn't they?'

Taggart nodded cautiously.

'They horribly mutilated him,' expounded Madrox, enjoying the feel of the words on his tongue. 'How long ago was all that now?'

'2176. Fifteen years. Five visits.'

'That long, eh?' He stood and walked around the table, his hands clutching the studded glove behind his back, eyes inspecting the far end of the ceiling. Keeping him guessing. When he came to a halt, he was standing behind Taggart. The junior Overseer cringed, just noticeably, but didn't dare turn and look.

'So what do you think? Could he still hold influence? Could he provide a rallying point again?' He produced the glove and rubbed it gently against his subordinate's ear. 'Might there be a mutiny in the offing?'

'I don't know.'

The Chief Overseer pressed his fist, through the glove, against Taggart's cheek. Now his threat was explicit in every word. 'So tell me: when did you last see Arthur Lakesmith?'

'It was months ago.'

'Months?'

'We haven't spoken for a long time. Not since the Cybermen . . . did what they did to him. I let him down. I haven't seen him since Patrol Four was last sent to check on him.'

'And yet he's not where he should be now.'

'I know, sir. We brought in his housemate. Why don't you talk to him?'

'Oh, I will.' Madrox grabbed what remained of Taggart's hair and pulled his head back savagely, provoking a gasp. 'But first, I want to be sure that you know where your loyalties lie, Overseer 4/3.'

'With – with you, sir.'

'Is that so? That wasn't the case fifteen years ago, was it?' There came no reply, so he yanked again. '*Was it*, Overseer?'

'No,' Taggart squeaked.

Madrox held tight for a moment longer, then let go and returned to his seat. He faced Taggart squarely, slipping back into his sincere act. 'We all want to see the Cybermen toppled.' That wasn't true. Hate them he might, but their defeat would rob him of his power. 'They like that. They know where they stand. They motivate people by making them scared. That's why they spared you when you worked against them. You saw what they did to Lakesmith; what they did to the colony. They know you wouldn't take the risk of betraying them.'

'I wouldn't.'

'Or would you? How long does it take to grow a spine, Overseer Taggart? Would fifteen years be long enough, do you think?' Taggart tried to speak, but Madrox waved him aside with a gesture. He placed both hands on the table and leaned forward so that his face was lit. 'Sometimes, it's tempting. We all hear rumours. Whispers of rebellion. Names and places. It's easy to keep quiet; to hope that, this time, it will actually work. Then we can stand back, watch the Cybermen fall and join the parties later. The chance of freedom, without the risk.' His voice hardened. 'But think about what happens if it goes wrong. The Cybermen won't only blame the rebels, you know. Last time, they wiped out every last Overseer. And you, Taggart – you, they already know. They know you were Lakesmith's partner. When the dust has settled and they're after revenge, who do you think they'll come to first?'

'I know that, sir.'

'Then think on it. Is it worth keeping your silence for the sake of an old man – a crippled old man – who failed to win his last war and wants another chance? He'll drag us all down with him if he tries anything. You know that.'

Taggart found his tongue. 'I do. But I honestly don't know what he's up to. I don't know where Lakesmith is, I don't know what he's doing. I swear, I haven't seen him in months!'

Madrox sat back in the shadows so that Taggart couldn't see how he had taken that. 'When do you come back on duty?'

'Tomorrow afternoon, sir.'

'Then I'm sending your patrol out tomorrow night – only this time I'll accompany you personally. We can search for Lakesmith and question known associates. You can guide us to those?'

'Well, some of them,' said Taggart.

'Good. Because, if we can't produce your friend, I might be forced to reconsider your position with us.' He didn't have to say more. Taggart might be approaching his fortieth birthday, but he would still be suitable for conversion and he knew it. Madrox dismissed him and, as he scurried out gratefully, the Chief Overseer sat back and thought over what he had learned.

Taggart had not been lying about Lakesmith, but he was hiding something. Madrox could tell. He was sure, though, that after tomorrow night, he would learn all. Cowards like Taggart were easy to control. That was why he had let him live for so long.

And, if Madrox found the alleged rebellion, could the Doctor's companions be far away?

Max Carter wandered in a trance, baked mud hurting her bare feet, sweating in the oppressive atmosphere and feeling every one of her thirty-three years. She knew that she was breaking curfew, but didn't much care. They

21

could do no more to her than they already had. They had taken Martin and they couldn't hurt her physically. Not with the child inside her. Not so close to the birth.

She had had no destination in mind, but she wasn't surprised to arrive at the hill. It rose, not very high, from the edge of the village, and it overlooked the carbuncle that was Population Control. She sat and looked across at the complex. Its dull metal walls were the antithesis of all that the original Tellurian settlers had wanted this colony to stand for. The ten villages of Agora radiated outwards from where it squatted in the settlement's dead centre; a permanent reminder that the Cybermen had razed that centre upon their first landing.

It was a large building, wings spread like legs on a giant spider, from a hollow, ring-shaped section. It was enclosed by a chain-link fence, surrounded and topped by barbed wire, and Max knew that mines and electronic deterrents lay within the perimeter. You needed an Overseer tech-unit to even get within reach of the heavily armed security watch. She dreamt of having the firepower to charge in there; to blast open its guts and snatch the prisoners. To free her brother. She knew that was impractical. But soon, she would change that.

Violent thoughts gave Max catharsis. They were taken from her by a sudden sound. A snapping of twigs. She jumped into a crouch, alert for danger. How could she have been so stupid? Of course she couldn't let herself be captured. What would Henneker and the others do then?

It wasn't a patrol, she saw thankfully. They were never so cautious. This was one person, as worried as she was. He had leapt for cover behind a black scrub bush. Max circled it, keeping down, then pounced with a speed made uncomfortable by her current bulk. She heard a squeak, in a male voice, and her foe thrashed as she pinned him with little effort. She saw his face: nineteen years old, he had tangled rust-brown hair, blue eyes and pale, slightly freckled skin. He wore a pair of corrective

22

spectacles not made on this world. Max recognized him and released her grip.

'It's you,' she said, her relief more apparent than she had intended. 'What the hell are you doing out here?'

'I felt cooped up in the bunker. It was hot. Besides, I've got a friend in there. I just wanted to, I don't know . . .' He tailed off and looked across at the complex morosely. Max had to sympathize.

She had not known this young man for long, but she could trust him. They had worked together since his arrival, when he had caused quite a stir amongst the rebels. An Agoran native, freshly returned from the stars.

Grant Markham had proved himself invaluable to the Project.

The route back to Taggart's quarters took him by the special cell. As he approached, he saw an Overseer peering through the viewing hatch in the door and leaving, apparently satisfied. That gave him a clear fifteen minutes before the next check. It still took a great deal of effort to persuade his arms to reach out and his trembling hands to undo the catch. He could almost hear Henneker's voice, deriding him for his lack of courage, telling him that he had to contribute to the effort. But he heard Madrox too, outlining the dangers of resistance and the fatal price of disobedience.

'Hello again.' The Doctor was still clamped immobile in the stocks, but his green eyes sparkled and he gave Taggart a friendly smile. 'Are you going to talk to me this time?'

He didn't know. His diaphragm was attempting somersaults. He told himself that this man was an enemy of the Cybermen. He might be able to help them. But then, if he could, why was he still trapped? What could one man do against such creatures anyway?

The prisoner was giving him a quizzical look. 'I think you want to do something,' he said. 'I think you want me to defeat your oppressors for you. Why don't you come in? We can talk.'

'I'm sorry,' Taggart muttered. He slammed the hatch shut and locked it, heart beating out a percussion line. He couldn't do anything, he insisted to himself. The Doctor's restraints could not be opened, not even by Madrox. Nobody could free him but the Cybermen themselves.

That didn't stop him from feeling guilty as he made the long journey to his bed. He had always considered himself to be a rebel. He hated the Cybermen and, when he could, he had used his position to help fight them. But he knew that such acts were too few and infrequent. He cloaked himself with all manner of excuses and hid behind the Overseers' black body armour.

Beneath that, Ben Taggart was simply a coward.

The Doctor sighed and began to settle back into his trance. The voice from the next cell interrupted. 'Who was that?'

'Someone who might help us – eventually.'

'Can he get me out of here?'

'I don't know.'

Plaintive, now: 'I'm scared. I don't want to be converted.'

The Doctor couldn't answer that. He had run out of promises.

'The Overseers say it isn't like death.' The boy was talking to convince himself. 'They say it makes you immortal; that once you're a Cyberman, you become invulnerable. Is that right?'

'In a way, perhaps.'

'I suppose I'll be changed though, won't I? I'll act like one of them, not like myself. Do you think I'll remember who I was?'

'I honestly couldn't tell you. Just keep on hoping.'

The boy remained quiet for almost a minute. Then he asked: 'Are you any closer to escaping yet?'

'Not that I know of,' said the Doctor despondently. 'As

I told you, I'm waiting for someone else.' As Madrox well knows, he thought. At least they hadn't found Grant yet, that was something.

'Then where has he got to? You said it's been three weeks since you were captured.'

'I know.' He let a trace of bitterness enter his voice. 'It's a new chap – he's not very good.'

'Oh. I see.'

There was nothing left to be said then, so with silent resignation, they greeted the night together.

The penultimate night before the Cybermen returned.

2

In the Making

The time ship perched on Arc University's landing pad, resembling nothing more than a giant insect head. Black eye windows reflected the sun's glare and a semi-organic membrane rippled in the breeze. The students had turned out to cheer on the expedition, but Jolarr couldn't understand why they had bothered. They hardly knew him, any of them. For most of the life segment he had spent here, he had studied alone in the library or at home, making use of remote communication facilities to increase the efficiency of his learning experience. He had become the institution's youngest ever graduand and one of a few to be granted access to the knowledge of the Arc Hives themselves. He still hadn't expected this.

He remembered how the Chancellor had broken the news. 'This is a great honour for the university,' he had said, all smiles and excitement. Jolarr had gazed back coolly, thinking: A great honour for me, you mean. He had already learned, from rumours on the WebNet, that the Chancellor had met with Hegelia herself and that the possibility of a time trip had been mooted. Jolarr knew what he had been summoned for before he was told. He only had to make himself believe it.

The Chancellor was waiting now, an inane grin on his face, as Jolarr was escorted to the pad to the accompaniment of whistles and applause. ArcHivist Hegelia stood by his side, even more grand than Jolarr had anticipated. He hardly listened as they were introduced. She was taller than he and her face was hard, severe and alert for all its ninety-plus years. Her cheekbones were high and prominent, her unblemished skin stretched tight across them. Green fire lit Hegelia's eyes and her glare made Jolarr feel that she regarded him with disdain. That couldn't be the case. She had asked for him to accompany her. He didn't know why, but he couldn't refuse her. Time journeys were rarely sanctioned and he might not get another chance of one.

Jolarr summoned his courage and reached out a hand. 'It's a great pleasure to meet you, ma'am,' he said.

Hegelia ignored it and gave him a slight nod of acknowledgement instead. 'Graduand.' Then she turned and swept towards the ship, regal in crimson robes and a silver headband which supported a bouffant of dyed red hair. The canopy was flung back to allow her access and Jolarr was ushered to the far side where he was hoisted into the seat beside her. It shifted to make him comfortable.

The rest of the ceremony passed in a blur. Jolarr had no interest in the Chancellor's speech. He sat in the cockpit and tried not to worry that soon he would be sealed in with the most respected of all ArcHivists. What would he say to her during their long journey?

He held his breath involuntarily as the canopy was pulled over to obscure his world. Hegelia ran through pre-ignition checks, not sparing him so much as a glance, and the ship vibrated slightly as the engines began to cycle. Jolarr tried to settle back, to prepare for the inevitable pressure of gravity. But then, the vessel rose a little and – with incredible, unexpected speed – surged forward.

For a fraction of a second, he thought they must have ploughed into the onlookers. His heart leapt and he almost yelped – but he managed to quell his ground-less panic. Hegelia seemed content enough with their motion. They must have slipped out of real space already. They were spiralling backwards through the centuries, yet it now felt like they were hardly moving at all.

'You can relax.' Hegelia's features didn't soften despite

her kind words. 'We have made it safely into the time-space vortex and our bearing and heading are perfectly correct. Estimated Time of Arrival is in one hour and fifty-five minutes. I trust that you are well prepared for this mission?'

Jolarr nodded dumbly. He didn't know which he feared most – the ArcHivist or the monsters which she had made it her life's work to study.

'So tell me, Graduand: what do you know of the Cybermen?'

The sun was struggling to mount the horizon and to make its presence felt through the clouds. Refracted rays washed Population Control in scarlet, doing little to shake Grant's mind from images of blood and wire. Bad memories, from a distant lifetime.

He hadn't wanted to come back here.

He remembered how he had felt, stepping out of the Doctor's police-box-cum-space-and-time-vessel: the gut-clawing sense of *déjà vu* at the sights and sounds of a world he had forgotten. Population Control, especially, had had his nerves screaming at him to run and hide. Even as he looked at it now, Grant's mind attached strong negative feelings to the complex, but failed to provide memories to explain them.

'Has anything else come back to you?' The query came from Max, who sat beside him on the brittle grass. They had been together all night, united by their woes.

'Only fragments,' he said, 'and none of them mean much. It was so long ago.' Something large and silver flashed across his mind's eye and he suppressed a shudder. 'I've always told people I left Agora by choice, to travel to New Earth where the technology was. I believed it myself. But now, it's making less and less sense. How could I have just gone? It was thirteen years ago – I was six years old, the Cybermen had taken over and you don't even have space travel!'

'Don't worry, it'll come.' To Grant's surprise, Max

squeezed his hand in a comforting gesture. He had worked with her for weeks now, but this was the first time he had seen her expressing affection for anyone. The determined set of her angular face had sagged and her normally scraped-back black hair was bedraggled, wisps falling over puffed-up eyes. Grant was privileged to witness a rare moment of vulnerability in Max Carter's life. He knew about her loss – the fate of her brother had been relayed in a strained, controlled voice, not revealing too much emotion – but he didn't know what to say that could ease her pain. She was holding it in and clinging to the idea that the Project might be successful. For that matter, he was too.

'They used to tell awful stories about technology, didn't they?' Max's tone was deliberately lighter and Grant discovered that a smile had crept onto his face.

'They still do. I heard one in the market-place yesterday.'

'Not the robot which grew bigger than the world and crushed it in one fist?'

He laughed this time. 'I think it was the Eternal Night Tale – you know, the engine blotting out the sun with its fumes?'

Max laughed as well, but their cheer subsided as they looked away from each other and the complex reinsinuated itself upon their senses. Grant's mind, at least, had turned to less pleasant things. 'You know,' he said, 'I've been frightened of robots for as long as I can remember.'

'I had noticed.'

'It's stupid. I've always been fascinated by technology; I just feel an unreasoning terror at the sight of . . . of lumps of metal, pretending to be alive. That's why I remembered the old stories. I always thought that somehow, subliminally, they were the cause.'

'But now you think it must be the Cybermen?'

'It wouldn't stretch the imagination much, would it? I must have seen one, back when I was young and living

29

here. I just wish I could remember more.'

Max had drifted into a hollow-eyed melancholia. 'Perhaps the old stories were right. Technology hasn't done much for this planet.'

Grant shook his head vehemently. 'It didn't cause a problem on New Earth. It's down to the people who use it whether it does good or not. I mean, think about what we're achieving with the Project. Think what our ancestors could have done if they'd had some sort of defensive system when the Cybermen first came here.'

'Maybe,' said Max, but she didn't sound convinced.

The sun continued to climb until the whole of its swollen red bulk was visible and making its way across the sky. Max shook herself and stood, massaging cramped limbs. 'Well, look at me. I'm operating today and I can hardly keep my eyes open.' She tried to smile, but only managed a sort of wistful expression. 'We'd best go. The patrols will be out soon.'

Grant nodded without enthusiasm and got to his feet. They began the long trudge back to the bunker. 'And by the way . . .' Max reached across and removed his spectacles, pressing them into his hand. 'If you must come outside, keep these off. The Overseers only have to notice one anachronism.' She forced a smile. 'Let's just hope Arthur Lakesmith's well this morning.'

'Then we can get on to the next stage, can't we?'

'We can hope.' Max took one last, sad look back at the prison which held so many friends – and, almost to herself, she added: 'If we couldn't do that, we'd go slowly mad.'

Jolarr focused his eyes upon a distant point and used well-practised memory techniques to bring the relevant data to the fore. Hegelia was testing him and he was determined to pass. 'The Cybermen,' he recited, 'originally came from Mondas, Earth's twin planet in the ancient cosmology. They evolved along similar lines to the Tellurians, until a freak accident dislodged their world from its orbit

30

and, eventually, from its solar system. They had to adapt to survive this catastrophe. They turned to cybernetics, replacing body parts as they became unreliable or superfluous. Eventually, they pursued such processes to their conclusion.'

'Their *logical* conclusion,' the ArcHivist interrupted. She seemed in awe of the idea. 'Just as they upgraded those parts of the body which were ineffective, so too they altered their very brains. They wiped out unnecessary feelings: love, compassion, hatred, fear. They fashioned themselves into a new race. Efficient, indomitable . . . near perfect.' She looked at him and her eyes were alight with zeal. 'How do you think it feels, Graduand Jolarr? To be invincible, to be unfettered by emotions? To devote your life to one cause – the continuance of your own race at any cost?'

'I don't know.'

'No, of course you don't.' Hegelia seemed to have brought her enthusiasm under control. She sat back and said no more.

Jolarr didn't know whether to continue his résumé or not. He was feeling ever more uncomfortable with his travelling companion. As interminable seconds ticked by, he started to fidget and he longed for the ship to reach its destination. No matter how his seat remoulded itself to suit him, he felt the overpowering need to stretch his legs. He wished he could at least see out of the closed-in cabin, but the portals had been made opaque to foil exactly that urge. The Time Winds would be too much for his limited mind to handle.

He found his thoughts drifting towards the Cybermen. In his time, they had become little more than shadowy creatures of legend; the subjects of fairy-tale and nightmare. Nobody had seen one for centuries – but neither was anyone sure that their threat was truly over. They had returned from apparent extinction before.

'Would you like to meet a Cyberman?' Hegelia asked, as if she had read his mind.

31

The question took Jolarr by surprise. 'That isn't possible, is it?' The Hive Custodians had strict rules about such things. 'I thought we weren't supposed to visit the actual time of occupation. I thought we were going to Earth year 2210.'

' "To gather archaeological and anecdotal evidence of the still recent events without fear of affecting an important temporal nexus," ' Hegalia said, directly quoting from the Hives' own guidelines. Jolarr thought he could detect a subtle mocking quality to her tone. 'And why,' she asked him before he could press the point, 'should the invasion of the colony world Agora be considered of historical import?' Another test. An easy one: Jolarr had spent most of the past week studying text files, most of which had been written by Hegelia herself.

'The timing,' he answered confidently. 'You've found evidence of Cyber activity on Agora in 2191 – but, at that time, their race was believed extinct.' Jolarr was mentally sifting through a mass of memorized information. He recalled how Mondas had been destroyed and how the Cybermen's subsequent attempts to invade Earth, using Planet Fourteen as a base, had failed, with massive Cyber casualties. 'Most were actually hibernating in frozen tombs on Telos – but you yourself postulated the existence of a further group, ArcHivist. You called them cyberNomads.'

Hegelia nodded graciously and indicated that he should continue.

'The Nomads had travelled out into the galaxy from Planet Fourteen, but they found themselves in a vicious and protracted war with Voga, the famed planet of gold. They lost and were presumed wiped out – until, three centuries later, a small, isolated group reappeared and tried to take their revenge on the Vogans. You also put forward a hypothesis that another such group might have reopened the Telosian tombs and helped to forge the new race – the Neomorphs – which proliferated during the twenty-sixth century.'

'So, in the year 2191 . . .?' Hegelia prompted.

'They would have recently fought the Vogan War,' said Jolarr. 'If we can find out what happened at that time, we might have another important piece of the jigsaw.' A thought occurred to him and he added, 'We might even come closer to knowing whether or not any Cybermen could have survived to our time.'

She smiled and Jolarr felt a warm glow of satisfaction at having pleased her. 'You are as bright and conscientious a student as your records indicate,' she said. 'I am glad to have you along on this expedition.'

'Thank you, ArcHivist.'

'However, you did not answer my original question. Would you like to meet a Cyberman?'

Jolarr considered that carefully, thinking over all the things he had learned about the monsters: their power and strength; their disregard for other life-forms; their ruthlessness. Of course he didn't want to meet one! Such a desire would be tantamount to an intention to commit suicide. But the ArcHivist, Jolarr suspected, was looking for a rather different response – so, obligingly, he gave one. 'It would be . . . interesting,' he said.

Hegelia smiled and turned her attention to the controls, checking the status monitors. 'Magnificent creatures!' she whispered – and her reverential tone filled Jolarr with foreboding.

The rebels' bunker had once been part of a cotton refinery which had been destroyed in the first invasion. This rough-hewn sub-level on the edge of Sector Two was all that remained and, in Max's eyes, it was too close to Population Control to be safe. It was protected, though, by a thin scrub covering and a primitive video-monitoring system, and Max had seen the logic in Henneker's view that 'right under their tin noses' was the least likely place to be searched. In any case, the rebel leader had a habit of getting his own way. Not that that had ever stopped Max from trying.

'I'm telling you,' she yelled at him now, 'it isn't safe! Lakesmith's implant didn't take.'

'He's all right, isn't he?'

'For the moment, yes. But if we're going to try again, I need to carry out fresh tests. I have to be sure he won't reject a second time – for his health as much as for the sake of the Project.'

'We can't afford to do that,' Henneker insisted. 'If we don't get more subjects started, we'll miss the arrival!'

'Then we'll miss it! Go ahead with a back-up plan!'

'We haven't got one!' Henneker pulled at his sandy hair in frustration.

'You can't lay this at my door,' stormed Max. 'You knew we weren't likely to finish on time – you should have made preparations. Get some men together, attack the complex, something. If you can stall them for a while . . .'

'I can't! You know what happened last time there was an uprising. It's difficult to recruit people as it is. I've made them believe in the Project. If they see nothing happening, they won't risk acting!'

Max dropped into a seat and sighed in resignation. She rubbed her fingers across tired eyes. 'Okay,' she said. 'If you find two people willing to undergo Stage One, I'll do them today – if Lakesmith's operation goes well. That's all.'

'But –'

'I'm not risking the Project, and their lives, for expediency's sake!' That was the last word. Max had already conceded too much. She wondered if she would have given in so easily had it not been for Martin. She hadn't told Henneker about that. It had already become just one more hurt to add to her silent burden. She hoped she would be able to remain detached and logical despite the situation. If circumstances demanded, she would need the strength to delay the Project rather than to risk failure. They could bring down the Cybermen next time. It would only cost five hundred more lives.

'I'll go and fetch our volunteers then,' said Henneker

peevishly. He crossed the cluttered bunker, casting an ink-jet shadow in the dim light provided by a low-voltage generator. He checked the rolling, monochrome picture on the security monitor – then, satisfied that it was safe, he climbed the short wooden ladder to the surface, pushed open the entrance hatch and heaved himself out.

Max watched him go and shook her head wearily. She turned to Grant, who had observed the heated exchange, as usual, in silence. 'Looks like we've got another busy day.'

'Looks like,' he agreed gloomily.

Max regarded the teenager sympathetically. 'You've got as much to lose as any of us, haven't you? More, perhaps. If we can't free your Doctor friend . . .' She left the sentence unfinished. Each knew as well as the other that, without the Time Lord and his craft – both currently held by the Overseers – Grant was stranded on a world he had once escaped.

'I never wanted to come here. I wanted to land on Earth.'

'Why didn't you?'

'The Doctor insisted. He kept asking questions about my past. He'd worked out something was wrong – and he might have known about the Cybermen, I'm not sure. He just went on about how I should face up to what I'd once run away from.'

'Perhaps he had a point.'

Grant shrugged. 'He made me come here, he said he'd protect me – and then what? We step out of the TARDIS, the Overseers swoop and I end up alone, not knowing what to do. I'd probably have been picked up myself if Henneker hadn't found me.'

Max attempted to divert the course of the conversation into more settled waters. 'You never told me how you come to be travelling with an alien. I suppose he landed on New Earth?'

'Well, actually no,' said Grant. 'It's a long story, but

basically, my town was caught in a transdimensional warp and I ended up on a television station three systems away. The Doctor was there.'

'That simple, eh?'

'He was good, and he knows plenty. If we could get to him, I'm sure he could sort out this mess for us.'

'You've been through things like this with him before?'

He nodded ruefully. 'A couple of days ago, we were fighting a living, homicidal computer virus. Now the Doctor brings me to my home planet and this happens. He must think I'm jinxed. I bet he never had such an exciting life before we met!'

Max smiled, seeing that Grant had cheered up a little. She gestured towards the red curtain which partitioned off her work area from the rest of the bunker and said gently, 'Come on. I think we'd best get started.'

The day dragged on.

Jolarr woke, surprised that he had managed to sleep at all. It took a few seconds for reality to reassert itself, then he remembered where he was – and who with. Hegelia was leaning over the controls of the time ship and tapping in information with well-trained speed.

'You are awake then,' she observed without looking up. 'Just in time. We are almost on the point of arrival.'

He experienced a wave of alarm at that news. He felt he was expected to make an intelligent comment, but his mouth was fuzzy and his vocal chords would not respond. Instead, he stared at the reflection of his white face and black hair in the window glass.

Jolarr felt only a gentle bump as the vessel returned to ground. He watched, not daring to interrupt, as Hegelia completed a series of checks. Then, as she sat back with a satisfied expression, he ventured: 'Are we there?' His voice was higher than normal.

'Of course. You do not think this ship capable of landing in the vortex, do you?'

'No,' he said quickly. 'But . . . well, this is my first

time journey. We're really in 2210?'

She didn't answer, and Jolarr wondered if he had imagined the flicker of a more sympathetic expression which crossed her face. Hegelia pulled back the canopy and he blinked in unexpected sunlight. Sweet, fresh air played around his nostrils and he realized how stale the ship's recycled atmosphere had been.

They climbed out of the cockpit and stood on the concrete-hard ground of a barren field. The sky was grey, but the sun forced rays through the clouds and the air was warm. Even before Jolarr had finished stretching his cramped legs, Hegelia pulled a handheld micro-recorder from the folds of her cloak and began to dictate. 'We have landed safely on Agora. The position of the sun indicates that it is late afternoon in the colonized sector. The ground here could not support crops and it seems that the preoccupation for which this settlement is prosaically named has long been abandoned.'

Jolarr heard the briefest of mechanical splutters. When he looked, the ship had disappeared. He knew that it had slipped into interstitial time: an elementary precaution, insisted upon by the Custodians. Time technology was too dangerous to fall into the wrong hands, especially before it was supposed to exist.

'I want you to take this,' said Hegelia, and Jolarr was surprised and proud to be handed the small, white recall unit. Her trust made him feel important, like his presence here was really valued.

He had already seen the distant silhouettes of short buildings on the horizon, and the ArcHivist now set off towards these. He fell into step behind her, which was what she seemed to expect.

Jolarr's misgivings were starting to fade. He was far now from the lonely, soulless world of academia, and he knew that his WebNet interface and HyperReality console could never have reproduced the excitement which was burgeoning within him. He revelled in the feel of the air, the distant sound of birds and other such humdrum delights as if they were totally alien experiences. In a way, they were. Jolarr was no longer observing history from afar, but living it.

Still, a pessimistic voice played over on a loop disc in his head, reminding him that imaginary environments had one advantage over their real-life equivalents.

They were safer.

Max Carter was back at home, back in her own bed, but enjoying no more than brief tastes of oblivion. Her mind was too full of the Project to allow sleep; too worried about whether the latest operations would prove successful in the long term; missing, too, the comfort of knowing that Martin was in the next room.

When she did manage to drift into something approaching a restful doze, she was haunted by memories of past indignities and hurts. She was lying on her back in the Overseers' surgery, a lighting panel burning purple rectangles into her retinas, paralysed by anaesthetic spray and listening in disbelieving horror as the living being within her was discussed like a saleable commodity. The scanners had detected a genetic deformity, they said; a minor defect, but impossible to correct and enough to label the child imperfect. It would not make good conversion material, nor would it be ideal for breeding stock. And now Max was leaving Population Control, cold despite the baking heat, her arms wrapped about her empty stomach, feeling as though a part of her self had been ripped out and the hollow space it left inside scrubbed clean with a scouring pad.

She was back in the present, still in bed, wet cotton sheets clinging. She felt the baby within her stir and, for a blessed moment, she thought it had all been a dream.

Then she remembered the truth and wanted to be sick.

Grant was equally restless; in his case, because Henneker was pacing the bunker, pouring out his worries to the only available ear. Grant tried to ignore him, burying his head in the rags which served as a pillow. Unlike the others, he had no home to go to; no obedient life to pretend to live. He had slept here for three weeks now and his makeshift bed never got more comfortable. Nor had he adjusted to being woken at all hours by the latest breakthrough or the latest argument.

He had dozed for only a few minutes this time, which made him feel more tired, not less. He had spent the morning and most of the afternoon assisting Max as she had worked to reverse their setback. He had not done much but hold scalpels, make the odd technical comment and mop the patient's brow. His part of the Project had passed and all he could really do now was wait and hope.

'I don't know what Carter expects from me,' complained Henneker. 'I thought, when you turned up, that we could make this thing work at last. But now she's telling me we need a back-up plan. A back-up plan! This close to the deadline?'

'We just need time,' Grant muttered indistinctly.

'There is no time!' Grant lifted a heavy eyelid at the rebel leader's anguished exclamation. In the sparse light, Henneker's youthful face was lined and gaunt. It was a contrast to the image of the 'Great Young Hope', which he preferred to project in his attempt to motivate a twice-defeated populace. That was why he had recruited Lakesmith: his name had meaning to many people. Like Max, however, he didn't mind Grant seeing a truer picture, although the teenager wasn't too pleased with the implied responsibility. He didn't think himself well cast in the role of confidant.

'Can't you think of anything?' asked Henneker, almost begging now. It was a familiar question. 'You've travelled in an alien ship – you must have picked up something!'

'Nothing useful,' he restated impatiently. 'As I said, the best thing I can think of is to free the Doctor – but this Taggart guy said there was no way of doing that, didn't he?'

Henneker looked as if he didn't believe a word that his

vaunted contact in the Overseers told him. Even so, he subsided into a sulky silence.

'It's up to Max,' said Grant, as his final comment on the matter. He rolled to present his back to Henneker and tried to settle into a much-needed sleep.

He knew before he did so that he was going to have the dream.

It was almost an hour before Hegelia and Jolarr reached civilization. Jolarr had become well used to his companion's brisk pace and he trailed only a short distance behind her as they crossed the village limits. She produced her recorder, although there wasn't much to report. 'The roads are dirt tracks, the buildings rotting wood. I can see no evidence of anything beyond a Level Two technology.'

She strode on, unconcerned by the looks they drew from the occasional quiet resident. The Agorans wore simple tunics woven from natural fibres and Jolarr felt conspicuous in his smart, green, one-piece graduation suit, tied at the waist by a synthe-leather belt. He wondered vaguely why Hegelia had bothered to appropriate antique recording equipment if they were to stand out so much.

Only once did a man dare approach them. He got halfway through his mumbled question before Hegelia informed him that they did not wish to join a rebel movement, thank you very much. He hurried off and they were not disturbed again.

They found a basic market-place, where more colonists gathered. To Jolarr's surprise, Hegelia paid them no heed. She continued her march onward and Jolarr, confused and footsore, began to resent her secrecy.

'Where are we going?' he asked her finally, hoping that she wouldn't take offence at his impertinence. When Hegelia ignored him, he added, 'Why didn't we talk to the people at the market? Couldn't they have told us something?'

'They can tell me little,' she said. 'I wish to discover the truth of things for myself.'

They had almost crossed the breadth of the village now, and it was clearly Hegelia's intention to explore beyond. Jolarr's mind was packed with questions, but he felt that he had tested his luck enough. He would have to wait until she decided to reveal more.

And then he saw it.

At first, he wasn't sure what it was. The roof of the building came into view over the top of a small hill, and it wasn't until they had left the village and were almost upon it that the hulking metal complex became fully visible. Hegelia stopped at the head of the rise and inspected her find with grim satisfaction.

'Opinion?'

Jolarr answered, even though his stomach was tingling with dread. 'It's at odds with the level of technology in the village. There's no evidence that the Agorans even have machinery for working metal, so we might assume that the building is of extraterrestrial origin.'

Hegelia was breathing deep with almost sexual pleasure. 'The efficient and symmetrical construction would suggest the Cybermen as its possible architects.'

'They left it behind here, you mean?'

She turned to Jolarr with an almost pitying look. 'I should warn you, Graduand, that I took the liberty of adjusting the time ship's navigational program. I have brought us several years further into the past than you were briefed to expect.'

For a moment, he couldn't believe it. The words sent a knife of uncertainty plunging into his heart. 'But doesn't that mean —?'

Hegelia's sympathy had run dry. Her voice was strident again. 'The best way to learn about history, young Jolarr, is to observe it. I would have thought that a boy of your intelligence would recognize that basic fact.'

His throat clenched; it was hard to coax words out. 'What about the Custodians? Their rules of non-intervention?'

'Ha! They expect me to enlighten them by studying dusty relics and collecting exaggerated accounts. No, this is where we need to be, Graduand. Agora, 2191. The final year of the Cyber occupation.'

She treated him to a thin half-smile and declared: 'I like to do my research up close.'

3

Shelter

Taggart had returned to duty in the early afternoon, still haunted by thoughts of Max's brother and, especially, of Lakesmith. He didn't know how his old friend fitted into Henneker's plans, but clearly he did. Tonight's search could imperil the rebellion; perhaps his own life too, if the truth came out.

The worry and the lack of sleep were making him nauseous. Madrox didn't help. He had summoned Taggart to a cell and made him witness to a brutal interrogation. The victim was the man in whose care the shattered rebel leader had been placed a decade and a half ago, to live out his days as an example to dissidents. Madrox had bullied him, bribed him and punched him, but his opponent had kept an obstinate silence. When finally he removed his blaster from its holster, Taggart felt like attacking him, disarming him, killing him. But he didn't.

'I'm going to ask one final time: where is Lakesmith?'

The prisoner spat at him. Madrox flicked his gun to the 'stun' setting, only for the sake of prolonging his enjoyment. He squeezed the trigger and an arc of electricity grounded itself through his target's chest. The man was flung back and his skull cracked on the wall, the echoes of the impact reverberating as he slid into a heap. Madrox fired again and the prone body twitched. One more shot, then he decided to finish it. He switched to 'kill' and aimed for the head. The microwave burst was invisible but effective. As boiling blood erupted across the floor, Taggart heaved and was almost sick.

He averted his eyes and leaned against the wall, legs

weak, bile rising. 'Why did you do that? He could have told us something.'

Madrox shrugged. 'Plenty of people can tell us things. We can find them tonight. I've made our job a little easier. We can loosen tongues by spreading word about the fate of collaborators.'

Taggart swallowed.

'By the way,' said Madrox in a cloying tone, 'with the sad death of our friend here, we're one short of our quota. We'll need to pick up someone else.' His thin lips curved into an insincere smile. 'Should we have to question a suitable candidate, that might give them further incentive to co-operate.'

Taggart was dismissed then. He closed the door behind him and raced along the corridor to escape the grisly scene, as if not seeing it would mean that the corpse was no longer there; no longer on his conscience. He knew why Madrox had required his presence. He suspected him and was putting on pressure. A voice inside him urged compliance. Another resisted. He had sold out one rebellion already and things had only got worse. If he could help it, he wouldn't repeat his mistake.

For the next hour, Taggart performed his duties un-thinkingly, his worries gnawing at his nerves. He wished he could get out to talk to Henneker, to warn him of what was to come. But he was rostered inside Population Control all day and he couldn't leave without Madrox noticing. There was only one thing he could try: a desperate gamble, for which he had spent three weeks unable to gather the courage.

It was pure luck that, today, it was his turn to water the special prisoner.

The robots were after him. Grant ran in blind panic across the battlefield. He ignored the explosions of mortar fire, the smoke and the sounds drifting closer. He stumbled, roots pulling at his ankles, and sprawled face-first, hands fighting for purchase on the soggy ground. He levered himself upright, coughing up mud, and staggered on. His neck hairs bristled and he knew they were closing in. He made the mistake of looking back. And then he was down again, encircled by wire; a fence he had not seen. His skin was lacerated, blood seeping down his forehead, and he gave up the struggle as he accepted that, not only was he entangled, but his pursuers had caught him.

They gathered in a half circle, leering down with ghoulish, too-human expressions. He recognized the advertising drones which peddled burgers in Newer York, and Bloodsoak Bunny, the manic star of a TV show which had been reprogrammed to kill him. He couldn't make out the details of the others. They were silver and humanoid, but their faces were obscured as if by drops of mercury on his glasses.

Another figure pushed through the crowd. Grant saw the gentle features of its heart-shaped face and smelt the lilac fragrance of its perfume. The robots cowered from this powerful, human woman as she reached out to protect the suddenly infant Grant from the terrors of the world. Grant let her take him and hoist him to her breast. Then the fleshy veneer fell away and he glimpsed metal behind her peeling skin as her grip tightened around his arms and she began to squeeze the life from him.

He woke in a sweat, his heart attempting to leap from his chest. He flinched from the feel of hands on his arms and focused his vision on Henneker, who was kneeling beside him and shaking him awake.

'Come on, Grant, we need you!'

Max was standing behind the rebel leader, arms folded in severe disapproval. Another man lurked by the ladder: a short, nervous-looking character who Grant recognized as a sympathizer to the cause. 'What's going on?' he asked blearily.

'Aliens,' Henneker whispered. 'Two more, in the colony. We have to get to them before the Overseers do.'

* * *

The Doctor beamed as Taggart peered through the viewing hatch. He fumbled with the keys and dropped them twice before opening the door.

'More water already?' The prisoner's cracked voice held a tired irony. 'Your hospitality spoils me.' Taggart gave him an embarrassed smile and raised the tin jug to the Doctor's lips. He sipped from it gratefully. 'I expect you're worried I might slim down until I can slip out of my shackles?'

Taggart merely grunted. Communication was forbidden. What if he was caught? He got up and walked towards the door. His courage had failed him again.

'Aren't you going to talk?' the Doctor called. Taggart paused on the threshold. He wanted to, badly.

'I'm the Doctor.'

'I know. Ben Taggart.' He glanced into the corridor. It was empty.

'Hello, Ben Taggart.' In a conspiratorial tone, the Doctor added, 'There won't be a patrol for another six minutes. I've been timing them. They're very accurate.'

Taggart knew that too, but it helped to hear it said. With sudden decisiveness, he crossed the cell, not giving himself time for second thoughts. He knelt by the Doctor's side and held the jug so it looked as if he might only be performing his duty. 'I need help.'

'You're not the only one.'

'You're supposed to be an enemy of the Cybermen, aren't you?' He tried not to let his voice betray how unlikely that seemed. He failed. The Doctor noticed.

'I have defeated them on several occasions,' he said pompously.

'How do you do it?'

'They have certain weaknesses. Their logical minds can lead them to adopt a blinkered view. They aren't as adaptive to the unexpected as organic beings, nor do they appreciate the value of intuition.'

'Oh. Nothing more . . . useful?'

The Doctor rolled his eyes before answering with a measure of contempt. 'They don't like gold.'

'But we don't have any. It doesn't occur naturally on Agora, and everything our ancestors brought from Earth went off in the colony ship with a splinter faction.'

'To New Earth, yes. Well, radiation affects some types of Cyberman too.'

'So we could flood Population Control with it!'

The Doctor's look was withering. 'The average human doesn't exactly have a high radiation tolerance either. Besides, by this time, I'm sure the Cybermen have evolved their way out of that weakness.' Taggart was deflated. 'No, on the whole, I think your best bet is to set me free. Then I can improvise.'

Taggart blanched. 'I can't.' He indicated the stocks. 'Only the Cybermen know how to open those things.'

'I'm aware of that. But get me a screwdriver, a pin or anything. I can get into the mechanism and spring it.'

The thought of that brought Taggart's worries back. If the Doctor escaped and Madrox found out how, his life would be forfeit, no doubt about it. It was too big a risk for too small a gain. He had confirmed his suspicions that this man was helpless. Even free, he could do nothing to save Agora.

Still, he had summoned up the nerve to get this far. He couldn't leave without achieving something. 'What's happening out there?' he asked in desperate hope. The Doctor looked puzzled, so Taggart elucidated: 'Do people know about us? Are they sending help?' He was almost begging now. 'We sent a message to New Earth, thirteen years ago. They must have done something.'

The Doctor's expression was hopelessly pitying. He imparted the news as gently as he could. 'New Earth doesn't have that sort of technology. They can't compete against a Cyber army. They probably sent a message to Old Earth, but . . . well, humans aren't well known for stepping in to end such conflicts on their own planet. I don't think Earth governments would be interested in a second-hand report about a far-flung colony that hasn't made contact since it was established. And, even with the best of intentions, they've had their own problems. It's been a hard time for Earth since 2157.'

'War?' asked Taggart disbelievingly.

'Of sorts. They won, don't worry, but they're busy rebuilding.'

Taggart's despair was total. His mind fixated on the stark, cruel fact that there was no help on its way. Of course, he had known that intellectually for years. He had known how futile it was to cling to hopes. But it still hurt to have it so categorically confirmed.

'Set me free,' the Doctor urged. 'I can get you out of this.'

Taggart didn't believe him, and the entreaty served only to snap his dismal thoughts back to reality. With renewed awareness of his tenuous position came a strong return of his fear of discovery. He had lost track of time, but the patrol must be due soon – and he would have to report to Madrox for night duty.

'I'm sorry,' he mumbled as he jumped to his feet. The Doctor looked astonished that he had chosen to abandon him. He shouted his name as he hurried away, but Taggart hardened his resolve against the calls. He slammed the cell door shut, blotting out the prisoner's expression of accusatory disappointment.

'Cowards die many times before their deaths, Ben Taggart!' the Doctor bellowed after him. Taggart knew the Shakespearian quote well; it had occurred to him before.

But things were hopeless. He could do nothing.

By the time Hegelia and Jolarr returned to the market-place, the traders' wares were being packed away, the stalls disassembled. An air of doom prevailed and people were vanishing from the streets with haste. 'It seems,' said Hegelia, 'that a curfew is in operation.'

'What should we do then?' asked Jolarr, careful not to sound frightened. 'We can't stay out here all night.'

'I am sure that will not be necessary.'

Jolarr wished he could share her confidence. At least, he reminded himself, the Cybermen were off-planet. For a few seconds, when Hegelia had told him the year, he had experienced a nauseous terror, expecting synthetic hands to erupt from the ground and seize him. The ArcHivist had dispelled that notion. She knew more about events here than she had admitted to the Custodians. The decaying journals of an Agoran native had enabled her to date the Cybermen's occupation precisely and had established that they visited only once every three years. At the moment, it was small comfort.

'What are you going to do?' he asked. 'Find someone to interview?'

'If you wish,' said Hegelia, but she made no move to act on the suggestion. Jolarr wondered if she was waiting for him to take the initiative. But before he could do any such thing, he heard footsteps; not the timid scamperings of the peasants, but rather the heavy, accordant tramp of military men.

Without thinking, he took Hegelia's shoulder and propelled her into the shadow of a nearby hut, his fear of such improper action outweighed by that of likely capture. For a moment, he squirmed beneath her disapproving glare. Then five men marched into view. They halted and their leader spoke with the people outside – the sort of speaking which requires a gun.

'He is asking for information,' Hegelia observed.

'About us?'

'I dare say it is possible.'

Jolarr quelled a groan and backed around the side of the building. He was dismayed to see that Hegelia remained at its corner. He wanted to drag her away, to berate her for imperilling their lives. He couldn't. She was an ArcHivist – and not just any one.

To Jolarr's relief, she eventually joined him. Her expression was thoughtful as she operated her recorder and dictated in a voice which was dangerously loud. 'As I predicted, the Cybermen have placed human agents in charge of enforcement. Their uniforms differ markedly from the normal garb of the Agorans and I

49

would postulate that these have been provided for them. Although I have observed them only from a distance, they seem to incorporate flexible armour. Machinery is contained within the chest area, perhaps something similar to the Cybermen's own units. Their guns –'

She was interrupted by a hissing sound which made Jolarr jump. He cast about for its source, then realized that the noise had been made by human vocal chords. An old woman, grey-haired and leathern-skinned, had pushed open the shutters of a window above them. She was leaning out and waving to attract their attention.

'You'd better get off the streets,' she called in a low voice. 'Go round the back and I'll let you in.'

Jolarr looked to Hegelia and thankfully welcomed her assenting nod.

When Madrox was convinced that there was nothing to learn from the traders, Patrol Four moved on. The red sun was sinking; long shadows presaged the onset of curfew and the streets were deserted in anticipation. Taggart marched behind Madrox and beside his Patrol Leader, hiding the misery which weighed down his thoughts. He had revealed as little as he could. The names he had given were of people who could only be peripherally involved, if at all. They had been leading lights in the old rebellion, but were too old and dispirited to take part in the new one. Madrox would see that. With luck, he would accept that Taggart knew nothing of recent developments.

The Chief Overseer hammered on a door. Taggart had expected him to simply barge in. A minute passed, then a familiar face appeared: Warner, an old friend. His grey eyes registered shock at the delegation awaiting him. Taggart hoped he could forgive him for bringing it.

Madrox gripped the front of the old man's nightshirt and swung his slender body out into the street. He prodded him with his blaster so that Warner was forced to skip backwards. Then he screamed theatrically: 'I hear you are involved in a rebellion. You will tell me all you know or suffer the consequences!'

'I – I –' Warner stammered.

Madrox flicked the setting of his gun to 'kill'. 'I want names, locations and details of plans. If you do not give them to me, I will destroy you!'

Taggart heard the creak of window shutters. They had attracted attention. They were in the centre of the village, visible from many homes. He felt a stab of fury as he realized Madrox had planned it that way. He knew Warner couldn't have done what he accused him of, but a public show of force might make others talk.

Madrox turned his weapon and swung it, striking Warner across the head. He fell to his knees and buried his face as the Chief Overseer drove another blow into his neck. 'Tell me!' he shrilled. Then, in a calmer voice: 'I will give you five seconds. Five.'

Taggart flinched as Madrox re-aimed his gun. 'Four.'

This was his fault. 'Three. Two.'

He couldn't do anything.

'One.'

'No!' Taggart stepped forward and knocked the gun's barrel aside. For a second, Madrox didn't look up. Taggart's anger subsided and fear replaced it. But when Madrox faced him, it was with a slight smile.

'Overseer?'

'I was wrong,' he said, voice trembling. 'Warner's not involved. He can't be. Look at him.'

'I agree.' The smile broadened and the gun was brought to bear again. One squeeze of the trigger would end Warner's life. 'But you can tell me who is, can't you, Overseer? Truthfully, this time?'

Grant and Henneker watched, concealed beside a ramshackle hut. There was nothing they could do against five Overseers, even if one might be willing to help. As Henneker had unhappily conceded, they had to bide their time.

Grant didn't want to be there at all. He had made that clear as he had followed Henneker into the open. 'What is the point of risking our lives like this?' he had asked.

'We have no choice. These aliens might have knowledge or technology to help us, like you did. We can't let it fall into the wrong hands.'

Grant had half-heartedly persisted, knowing that his was a doomed argument. Henneker could be more stubborn than Max. He wished he had had the surgeon's courage. She had told their leader that she was too busy to be running his fool's errand – and even the villager who had stumbled into the bunker and breathlessly imparted his information had backed away with a series of excuses.

Grant had given in – and so he was here, lying flat on his stomach in the centre of Liberty (or Sector One, as it had been renamed), regretting that he had heeded Max's advice to leave his glasses behind as he squinted myopically into the darkness. 'They'll pay for this tomorrow,' vowed Henneker. 'Madrox especially.'

Grant wasn't so sure, but this was no time to differ. He tugged at his colleague's sleeve. 'At least they can't know about the aliens, else they'd be looking for them too.'

Henneker nodded and turned away reluctantly. Grant guessed that force of habit alone added confidence to his next words. 'Come on then, let's carry on searching. We're a step ahead of the Overseers, at least.'

Taggart had not given Henneker away. But he had, under threat of an old friend's death, revealed the names of some people he knew to be helping him. The second of these had avoided the brutal, public and messy fate of the first by making even Taggart seem tight-lipped. He had not known the location of the bunker, but Madrox didn't care. He had the name of the rebel leader and, jubilantly, he led the patrol to Henneker's home.

He was disappointed (and Taggart was secretly relieved) to find nobody in residence. He discharged his gun into the ground and ranted until Taggart feared that he would drag each one of the missing man's neighbours outside and kill them to relieve his frustration. It was at times like this when Madrox was most frightening. His anger was typically uncontrolled, bordering on the fanatical; he could snap at any moment and sometimes did. This time, however, the tirade ended without casualties. The Chief Overseer stood, breathing deeply to bring himself back into harness. His stony face was set harder than normal and his lank brown hair shone with perspiration.

That was when an elderly woman stepped from the shadows and coughed politely. Alert and dangerous again, Madrox whirled and brought his gun up to cover the newcomer. 'You are breaking curfew, citizen!' he shouted with unnecessary venom. He switched the weapon to 'stun'; more, Taggart thought, to make a threatening click than because he felt merciful.

'I'm sorry, sir,' the woman said, 'but I thought you'd want to know as soon as possible. There are aliens in the colony.'

Madrox's expression froze. He took another measured breath, his nostrils flaring, and lowered the gun slightly. 'I took them into my home,' the woman said, a little more confidently now that she had her ruler's interest. 'I thought it was best to keep them there until I could contact you.'

The change in Madrox was total. He relaxed and let his gun hand fall to his side. 'You did right,' he said, and a nasty smile of triumph spread across his features.

'I've got you, Time Lord,' he whispered, staring into the distance as if at his absent foe. 'Got you!'

Jolarr wriggled uncomfortably on a lumpy mattress. In the next berth, Hegelia lay fully clothed on her back, asleep despite everything. They had not learned much from their host – the ArcHivist had been particularly irritated by the woman's refusal to discuss the Cybermen – but at least, for tonight, they seemed safe enough. Jolarr hated to think beyond that.

Awake and restless, he climbed off the bed and stood

by the window, staring through the slats of the shutters at the landscape of a world not his own. He shivered and considered another advantage of HyperReality: the machine's 'off' node, to provide immediate withdrawal from unpleasant situations.

He withdrew instinctively when he saw the security men – Overseers, the woman had called them – marching across the empty market square. It took him a second or two to realize that his supposedly gracious host was accompanying them. More time slipped through his grasp as he tried to convince himself that he was imagining things. And then he heard the downstairs door crashing open and his most pessimistic thoughts were proved well founded.

Jolarr rushed to where Hegelia lay and shook her. She didn't wake and he didn't have time to try again. He rushed out onto the landing, but one of the Overseers – a hazel-haired man with a stern face, flared nostrils and eyes which rivalled Hegelia's for intensity – was on the stairs and fast approaching. 'I am Chief Overseer Madrox and you are under arrest. Don't try to resist!'

He backed away. Madrox closed the gap between them and reached for him, but Jolarr lashed out instinctively and his would-be captor stumbled backwards. The rest of the Overseers – presumably his subordinates – crowded the stairway as if eager to be seen to help.

In desperation, Jolarr vaulted the wooden banister. He made a jarring landing in the hallway far below and fell against the wall. Necessity made him ignore the pain. He recovered his balance and went for the door, shoving off the Overseer who moved to block him. He was centimetres from freedom when a shot rang out and a stabbing sensation numbed the muscle in his left shoulder. He grunted, twisted and hit the door frame. Two Overseers closed in but he thrashed his arms and, somehow, his lithe form managed to slip through them.

He was clear then, racing into the night, his grazed arm hanging like a dead weight, limping to favour his injured foot. Unfamiliar buildings flashed by. He didn't know

54

where he was going. All he could think was that Hegelia was surely a prisoner. He couldn't hide behind her wisdom any longer. Jolarr had seen no signs of pursuit, but still he ran. There was nothing else to do.

Two figures loomed before him and he swerved to avoid them. Too late. He was held in the muscular arms of a tall, broad man who hissed at him to be quiet and still; he was amongst friends. It took a few seconds for that to register, then Jolarr ceased his struggles and was set free. He stepped back, head aching and legs feeling hollow in the aftermath of adrenalin-fuelled activity. The man who had held him was in his mid-twenties. Blond hair fell down in a straight fringe, cutting across one calculating blue eye. His face was strong and determined. His companion was only a few years older than the Graduand himself. He stood back, waiting on the other's lead.

'There were two of you,' the older man said. 'What happened to the woman?'

'Your security people – the Overseers – caught her.'

'Right. Let's get you to the bunker. We can talk there.' He set off at a trot, without checking to see if they were following. He was used to being obeyed, Jolarr concluded – and, despite his weariness, he fell into step beside the teenager. They jogged in silence for an indeterminate time and it occurred to him that they were heading towards the complex at the colony's centre. They didn't get there.

The blond man stopped and chivvied them into the darkness between two houses. Four Overseers appeared in the street. They were running and their ranks were broken, in contrast to the military precision of the group he had seen earlier. This was no routine patrol. They were searching. The fugitives backed down the passage and emerged into a square, surrounded by windows. Jolarr couldn't shake the idea that the buildings had eyes and were relaying his location to his enemies. He was relieved when they passed quickly through the place, and soon he noticed that the leader was attempting to bring them around in a circle. Once again, they were kept from their destination.

The man cursed as he turned and led them back, his speed increased by urgency. 'I don't understand,' he said, once they were unobserved, huddled by the blind side of a storage hut. 'They're blocking us all ways.'

'They couldn't have found the bunker, could they?' his companion asked with a hint of panic.

The leader shook his head, but the denial was hardly wholehearted. He was scared too, and his fear grew visibly as they all heard footsteps, perilously close. 'I don't believe this!' He led them away, keeping low as they darted from shadow to shadow, alert for signs of movement. They changed course several times, veering one way then another, always finding the Overseers one step ahead, slowly herding them into a corner.

They emerged onto the sloping grassland which separated the village from the Cyber complex. The blond man hesitated and cast about in agitation. Then he looked at Jolarr, saw the ragged sleeve of his suit where the gunshot had hit, and cursed again. 'They've tagged you!'

To Jolarr, the words were like the pronouncement of a death sentence. He listened dazedly as the man informed him that they couldn't help. Their only hope was to separate, so that maybe one of them could get through the blockade. He gave Jolarr no time to argue. He pushed him back towards the village and sent his colleague to the right. He raced in the opposite direction himself and Jolarr was left conspicuously alone.

He took a few staggering, automatic steps before he came to a fear-frozen halt at the village border. A cluster of figures loomed out of the darkness and Jolarr stared down the muzzles of four guns.

Grant stumbled on through the undergrowth, the coiled wire which surrounded Population Control his only point of reference through the darkness and his short-sightedness. It occurred to him that Henneker had sent him away from the bunker, towards which he himself had headed. Was he really so expendable, he wondered?

For a minute he thought he was going to make it anyway. The patrols had closed in on the alien, allowing him to escape. He could slip through their net. Then a powerful light stabbed out from the metal building, obscuring his vision with balls of yellow. He tried to keep going, but fell against the wire. A barb cut through his thin Agoran clothing and gouged a bloody line into his leg. He tore himself free with no thought to the pain and carried on running. The ground rolled beneath him at a terrifying speed and his mind insisted that he could fall at any moment. His subconscious countermanded any such concern and drove him on. His lungs were bursting, his legs ached and he experienced a flashback to the nightmare battlefield, imagining dreadnoughts hard on his heels.

Grant was no longer conscious of his surroundings, just of the imperative to keep running for survival.

As usual, it was all Ben Taggart's fault. He had seen the alien in his sights and hesitated, but had been only too aware of Madrox's presence. He had thumbed the switch on his gun to the third and least harmful setting, then fired. The pellet had hit, sending a mildly radioactive dye into its target's bloodstream and ensuring that he would show up on scans. Madrox had called out every patrol to apprehend the fugitive. The Chief Overseer had been in his element, rapping orders into his tech-unit, acknowledging news of the alien's capture, arranging for a floodlight to help find the others and co-ordinating his underlings to close inexorably in on the conspirators. He enjoyed cat and mouse games, particularly when he couldn't lose.

They heard the shouts of the Patrol Three Leader first and saw the boy seconds later, by the fence of Population Control. He seemed to be a colonist, but with the light behind him, it was hard to tell. He doubled back from the first patrol towards Taggart's and, finding himself surrounded, was paralysed like a threatened rabbit. The

Overseers closed in and Taggart shaded his eyes, his own vision not yet adjusted, to make out who they had caught. Please don't let it be Henneker, he prayed.

Madrox operated the bio-scan mode of his tech-unit. 'An Agoran native,' he confirmed, 'but one whose identity is not registered.' He folded the unit back into its housing, deciding that the problem could wait. He sneered triumphantly at his captive and produced the studded leather glove from his belt strap. He slipped it on and delivered a blow to the boy's face. His victim fell, nose bleeding.

Patrol Six arrived, the boy from the house cuffed to its Leader. Madrox didn't need to scan him. The strange material of his clothes would have marked him out as an offworlder even if his white skin, his thatch of short black hair and his deep, black, almond-shaped eyes had not. 'So we have the Doctor's other companion, yes? Well, we have certainly met our quota for this period.' The Agoran native had been hauled to his feet and Madrox looked him in the eye. 'In fact, we seem to have more bodies than we can use.'

The boy didn't meet his stare. His head dropped and turned so that his profile was illuminated. Taggart studied his face, clearly visible for the first time – and, unexpectedly, a dam burst in his mind and allowed a startling truth to flood in.

At first, he tried to deny it. He looked for some feature to disprove his mad theory. It had been thirteen years, after all. How could he be sure that this was the same person? But the more he stared, the more obvious the resemblance was. It was him.

This wasn't fair. What was the boy doing here? Why now?

After all this time, why had Grant Markham made the fatal mistake of coming home?

4

New Man

Hegelia had heard the approach of her captors in time to get to her feet, pat down her crumpled robes and adjust her hair. She had greeted them, arms folded, looking like a queen in her finery. 'At last!' she had said. 'Do you know how long I have waited?'

Truth to tell, the ArcHivist had half expected this. She had not been surprised to hear the pleadings of the old woman as she was led past her: 'You will remember I've been loyal? I have a young son. He's my last.'

Despite her vehement objections, Hegelia had been handcuffed. She had approached Population Control, nevertheless, with customary dignity. It would seem to spectators, she decided, that she was the jailer, her guard the prisoner. They stopped at the gates and she watched as he sent out an ultrasonic signal from his tech-unit. A camera swivelled to observe them, then the wire-mesh barricade swung open.

They followed an erratic path across the grounds, the Overseer studying his unit as it guided them through ground-based defences. Hegelia was careful to tread only where his footprints had flattened the grass. Another signal and another camera gave them access to the building proper. She marvelled at its construction: simple, efficient and logical. It was typical of Cyber architecture, and it thrilled her to observe it as its creators intended, instead of sifting through rusted ruins.

The Overseer left her in a rectangular cell. She saw, with some irritation, that it was not empty. Her cohabitant was a youngish man with fair hair and gaudy clothing, from which she inferred that he was not an Agoran. His wrists were manacled and his neck held in restraints which forced him to kneel. His face was dirty and bruised and the ArcHivist's impression was of some sort of vagabond.

'Are you here to question me?' he asked, when they were alone. 'Beat me up?' He raised a hopeful eyebrow. 'Free me, perhaps?'

She sniffed. 'Our imprisonment is the only thing we have in common. I suggest we do not waste our time in chatter.'

'Quite right,' he said in an ebullient tone. 'Why don't we get straight down to the business of escaping?'

'I have no wish to leave.'

'You don't?' He seemed puzzled. Then he brightened. 'Perhaps you could just help me then?'

She rounded on him. 'Young man, I do not think you have listened to a word I have said.'

'And I'm the Doctor. Nice to meet you. Excuse me if I don't rise.'

'No – you can't be!'

Her fellow prisoner shrugged with false modesty (no mean feat, held as he was). 'I have been told that my youth belies the reality of my reported exploits.'

She wasn't convinced. 'The same Doctor who is spoken of in the history of the Cybermen?'

'I rather hoped they would be spoken of in mine.'

'You repelled the invasion of Earth in 1970?'

'Not to mention 1986, when Mondas returned to its solar system.'

'You are the same Doctor who sealed the tombs on Telos?'

'Not quite the same, but –'

'Which regeneration?'

Hegelia had caught him offguard with that question. He clearly hadn't expected her to know so much. 'Well . . . number six.'

'You fought them in Antarctica when they tried to sabotage the FLIPback project!'

'I really don't think you want to be telling me that.'

60

'Your future,' Hegelia guessed. 'I remember you now, from the description. Of your jacket, at least. You are the one who returned to Telos when the Cybermen discovered time travel.'

'Guilty as charged.'

Hegelia brimmed over with resentment at a role model destroyed. 'Then how can it be that you, the so-called arch-foe of the Cyber race, can in reality be such a facetious buffoon?'

The Doctor frowned. 'You know, if you weren't such a fan, I could get quite upset about remarks like that.'

Grant had been left with the alien boy in a metal box-room, the dimensions of which gave them barely enough space to both sit at the same time. His cellmate had introduced himself as Jolarr, but had said little since. Grant wondered if he was shy or just antisocial. He wasn't too adept at small talk himself, so after a startlingly misjudged comment along the lines of 'I hope the Cybermen turn up soon – I'm getting cramp,' he decided to make do with an awkward silence.

Amidst the background clangour, he failed to hear footsteps approaching. A viewing hatch was pulled back and Grant recognized the fervid eyes of Madrox. The door was yanked open to reveal him in full, with another Overseer at his shoulder. This one had black hair and a moustache and the lines of his face suggested that his miserable expression was habitual. Grant had seen him in the village.

'Out,' said the Chief Overseer curtly. Both prisoners struggled to their feet, but Madrox pushed Jolarr back. 'Not you.' He turned to Grant. 'I want to ask you a few questions. Bring him, Taggart.'

He turned and marched away. The man who had been identified as Taggart locked the door and took Grant's arm. As he did, he whispered, 'Don't give him your real name.' Grant nodded, recalling that Henneker had mentioned a 'Taggart' on many occasions. It was comforting to have an ally present, although Henneker had often complained about this one. He couldn't be relied upon.

Grant was led down metal corridors, all boringly similar, until he suspected that Madrox was taking him in circles deliberately to prolong the suspense. The monotony was broken as they descended two flights of a winding staircase. Then it was back to identical corridors for a further time. Eventually, they reached a small room, furnished only with a table and two chairs and lit by a bare bulb which concentrated light upon its centre whilst leaving the corners shadowed. It was an interesting contrast to the small, efficient lighting panels which punctuated the ceilings elsewhere.

Grant was ordered to take one chair, whilst Madrox sat in the other and leered across the table. Taggart stood by the doorway, not quite managing to look like a smart and efficient guard. When questioned, Grant took his advice and proffered a pseudonym. He chose 'Stuart Revell', but wished he hadn't. That had been the name of his best friend on New Earth. He had died, minutes before Grant had left his adoptive homeworld. Thrown from one dangerous situation to another, surrounded by unfamiliar things, it was easy to forget that one part of his life had gone for ever. He hadn't yet grieved properly and the memory of Stuart opened up a well of misery.

He steeled himself and tried not to think about it as he used a cover story prepared by Henneker. He said he had been born in the Outlands, the wilderness beyond the colony. It was a plausible lie. Several people had fled there over the years, as Madrox knew. He sent out odd patrols to bring some back, but only as a token gesture. When the Cybermen had taken over, they had done something to Agora's sun which had altered its climate. It was hotter than before and rain was less frequent. Crop growth was difficult, and away from Population Control's alien food synthesizers, life was tough. Desertion, therefore, was a minor problem. The colonists stood more chance of surviving by keeping their heads down and following orders.

That was why, Grant said, he had opted to rejoin civilization as soon as he had grown up and left his parents. 'Perhaps you need a little time then,' Madrox growled with irony, 'to become accustomed to our laws – particularly those pertaining to curfew hours and to fraternization with dissidents.' Grant had no answer to that.

'Who else was with you?'

Madrox had to ask the question again, and even then Grant only managed to answer with a mumbled: 'I'm sorry?' He could feel himself beginning to tremble. He couldn't handle this. Whatever he said, he was going to give himself and the rebels away.

'There were two of you with the alien,' said Madrox, more fiercely. 'Who was the other man?'

'I still believe it must have been Henneker,' Taggart put in. Madrox shot him a furious glare.

Grant seized upon the lifeline, nodding eagerly. 'It was. I remember now, that's how he introduced himself. I just . . . I ran into them both while I was exploring.'

Madrox leaned back and his face slipped into shadow. All Grant could see was the insane light of his eyes. 'I should kill you.' He fingered the muzzle of his gun, then added, 'I would be loath to waste such a specimen, though. Your tech-scan shows you are in fine condition apart from a degree of short-sightedness. We can correct that with laser surgery.' His mouth curled into a cruel half sneer. 'The Cybermen replace most of the eye during conversion anyway.'

Another pause, then Madrox made an attempt at a more genuine smile. 'Of course, you are also at a prime age for use as breeding stock – and, fortunately for you, we have now filled our last vacancy in Population Control. According to his scan, your friend is not so alien as to be unsuitable. I would suggest that, as you have a three-year reprieve, you use it to impress me. It could save your life.'

If I'm still here in three years, Grant thought, you can have it.

Hegelia was becoming tired and impatient. The absence of furniture forced her to stand, for to sprawl upon the floor would have been unseemly. She had hoped to have been attended to by now; to have had her demands for a transfer heeded. The last thing she wanted was to have to cope with the unceasing inanity of her present companion.

He never gave up. 'I'm only asking for a hairpin. Rassilon knows, you're wearing enough to keep a voodoo enthusiast satisfied into the next decade.'

She tried again, making her fraying patience obvious. 'As I have attempted to explain, I have travelled to this world from the far future. I cannot risk actions which could alter my past.'

'That's preposterous,' he retorted. 'By being here at all, you're risking that. If you hadn't been placed in this cell, I might have ended up sharing with someone more obliging. You could be keeping me trapped here when I should be out defeating Cybermen!'

Hegelia wanted to refute his argument, but found that she couldn't. The Doctor noticed her consternation and pressed his advantage. 'If I die now because of you – before I've averted this flipflop disaster, or whatever it was – you might not have a present to return to. Are you so keen on the idea of letting the Cybermen destroy Earth and perhaps go on to conquer the galaxy?'

He was swaying her. But no. He was appealing to emotions and they could provide no basis on which to act. Cold rationality was the only way to decide. The only way to ensure efficiency. 'I know little about the events of this epoch, Doctor. However, history dictates that you do not die here, and that the Cybermen will return to Agora only once more. It will happen without my interference.'

'But with what consequences? How many deaths?' Her fellow prisoner was losing his temper. How improper of him, Hegelia thought. 'You might well be right. The Cybermen may not come back after this next time. If they were to leave the colony a radioactive cinder, there'd be no point, would there?'

'The problems of a primitive few in this era are of no long-term importance.'

'A "primitive few"?' the Doctor exploded. 'The Cybermen are due here in a matter of hours to harvest five hundred poor unfortunates from inside this building.' He jabbed a finger as best he could to his right, to the back of the cell. 'There's a boy on the far side of that wall, alone and terrified of what they're going to do to him. Do you want to try explaining to him how his fate won't matter in a few centuries' time? That he's going to die because of your supercilious indifference?'

Hegelia felt her own feelings stirring in response to his misapprehension. 'He is not going to die, Doctor. The Cybermen kill only those who resist them. That boy, along with all other occupants of this complex, will simply be converted.'

'Into one of their own soulless kind!' the Doctor snapped.

'Is that such a bad thing?' She caught his scandalized expression and stooped to bring their eyes level. She orated with passion, 'Imagine that you can live for ever and life is totally free from pain. You can see all things with clarity and always make the right choice, unblinkered by irrelevant details. You know what you want and you have the intelligence, the power and the drive to achieve it. You will never regret your actions, never become confused. Never fear, never sicken, never lose control. That, Doctor, is what the Cybermen are offering.'

'The opportunity to become a faceless member of their army,' he countered scornfully. 'To follow orders, to live without emotion, to sacrifice the experiences which make existence worthwhile.'

'It is not such a sacrifice.'

'In that case, why don't they give their victims a choice?' He pointed again to the rear wall. 'My friend through there wouldn't let them rip out his heart and lungs and replace his frontal lobes with machinery!'

'He will feel quite differently once he is converted.'

'Well, yes,' said the Doctor, 'that's my point exactly.'

She had no response to his acid observation. She thought of the fear amongst the people of her own time, the haunted looks which shadowed their eyes when the possibility of a Cyber return was mooted. She had intended to treat this exploration with the detachment she employed in poring over old, corrupted files. The thought that she was amongst real people – real, frightened people – was one which unsettled her. She had hoped to deny it.

She changed the subject to an easier one. 'Why do you require my assistance anyway? I had heard you were a passable escape artist.'

'Oh, yes. The Cybermen heard that too. They took precautions. The Overseers searched me for sonic devices, locked me into this thing and didn't even equip my cell with a camera to strip down for spare parts. If you were to collapse with a critical illness, I doubt they would even open the door. They know my tricks too well.'

'Then has it not occurred to you,' said Hegelia haughtily, 'that they would not have placed me in here if they believed I could help?'

'Of course it has. But there's no harm in trying, is there?'

'Perhaps so, if this is some sort of trap. It may be the Overseers' intention to allow you to break free. Have you considered that?'

'I agree,' said the Doctor, 'but on the whole, I'd rather take my chances against whatever they're planning without the shackles. At least I'd be able to scratch my neck.'

Hegelia glared at him, but was met only by a compelling expression of optimism. She sighed, reached up and yanked a pin from her carefully sculpted *coiffure*. 'The locking panel is under a small cover next to my right ear,' said the Doctor hopefully.

Hegelia gave him the pin with bad grace. 'I believe you can reach it.'

'Thank you very much.' He grinned a madman's grin.

'I have to say,' said Hegelia, frowning in a mixture of disapproval and respect, 'that you are hardly what I expected.'

By the time Taggart and Grant left Population Control, the morning was well advanced. The sun, however, was invisible and the clouds which obscured it had darkened. Within the day it would surely rain, for the first time in months. Taggart was saddened by the unbidden memories of another deluge, fifteen years past, and a desperate battle which his cowardice had lost. He hoped things would work out better this time.

At least something had gone right. Madrox had ordained that 'Stuart Revell' should find a home, and Taggart had been charged with finding a space for him and adding his name and new address to census records. Once they were past the perimeter fences, this gave them a chance to talk in private. The uppermost thing on Taggart's mind was to confirm his suspicions once and for all, although he was sure of them. 'It is Grant, isn't it?'

The boy nodded. 'I suppose Henneker mentioned me?'

Taggart mumbled something non-committal. The truth was, Henneker told him little. 'What was the false name in aid of?' Grant asked.

'Madrox might have remembered your real one from before you left.'

'He might?'

'You don't remember what happened? No, I suppose you wouldn't. You were very young.'

'What did happen?' the boy asked eagerly.

Taggart didn't have time for this. He could only

stay outside for so long before his colleagues became suspicious. There were only a few that he could trust to cover for him. 'We got you off this planet,' he said quickly, 'you and a few others. We wanted at least someone to be free of the Cybermen.'

'I see,' said Grant, although his tone suggested that he didn't. He was plainly going to ask more questions, so Taggart leapt in.

'What the hell are you doing back here?'

'I was travelling with the Doctor. Didn't Henneker tell you?'

Taggart stopped, astonished, and stared at Grant as if to check for any indication of a lie. 'So you're the mysterious companion that everyone's looking for?' He remembered the two new prisoners and corrected himself: 'One of the companions.'

'The only one. I don't know where the aliens came from.'

Taggart was confused. Still, he needed to get a message to Henneker, that hadn't changed. The rebel leader was probably unaware that Madrox was wise to him. He could go back to his home at any time and run into the patrol which had been left to guard it. That would be disastrous.

'Listen,' he said, 'there's something Henneker needs to know.'

'I'll bet there is,' said Grant. 'What did you give him away for in there, anyway?'

'Madrox knew about him already. I don't know who you were really with last night, but I didn't see the point in tipping him off about someone else.'

Grant nodded understandingly. 'It was actually Henneker.' He thought for a moment, then said: 'The bunker's not far. Have we got time for a detour or will Madrox notice? We can tell Henneker what's happened and see how things are going.'

For a second, Taggart thought about telling Grant that he didn't know where the bunker was. But it had always rankled that Henneker wouldn't trust him with the information, and it would be comforting to see the rebel leader face to face. He glanced back at the complex, an illogical worry telling him that Madrox was standing behind him, staring icily. He wasn't, of course.

Taggart shrugged. 'Lead on,' he said.

They took a sharp turn which led them away from the nearest village and set them on a parallel course to the fence. As they walked, an ominous roll of thunder rent the stillness and Taggart shivered in a sudden rush of freezing air.

The monitor's flickering image showed two figures pushing through the stunted black growth above the rebels' hideaway. Max started when she saw that one wore an Overseer's uniform. She was about to raise the alarm when she recognized the other one as Grant. Then the trapdoor was opened, weak sunlight filtered into the musty bunker and Ben Taggart climbed onto the precarious wooden ladder.

Max's relief was contrasted by Henneker's explosive reaction. 'How the hell did you find us?'

'I needed to talk to you,' said Taggart, sidestepping the question. It seemed obvious to Max that, in fact, Grant had brought him here. One look at the teenager's face showed that he had not known he was breaking a confidence.

Taggart didn't leave time for objections. He launched into his story, to which Max listened with interest. He told them about the aliens, about how Madrox believed they were the long sought-after companions of the Doctor. He then explained how much Madrox had learned of the rebellion and he warned Henneker about a permanent guard on his house. Henneker clearly blamed him for giving away as much as he had, although Max found herself wondering what else he could have done in the circumstances. She had to admit, though, that he posed a problem – which Henneker put into words.

'How do we know you won't give away the location of this place?'

'I won't, I promise,' said Taggart. 'Besides, I think Madrox will leave me alone now. He thinks I've told him everything.'

'We could keep him here,' suggested Max. 'The Cybermen are due today. The Overseers wouldn't have time to miss him before it hits the fan.'

Henneker thought about it. Max saw that Taggart was terrified by the mere prospect. 'No,' the rebel leader said finally, 'we can't afford to let the Overseers know there's anything wrong yet. Anyway, there's something he can do for us.'

'What?' asked Taggart cautiously.

'Free the aliens.'

He immediately turned white, and Max didn't blame him. 'What was that you were saying about tipping our hand?'

'They might not notice a couple of missing prisoners,' Henneker countered. 'Not until it's too late, anyway.'

'You're mad! We don't need to do this. The Project –' She checked her words. They didn't need Taggart to learn even more than he already had done. 'You know how far we progressed last night,' she rephrased carefully. 'What do we need the aliens for?'

'Because, in case you hadn't noticed, we're behind schedule. We won't be ready before the Cybermen arrive, maybe not before they've gone. These people might have weapons or machines which can help. They've certainly got a ship – we know they didn't travel here with Grant – and the Overseers aren't even looking for it.'

'So you're prepared to risk Taggart's life on an off-chance!' Max wondered why she was sticking up for the Overseer. She thought about his patrol taking Martin away and sternly told herself that she had no reason to care about what happened to this traitor. But Henneker was wrong. She had only recently berated him at length for losing Grant, and now she could see

70

him making the same mistake again.

'I'll do it,' said Taggart suddenly. Max suspected that he had meant to appear decisive, but his voice came out small. 'But just the boy,' he said. 'I got the impression that the woman wanted to be captured. I'm not sure she'd co-operate.'

'The boy will be enough,' said Henneker. He smiled victoriously and crossed the room to a corner in which cardboard boxes and paper bags held a plethora of disassembled machinery, mostly junk. He delved into a yellowing bag and pulled out an ageing, weathered Overseer tech-unit. He proffered it to Taggart. 'Here, you can give him this. Get him out of the building, show him the best route to avoid the guards and he'll be able to use it to get the rest of the way to the fence.'

Max snatched the unit from him. 'Where did you get this?'

Henneker seemed inordinately proud of the acquisition. 'Remember when an Overseer patrol disappeared four years ago?'

She did. 'And a dozen young men from Sector Five were tortured and marched off to Population Control in revenge. That's typical of you – it doesn't matter who gets hurt, so long as you get what you want!'

'The Overseers would have filled the complex anyway,' Henneker argued, 'just a little later, that's all. And we can save many more lives by stopping the Cybermen!'

They glared at each other for a long moment. Max was fuming with resentment. So long as he survived, anyone else was expendable, that was the deal. Reluctantly, she had to admit there was some logic to it. Henneker had put a lot of effort into becoming a new figurehead around whom the shattered Agorans could rally. It had taken over a decade to replace Arthur Lakesmith; how much longer to find someone else if Henneker was defeated too? But Max still hated his attitude.

Taggart broke the deadlock. 'I think I'd better go,' he

mumbled. 'I don't want Madrox realizing how long I've been gone.'

Henneker nodded. 'Send the boy as soon as you can. We've only got a few hours.'

Taggart hurried out and, for a minute, a tense silence filled the bunker. Then Grant retrieved his spectacles, with a rueful nod towards Max, and headed towards his makeshift bed with a yawn.

'Wait a minute,' said Henneker. He smiled. 'Max made something of a breakthrough whilst you were gone.'

The reminder of success lifted Max's spirits. She stepped over to the curtain and called, 'Grant's here. Ready to be shown off?'

The boy tensed visibly in anticipation of the unveiling. Max knew why, although she couldn't understand his apprehension. If it hadn't been for him, after all, they might not have reached this stage. He possessed something most Agorans lacked: experience of using technology on a daily basis. He was also well read. The New Earthers had taken all the scientific texts in the colony ship with them, and Grant had pored over a good proportion of them in his time. His knowledge was extensive, if not overly practical, and he had been able to greatly speed up the realization of Henneker's dream.

Once, they had believed it would be another three years before they could think of challenging the Cybermen. Now, they were anticipating immediate action. Of course, there were still problems, and the time factor figured most prominently amongst them. But, for a few seconds, looking at her achievement as it emerged from the work area, none of those things mattered. Max saw the wonder and terror in Grant's eyes and she swore to herself that today would be the day of reckoning.

The invaders would not dare to blight her life again.

The viewing hatch was pulled open to reveal the top half of Madrox's face. 'I thought you might like to know, Doctor,' he sneered, 'we have your other companion; the pale-skinned one. As punishment for your insolence, I have decided to give him to the Cybermen.' He slammed the panel shut with a satisfied clunk.

'Jolarr!' Hegelia whispered in horror, unfolding from the squatting position she had grudgingly taken.

'If conversion is such a life-enhancing process, why the upset?'

'Jolarr is special.'

'All life is special to someone.'

Hegelia refused to rise to the bait. She looked at the Doctor, who had managed to gain access to the controls of his restraints and was prodding about with her hairpin, working by touch. 'He saw you doing that, you know.'

'I know.'

'The fact that he did not say anything proves that he is planning a trap.'

'Not necessarily.' The Doctor sighed. 'The only way to trigger the release mechanism is to input a six-figure combination which changes to a different, random one each second. The Cybermen could do it by communing with the device's AI circuits, but my only hope is to keep guessing.'

Hegelia pursed her lips. 'So what you are saying is that you have an ongoing series of non-cumulative one in a million chances to escape?'

'Exactly.'

'Then it is little wonder that the Chief Overseer did not bother to stop you.'

Rain spotted Taggart's face as he returned to the surface. He hardly noticed. He wanted to turn straight back around and tell Henneker that he'd changed his mind, that he wasn't prepared to throw his life away. Such an action, he knew, would for ever confirm the label of 'coward' with which he had been branded for fifteen years. He would be known as the man who had stolen two chances of freedom.

It was with both irritation and a measure of relief, then,

73

that he realized he had forgotten to arrange Grant's home. It needn't be a problem: Henneker would know of a sympathizer who could provide a bed for the boy without curtailing his illegitimate activities. All Taggart had to do was to get the address and tap it into his unit. Madrox would never suspect foul play. Furthermore, it gave him an excuse to return to the bunker, where something more might be said. Perhaps Max would stand up for him again, relieving him of his unpleasant burden. This time, he wouldn't be stupid enough to argue. He hurried back to the entrance and, casting a glance around, pulled it open and scrambled through.

As he dropped to the floor, he opened his mouth to apologize for this second intrusion. He choked back the words. His eyes, readjusting to the gloom, took in the sight of Henneker, Max and Grant, all standing in a row, their expressions startled, their mouths hanging open. Next, he focused on the unfamiliar figure which lurked in the shadows behind them.

His first impression was of a grotesque statue, composed of a tan metal which was freckled with red as if partially rusted. It was almost six feet tall and humanoid, but it possessed a considerable bulk. Its limbs gave the impression of powerful pistons and, running along each forearm, was a tubular excrescence which could only have been a gun. Its head was fat and angular, its mouth a letter-box slit and its eyes were black slivers beneath a ridged and slightly arched protruding forehead. Its dispassionate expression reminded Taggart of the Cybermen, calling to mind his encounter with those monsters long ago. For a second, he thought this monstrosity must be connected with them. But logic told him that it had to have been in the bunker all along, concealed behind the red curtain. He realized that, finally, he had stumbled upon the truth of Henneker's Project.

'You might as well say hello to your old partner-in-crime,' Max Carter said. 'Meet Arthur Lakesmith, former rebel leader and now the first of our Bronze Knights.'

The figure moved. It seemed to be an effort for it to shift its legs and it jerked, off-balance, as its leading foot crashed into the floor. It lurched towards him ponderously and Taggart backed away until he felt the wooden rungs of the ladder pressing into his back. The creature closed in and he wanted to appeal to Max or Henneker to call it off. He couldn't speak. A hand swung upwards with unexpected speed and took his throat between a pair of cold, rough fingers. Taggart didn't doubt that, just by making a fist, it could snap his bones and crumble them to powder.

'This one knows too much. He has betrayed us before.' The voice was routed through a mechanical filter but, in contrast to the Cybermen's synthesized tones, it retained a trace of humanity. Taggart recognized the inflections of an old friend.

'He cannot be allowed to betray us again,' the Bronze Knight said with chilling certainty. 'I will kill him.'

Ben Taggart found his voice and screamed as the cyborg monster tightened its grip.

5

Return of the Cybermen

The storm broke at midday. The crash of rain on the tin roof drove itself into Madrox's brain like a never-ending static burst. He patrolled the corridors at random, not caring where he was and wishing fervently that the day was over. He was tired and his head throbbed. He hadn't slept properly for two days. One reason for attaching himself to Patrol Four had been that he would otherwise have spent the night awake, tormented by anticipation. The Cybermen were due in a few hours' time and, contrary to opinion, Madrox hated their visits as much as anyone.

He looked in on the alien boy, but couldn't even work up the enthusiasm to taunt him. Jolarr sat against the far wall of his cell. As the viewing hatch opened, his black eyes turned upwards and he begged, 'Please set me free. I'm from the future, I can't die here.'

Madrox walked away, his footsteps lost to the sounds of the weather. It had been raining that time too, he recalled: 2176, when Vincent Madrox had been sixteen and worried by his status as prime conversion material. Everyone had heard talk of Lakesmith's rebellion and most Agorans were getting their hopes up, looking forward to freedom. Madrox knew more about it than most, but he had a different goal in mind.

His father had gone out to fight for the rebels at dawn. Within six hours, news of their defeat had filtered back to his village. Madrox had slipped out into the downpour and headed in the direction of the loudest screams. The Cybermen were taking bloody vengeance for the uprising, sweeping through the streets and gunning down all who got in their way. Madrox had gaped in awe at the giants, framed by lightning forks which split the sky.

He remembered the fear he had felt as he stepped out boldly in front of one. It had instantly raised its gun to kill him, but he had told it that he wanted to serve. He had knelt respectfully in the squelching mud and awaited its answer. Life or death.

Fifteen years on, Madrox had risen through the ranks of the new Overseers until he had the power he had always yearned for. His secret was blind, unquestioning obedience. There was no way of defeating the Cybermen, so he reasoned that he may as well get something from them. But, along with the position they had given him, came the danger inherent in failing to please them. Madrox was the longest serving Chief Overseer. He had been given the job nine years ago and he had survived two visits; two debasing and terrifying demonstrations of how little influence he really had.

For thirty-five Earth months out of each thirty-six, he knew it was worth it. Whilst he was ruling uncontested, life was good.

But then they came back. They always came back.

Grant's nerves had wound too tight for him to move. One part of him wanted to leap forward and stop the armoured juggernaut which had been Arthur Lakesmith from committing murder. Other, larger, parts were telling him that the others wouldn't welcome his intervention. Above all, Grant felt the quickened pulse and the petrifying attraction/repulsion of a familiar phobia. Lakesmith was a cyborg rather than a robot – but then, so were the Cybermen, from whom his fear was apparently born.

Max was under no such inhibitions. 'Henneker, stop this!' she ordered fiercely. The Bronze Knight hesitated and looked to the rebel leader, who – with, Grant thought, a little reluctance – nodded his assent. Lakesmith released his grip and his former friend stumbled against the wall, breath coming out in ragged wheezes.

Lakesmith lumbered back to his corner, unconcerned by Taggart's condition.

'What – what is that thing?' the Overseer croaked.

'She already told you,' said Henneker, nodding towards Max.

'You might as well know,' said Max. Her sigh broke the tension and made Grant, at least, feel more comfortable. She picked her way through the bunker's clutter and located a splintered wooden chair, from which she had to sweep a pile of papers before she could sit. 'We – or rather, our predecessors – decided that the only way to defeat the Cybermen was to play them at their own game. In other words, to abandon Agora's principles and to use technology against them.'

Taggart was not quite able to support his own weight yet and he propped himself up with one hand against the wall. His eyes were drawn towards Lakesmith. 'I know. I was there, remember? We smuggled items out of Population Control – small things – and started to make bombs. We got guns from the Overseers.'

'Of course,' said Max, 'but what you won't know is what happened after the rebellion.' Taggart bowed his head guiltily. Grant edged around the bunker until he reached the furthest corner from the Bronze Knight, where he lowered himself on to a stool to listen. 'Population Control was looted during the fighting,' Max continued. 'Schematics and components were more readily available in its aftermath. Henneker here began to work on a way of using them. What we didn't have, we arranged to be brought to us – by people like you, Taggart. The problem was, all we could get our hands on was Cyber technology. We wanted to make more guns and more powerful bombs, but our resources were geared towards the cybernetic sciences. We accepted that and we drew up a plan to create an army of creatures to rival the Cybermen. We performed implants, grafts and brain alterations, and now at last our fighting force is taking shape.'

Max would have gone on, happily relating the details of her achievement. Henneker, however, was more concerned with the present. 'We hope to have thirteen Bronze Knights converted before the Cybermen leave. They never send more than eight troops themselves. We should have the advantage of numbers.' His voice took on a hard edge. 'The problem is, as Lakesmith says, what do we do with you?'

Taggart was visibly worried. He steadied himself and answered in a tone of strained confidence. 'Nothing's changed. Madrox thinks I've told him all I know. He'll be occupied, anyway. He gets more worried than anyone when the Cybermen are due.'

Grant found himself looking at Lakesmith again. The first Bronze Knight was facing Taggart with what he fancied was a threatening expression. It wasn't, of course. The sculpted face was incapable of showing emotion. Grant tried to remember that, within the casing, stood a human being, albeit transformed. It would have helped if the Knight had moved at all. Its foot could have shifted, its eyes could have scanned the room, its chest could have pumped with the rhythms of breathing. The absence of such signs of humanity made Grant feel an insane urge to flee. He ignored it, but not without effort.

'I still have the alien boy to free,' said Taggart. 'If you keep me here, or . . . or do anything to me, I won't be able to help you.'

'That's true,' mused Henneker. He turned to Lakesmith. 'What do you think?'

The Bronze Knight answered immediately. Grant didn't know whether its eerie, part-human voice was better or worse than a completely artificial one would have been. 'His mind is inefficient and ruled by fear. He cannot be trusted.'

'I think he can,' Max put in firmly. 'Look at him, he's more scared of you than of the Cybermen!'

'He has reason to be,' the Bronze Knight said.

Grant felt a numbing coldness and shrank back into his

seat. He closed his eyes and wondered how he had come to help create his own worst nightmare.

Madrox had decided to interrogate the Doctor's female companion; not because he needed to learn anything, but rather because he wanted to pass some time in enjoyable activity. Things weren't going as well as he had planned.

'All I am asking,' said Hegelia, 'is that you release my assistant and put me through the conversion process in his place.'

Madrox looked at her incredulously. 'A female of your age?'

'I would still be suitable,' she said primly.

'You're too great a risk. The Cybermen expect prime candidates. Now, I'm sure your friend appreciates your intentions, but let me remind you that you're not exactly free yourself! I'm leaving it to the Cybermen to decide what should be done to you.'

Hegelia rolled her eyes and looked at him as if he was a dim child. 'As I have already explained, Jolarr and I are not in any way associated with the Doctor. You have arrested the wrong people.'

'I don't want to hear that!'

'Then you are deafening yourself to the truth.' She towered above him, having refused to be seated. Madrox had perched himself on his desk, to at least gain some height whilst appearing relaxed. Even so, he was losing control of the interview.

'We are researchers,' Hegelia said again. 'We have come here from the future because we are interested in the Cyber race.'

He glared at her. If this was true, he had failed the Cybermen. He couldn't accept it. 'We have scoured this colony and you and the boy were the only aliens present. Do you expect me to believe that's a coincidence?'

'Did your masters tell you nothing, man? Do you have no idea who you are searching for?' Hegelia sighed, pursed her lips and looked into the distance as she searched her memory. 'You have the sixth incarnation of the Doctor in custody. When he appears in Cyber records, he is accompanied by a young woman named Perpugilliam Brown.' She looked at Madrox, who shook his head. What was she hoping to gain from this?

'There were others, too. I learned of them whilst cross-referencing the Cybermen's timestream with the Doctor's other activities in his section of the Hive. There was a computer programmer from Earth – Melanie, I believe her name was. Before that, a human colonist. Grant. Grant Markham.'

This time, the widening of Madrox's eyes was enough to staunch Hegelia's recital. The name immediately registered as familiar, but it took him a few seconds to remember why. As soon as that happened, the Chief Overseer knew where he had seen Grant Markham recently.

All this time, he had been searching for aliens. All this time, the Doctor's friend had been beneath his nose. An Agoran native. He felt his shoulders tremble with the familiar onset of impotent rage and he buried his face as purple spots rushed in to crowd his vision.

Taggart! He had been present during questioning. He had taken the boy away later. Of all people, he must have known who he was. He had won the contest. He had kept his secrets hidden, after all.

Madrox released a scream and attacked the desk with his gun barrel. When that failed to relieve his frustration, he struck the wall hard enough to make the room shake. Then he stood and controlled his breathing, listening to the ringing reverberations.

'Have you quite finished?' asked Hegelia sarcastically.

Madrox scowled at her and raised his blaster, perturbed to notice that it had been bent out of shape. It now pointed downwards. 'As far as the Cybermen are concerned,' he growled regardless, 'you and your friend arrived with the Doctor. Should you tell them differently, they will not believe you – and I will ensure that you are painfully executed!'

'Perhaps if you were to release my assistant, I might be more minded to co-operate.'

Madrox yanked the door open so fiercely that it almost came off its hinges. Its Overseer guard jumped back in surprise. 'Get her out of here!' he ordered.

'You will gain nothing from this, Chief Overseer!' Hegelia shouted, striding from the office in preference to being dragged. Madrox slammed the door. He was in no doubt now that she had been telling the truth. But he had no time to detail a patrol to look for Markham, who would certainly have vanished. He had no choice but to lie to the Cybermen. They had no reason to disbelieve him, after all. If he could fool them – if he could keep calm and not panic – he could do this. He could survive.

Then, as soon as his masters had left, he would hunt down Markham and Taggart and kill them.

In contrast to the Doctor's special cell, Jolarr's was opened by a simple master card. Taggart swiped his through the appropriate slot and checked both ways as the door clicked open. No patrols were scheduled, but he couldn't shake the fear that Madrox might march into view.

Jolarr was slumped in a corner of the tiny room. He didn't look up. Taggart switched his tech-unit to bio-scan mode and checked that the radioactive trace had worn off. It had, of course. He felt cheated. He had lost his final chance to back out of this with grace. 'Come on,' he forced himself to say. 'We're getting out.'

Jolarr raised his white face from between his arms. He looked at his would-be rescuer blankly. Taggart checked the corridor again, apprehension making him fret at the minor delay. 'I said come on. Do you want to escape or don't you?'

Jolarr stood but didn't make a move. He stared at the Overseer's uniform, surprise, distrust and hope alternately moulding his expression. Taggart grabbed his wrist and dragged him into the corridor. He closed and locked the door, hyper-conscious of his heart's heavy pounding. He had gone too far to back out now. He was committed. His life was at stake.

He had spent an hour studying the rosters and he had worked out the optimum escape route through the complex. He dragged the compliant alien along it now, their footsteps echoing like jackhammers against the metal floor. Speed was more important than stealth, but there was always a chance that an Overseer might detect the sound of running, even through the storm. Taggart was relieved when they reached the bottom of the last flight of stairs and ducked into the relative safety of an automated, rarely visited food refinery. He bustled Jolarr behind a rumbling machine and thrust the purloined tech-unit into his sweating hands.

'We wait here for five minutes,' he said, 'until the next patrol goes past. Then we've got a clear run at an exit. The only problem will be a security camera, but I can fix that. Here, I'll show you how to use this thing to get across the grounds safely.'

'No!' said Jolarr.

Taggart felt his stomach cartwheeling. Whatever the problem was, he didn't want to hear it. Why couldn't things ever be simple?

'I came here with a colleague. We have to go back for her,' Jolarr explained.

Taggart shook his head. 'We can't. There isn't time. This is risky enough as it is.' He reached to operate the tech-unit, to begin his demonstration. Jolarr pulled away.

'I can't leave her. She's my only way off this planet. And you don't want to know what will happen if she changes history by being here.'

He was right; Taggart didn't want to know. But Jolarr had already turned and was heading back towards the door. Taggart entertained the fleeting notion of abandoning him, but it was swiftly replaced by an image of Jolarr being interrogated and telling Madrox exactly how he came to be wandering about the complex. He hurried after him, too late to prevent the alien from leaving the room. He followed him into the corridor, where Jolarr had faltered and was weighing up the possibilities offered by each direction.

'Where is she being held?' he demanded as Taggart appeared. As a matter of fact, Taggart realized, Hegelia wasn't far. She was with the Doctor, in the special cell, on the ground floor. This level. Too close to the control centre. Before he had decided whether to answer, Jolarr had picked a direction – the wrong one – and hurried off. Taggart felt a cold flash of panic as he remembered the imminent patrol. He hurled himself after his charge and gripped the back of his tunic. Jolarr struggled and Taggart, using strength he hadn't known he possessed, clamped a silencing hand over his mouth and hauled him bodily around a corner. They both shrank into the shadows as, seconds later, two Overseers marched past the intersection.

Taggart waited another full minute before relaxing his hold. He half expected the boy to run away again, but thankfully Jolarr had been subdued by their close call. 'Do you see now why we have to get out of here?' he whispered. 'If anyone finds us, I'll be dead and you'll be back on your way to the conversion chamber.'

To Taggart's dismay, Jolarr shook his head. 'I know it's dangerous, but I can't leave the ArcHivist.' The alien's determination had been tempered by caution, but deter-mined he still was. Taggart looked into the dark pits of his eyes and began to accept, with a weary resignation, that he was not going to be given a choice.

He considered his options. As he had observed, Hegelia's cell wasn't too far – and, with his carefully laid plan already in shreds, one route through Population Control would only be as dangerous as any other. 'Are you sure she wants to be rescued?' he checked, before committing himself. Jolarr's expression made him feel idiotic for asking.

Taggart said no more. With a reluctant grunt of assent, he led Jolarr back into the main corridor and followed in the path of the patrol. At least, he tried to convince

84

himself, he might come out of this a hero. By freeing both aliens, he would exceed even Henneker's expectations. If he succeeded, that was.

He had no such luck. They reached the special cell and Taggart yanked open the viewing hatch, to find that Hegelia was not present.

'Where is she?' Jolarr asked, too loud for comfort.

The Doctor looked up from his shackles. 'If you mean my cellmate, she was taken for interrogation. Do you want to wait?'

'That's it,' said Taggart. 'We've got to go!'

'But what about the ArcHivist?' asked Jolarr.

'And what about me?' the Doctor called. 'A laser probe would be useful right now, if either of you have one.'

Jolarr reached for the hatch before Taggart could. 'I can't help you,' he said apologetically. 'I can't change history.'

The Doctor groaned. 'Not you as well. Was it Winston Churchill who talked about evil flourishing when good men choose to do nothing?'

'No, it wasn't,' Jolarr responded.

'Oh.' The Doctor looked crestfallen. 'Well, perhaps he should have done. It would have been inspirational.'

Jolarr closed the hatch and turned to Taggart. 'We'd better go,' he said reluctantly. Taggart nodded. He tried to look sympathetic, but couldn't quite disguise the relief which washed over him.

A small explosion rocked the bunker. Max jumped to her feet, pulled back the curtain and launched into a tirade against Henneker, reminding him how delicate her process was. 'We have to carry out tests,' he defended himself, indicating the smoking remains of a chair. Lakesmith stood before it, the blaster on his right arm still aimed at the debris. 'That was the lowest setting,' boasted Henneker.

Max tutted, let the curtain fall and slumped back into her seat. Grant watched sympathetically, knowing how tired she must be. The onus to complete the Project was on her, and she had toiled almost non-stop since the early hours. He had helped where he could, but the remaining work was essentially surgical and Max was the only one with the relevant skills. Grant had to admit that half his reason for being in her work area at all was to avoid the disconcerting proximity of Lakesmith. Soon, there would be no such place to hide.

The fourth and fifth volunteers were waiting in the main part of the bunker. The second and third were already here on the tables, encased by plastic moulds. A thin tube snaked from each to a large vat in which a rust-coloured liquid spat and bubbled. The formula for this synthesis of plastic and metal had been partly extrapolated from a dead Cyberman, long before even Max had begun her work. Henneker had once explained how his people had spent a year attempting to duplicate the substance with which their enemies were sheathed. They had failed to do so accurately, but by introducing malleable copper into the process, they had been able to facilitate the fusion of the other disparate elements into a compound which, whilst not as hard or as flexible as that used by the Cybermen, would suit their purposes.

Another crash resounded as Henneker determined the (narrow) limits of Lakesmith's manoeuvrability. Max groaned.

'How long before they're ready?' asked Grant, nodding towards the two subjects.

'The moulds come off in a couple of minutes. After that, it's just a case of welding the weapons on. You can do that, can't you?' Max asked. 'The nerve connections are in place.'

Grant nodded, although he didn't relish the idea of getting so close to the creatures. Max rubbed her eyes and suppressed a yawn. 'I need to clear this pair out and get the next two in for brain ops.'

'What do you actually do to them?' asked Grant.

'I thought I'd explained.'

'You did. Well, sort of – I just didn't expect Mr Lakesmith to turn out as he has.' Max looked at him questioningly and Grant tried to elaborate. 'He doesn't act the way he used to. I mean, I know you've wired parts of his brain to the armour and I know you've messed with some of the chemicals it produces, to stimulate aggression and block fear, that sort of thing. But it's more than that. He's acting like . . . well, like a robot. Like he isn't the same person.'

'Perhaps he isn't. You never can tell with brain operations. I can describe what I've done to Lakesmith physically, but there's no objective way to measure what I might have done to his mind. Even he couldn't tell you that.'

'He couldn't?'

Max shrugged. 'It's one of the problems of this whole idea. I've had to make it clear to everyone who's thought of volunteering. By operating on Lakesmith, I've made him act, maybe even think, differently. Does that mean he's a different person? What does he feel inside? Have I left his identity intact?'

Grant turned the problem over, but came up with no easy solutions. Max was warming to her theme; she didn't often get the chance to talk about her work. 'Let me give you an example. I've separated the hemispheres of Lakesmith's brain. They can't communicate directly. Now, you put something in his left hand and keep it out of his sight, and he won't be able to tell you what the object is. The data is being collected as usual in the right hemisphere, but it's the left which controls speech. Part of Lakesmith will know what he's holding, but not the part which could relate the information to us.'

Grant was struggling to cope with this. 'So what you're saying is, he's become a split personality?'

'No, the halves of his brain are still working in conjunction, even though they aren't joined any more. You can only really see the difference in artificial test conditions.'

'So is this what the Cybermen do to themselves?'

Max shook her head. 'All the information we have about the human brain was downloaded from their medical computer in Population Control – but they learned this procedure from Old Earth back in the 1970s. It was used to treat disorders like epilepsy. What I've done is to incorporate some of the Cybermen's own theories into the operation. You know how much of our brains we normally use?'

'It's only about half, isn't it?'

'More like a quarter. So, as well as separating the hemispheres of the brains, I've augmented and stimulated each one to perform with heightened efficiency, encouraging them to act independently in certain tasks and increasing that figure to almost double. Our Bronze Knights have a vastly improved reaction time and greater awareness. You'd be hard pressed to sneak up on one.'

Max left Grant thinking about that whilst she crossed to the two subjects and began to peel their plastic moulds away, revealing two fully functioning Bronze Knights. Grant was so absorbed by the thought of what had been done to them – and how they might feel about it – that it was almost a full minute before he remembered to be scared.

An Overseer marched the protesting Hegelia back to her cell and pushed her roughly inside. As the door clanged shut behind her, she felt like punching the wall in frustration. She could not act so, however, in company.

'Madrox wasn't too friendly, I take it?' Even as he spoke, the Doctor was working autonomically with the hairpin, taking his chances of freedom no matter how slim they might be.

Hegelia seethed. 'He is a stubborn, irrational simpleton!'

'No. He is a frightened human being, with a human's greed and a human's ego. Both somewhat overdeveloped, maybe.'

'The eradication of such destructive emotions could only be a blessing.'

'Well, if you say so. By the way, a friend called whilst you were out.' Hegelia looked at him with a frown of disapproval. What was he prattling on about now? 'Young man, pale skin, untidy hair. One of the Overseers was taking him out to play and he wondered if you could come too.'

'Jolarr is free?'

'Isn't that what I just said? He was on his way there, anyhow.'

The ArcHivist felt a grin forming as joy suffused her body. Everything was perfect now.

'Well, I'm glad you're happy,' said the Doctor, reacting to her expression. 'Myself, I could do with hitting the right combination and getting out of here.'

'Time is running out,' Hegelia warned. She was almost beginning to feel sorry for him. The other prisoners would only be converted, but the Doctor was a bitter foe of the Cyber race. What they might do to him almost didn't bear thinking about. 'I was given the impression by Madrox that the Cybermen will be here within minutes.'

'Thank you for that cheering thought,' the Doctor muttered. He set to work with renewed determination. She watched him for a while, then let her vision turn inwards, to memories of past achievements and dreams of future glorious discoveries.

The rain beat down on the complex and its rhythmic clattering lulled Hegelia into a trance-like state. Time passed, and the storm eased off until it was almost inaudible. The background noises of Population Control had lessened as its occupants became subdued in anticipation of the visit. The Doctor's voice punctuated the eerie calm with increasingly frequent grunts of annoyance. And Hegelia surfaced from her reverie as a new sound insinuated itself upon her eardrums: a low-pitched, rumbling whine of starship engines.

The Doctor heard it too. He had ceased his vain endeavours and was craning his neck to look upwards. He needn't have bothered, Hegelia thought pragmatically. He could see nothing but the metal ceiling. Apart from which, it was obvious to anyone what was happening beyond that barrier.

'Time's up,' announced the Doctor glumly.

The atmosphere in the control centre was equally tense. Patrol Two were the unlucky ones on duty; they had been performing their functions in heavy silence since Madrox had arrived and taken the Chair.

The Chair was situated in the centre of the circular room, the grey consoles arranged about it in a spiral pattern. It faced a mushroom-shaped communications device, tuned to receive interplanetary transmissions. It had been three years since anyone had last had to use it; three years since Madrox had last sat here, skin itching as he sweated beneath the metal reinforcement of his uniform, waiting for the monitor in the mushroom's helmet to come to life.

This was the worst time of all, he thought. Arriving far earlier than necessary, so terrified was he of the penalties for tardiness. Sitting here, his power stripped from him, exposed as illusion. And waiting for his masters, his race's oppressors, praying that they wouldn't find fault with his service.

The screen was lit without fanfare and Madrox tightened his grip on the Chair's metal arms. As always, the sight of the Cyberman's silver face filled him with dread. In common with all its kind, its eyes were blank and its mouth a straight line, incapable of smile or frown. Its head was made oblong by the addition of blocks like earmuffs to each side. From these, ridged pipes extended, turning upwards and inwards at right angles and meeting at the top of a bulge above the creature's forehead. Madrox's gaze was drawn by the hole in the middle of this, through which could be seen the circular ends of four tubes. Conversing with a Cyberman necessarily entailed staring down the multiple barrels of a loaded gun.

90

'We are ready to land,' the Cyberman said without preamble, its machine voice almost bereft of tone or inflection. 'Is everything in order?'

'It is,' said Madrox.

'We have scanned your computer. The security camera on Circuit Three was rendered inoperational 17.4 minutes ago for a duration of 8.3 minutes.'

'I know. I sent a detail to attend to it. We think it was a simple mechanical failure.'

'It was sabotage.'

Madrox swallowed. The matter-of-fact report was more unsettling than any straightforward accusation would have been. 'I'll investigate,' he promised, conscious that he had failed his masters once. How much would they tolerate before deciding to replace him?

'There has been no defiance of your authority?'

'No.' The Cyberman neither answered nor moved, and Madrox, feeling his face perspiring, decided that something closer to the truth would be safer. 'There were rumours of a rebellion, but I took a patrol out last night and dealt with the ringleaders.' If only today's patrols had been able to find Henneker, he thought. Still, what could one man do? 'Perhaps this sabotage was part of an attempt by the last few dissidents to attack the complex. If so, it didn't work.'

Madrox was aware that his voice was speeding up. Still, the Cyberman didn't comment. Feeling that it was somehow disappointed, he played his trump card earlier than he had intended. 'I've arrested your enemy as well. The Doctor. He and his companions are in custody as per instructions.' Nerves kept him talking. 'One companion was suitable for conversion, so I have placed him in a normal cell. The other was female and too old. She is being held with the Doctor.'

If he had been hoping for an expression of approval, he was disappointed. 'We will land,' said the Cyberman simply. The screen blinked off and Madrox sat back with a heartfelt sigh of relief.

The building was completely silent now, all ears turned outwards to the sound of reverse thrusters, growing in volume as the ship came steadily closer.

Madrox knew that he had surmounted but the first of many hurdles. The Cybermen were here now, and his ordeal – like that of the people he usually ruled – was just beginning.

6

Total Control

Jolarr heard the engines, but didn't dare remove his gaze from the flickering display of the old tech-unit. The Overseer, Taggart, had hurriedly told him how to use it before thrusting a thick towel into his hands, leaping up to slash at the wiring of a swivelling camera, pushing Jolarr out into the open and hurrying back into the complex with all speed. He had temporarily deactivated some of the remote-controlled defences – enough to provide a safe route which would not take the escapee within sight of manned guardposts – but Jolarr would still need the unit to circumvent others. He didn't trust the primitive device, and his slow journey across the grounds had been fraught with the worry that he would step on a mine at any moment.

He wished Hegelia could have been with him. He had been dismayed to find that she was not in her cell, but he'd had no choice but to accept Taggart's word that he would send her to join him as soon as possible. He didn't believe it.

The tech-unit told Jolarr that a direct route to the fence was now clear. He sprinted the last few steps and turned back, anxious to see what was behind him. The rain had slowed to an unpleasant drizzle, but the sky was grey and light was sparse. At first, he couldn't see anything abnormal. But then his gaze turned upwards and, hanging against the clouds, he saw the ship. And recognized it, from his research. It belonged to the Cybermen.

Jolarr scrambled up the fence, driven on by the illogical idea that the arriving aliens could see him. In his haste, he cut his hand on the barbed wire strung across the top of the barrier. He unfolded Taggart's towel and tossed it over the uppermost strand. It protected him from further harm as he pressed the wire down and awkwardly straddled it.

The great silver vessel was approaching on a vertical descent. It was shaped approximately like an old Earth rocket. A pair of angled fins protruded from a bulky rear compartment, whilst a sleeker forward section (currently at the top) culminated in a slightly bulbous cockpit housing. As Jolarr watched, the ship came in to land at the centre of Population Control, settling into and neatly interlocking with the building's circular indenture. Its drive was disengaged and Jolarr was heavily conscious of the ensuing silence.

Overtaken by fear, he hauled himself over the wire, clung to the fence for a moment and then leapt the ten feet or so to the ground, pushing himself forward so as to clear the barbed wire loops beneath him. He landed and rolled into the mud, then picked himself up and ran. He had been told to follow the fence until he reached the rebels' bunker (Taggart had described its location as best he could), but for now, he just wanted to get as far from the Cybermen as possible.

Hegelia had lied. At best, the ArcHivist had cruelly misled him. Thanks to her, Jolarr had thought himself safe, believing that the planet's conquerors would not be present during their mission. His comforting illusions had been shattered.

The Cybermen were here. And nobody on Agora was safe any more.

Madrox stood to attention and saluted as five Cybermen marched into the control centre. The gesture was neither necessary nor appreciated, but he felt that a display of respect could only help his cause.

The creatures towered at least a foot above him. They were swathed in a plastic-metal compound which, Madrox knew, was a lot tougher than its flexibility made it seem. Hydraulic muscles were serviced by piping which lined their arms and legs, drawing fluid from a tank hidden beneath their armour. Attached to the chest of each was a control unit, with which they could activate various functions manually: their in-built weapons, for example. The foremost of the giants was marked out as their Leader by the black coloration of the blocks and pipes which surrounded its face, as well as by the thin, cylindrical gun which it wielded. It halted before Madrox and asked: 'Have you obeyed all orders pertaining to the Doctor?'

'We have.'

It dismissed its entourage with a jerk of the hand. Three Cybermen turned and left in silence. The fourth crossed the room by the Cyberleader's side, nervous Overseers backing out of the path of the imposing pair. The Cyberman seated itself, a little stiffly, before one of the consoles, the Leader standing at its shoulder in a supervisory position. Madrox made himself shuffle closer. 'Is everything to your satisfaction?' he asked ingratiatingly. The Cyberleader didn't answer. It didn't need to. If it found fault, Madrox would hear about it instantly.

Heavy, prosthetic fingers stabbed buttons and pushed levers. Strings of numbers scrolled across a computer screen, too fast for him to read. Then, finally, the Cyberman reported: 'The chamber is operational.'

'Excellent!'

'The three units are in position.'

To Madrox's relief, things seemed to be going well. Even so, he couldn't help but shiver as the Cyberleader sealed the fates of five hundred of his own kind with its usual chilling pronouncement.

'The conversion process will begin immediately.'

'They're here, aren't they?' said the boy on the far side of the wall. His voice was dead, resigned to his fate.

'I'm afraid so,' the Doctor called back to him. 'I'm sorry.'

His regret was genuine, and Hegelia was beginning to think she had misjudged her cellmate. The Doctor's occasional clowning was a mask, concealing a very capable and compassionate being. She almost wished she could care as much, but her present position made it impossible. She mustn't interfere. She felt inexplicably guilty about that.

She moved across to the wall and leant an ear against it. 'It is not like dying,' she said gently. The boy didn't answer.

The Doctor was still working on the circuits of his restraints. 'You don't know that,' he said pointedly, his voice low enough not to carry. 'You can't imagine what it would be like to die – or how it might feel to be converted into a Cyberman.'

'Indeed not.' Hegelia was pleased that he was showing signs of understanding. 'The mind is still a mystery to us. Do we, in having our emotions removed, retain the fundamental essence of who we are? Do we become different people, or would we merely be the same person advanced to a new level of being? How would we feel?'

'Either way,' said the Doctor, 'we'd become heartless destroyers with no respect for life. Inhuman abominations, dedicated only to the continuance of our own worthless kind!'

Hegelia scowled. She had been mistaken. He didn't understand at all. 'How can you not find the idea of the Cybermen alluring?' she said. 'Do you not see the elegance, the beauty, in their design?'

Whether he saw it or not, she was never to learn. With a sudden exclamation of 'I've done it!' and a profoundly surprised expression, the Doctor pulled his head free from the stocks and fell back gratefully. His manacles clicked open and he rubbed his hands through his hair in relief. He massaged his wrists and ankles for a few seconds, then sprang to his feet as if his circulation had never been hampered, and dashed across to the cell door.

'Congratulations,' Hegelia said drily. 'Now what do you intend to do?'

'Escape,' he answered. He made a cursory inspection of the lock, then muttered, 'As I thought,' hurried back to the restraints and set to work on their innards with the hairpin again. 'It's a crude magnetic system.' Hegelia didn't know if he was addressing her or if he just enjoyed the sound of his own voice. 'At the root of it is a logic problem in binary code, to which the key would provide, if you like, the solution, not through its shape but through a precise magnetic coding.' He straightened up and crossed the room again, gingerly holding the pin by one end. He rammed it hard into the keyhole and watched with satisfaction as the door slid open. '*Voilà!* Witness a typical failing of the Cybermen: refusing to believe that people with emotions can think as logically as they.' He paused on the threshold and looked at Hegelia. He seemed hopeful, but also a little sad. 'Are you coming?'

She shook her head. The Doctor accepted her decision, although he obviously didn't approve. He left without another word, leaving the door conspicuously open.

Maybe, Hegelia thought, he had deduced more than she gave him credit for.

The Doctor stopped in the corridor, trying to get his bearings and alert for any signs of movement. Normally, he would have trusted to luck and to his (sometimes) unerring sense of direction and made a run for it. But after three weeks as a prisoner, he was in no mood to risk his newfound freedom so recklessly.

His cell was situated on one corner of a four-way junction. Stretching each way on the same block were two rows of simple metal doors, all locked and operated by card readers. Evidently, behind these dwelt Madrox's offerings to the Cybermen. The Doctor felt a black tide of disgust lapping at the edges of his stomach.

He followed the corridor around until he reached the cell behind his own. He delved into his pocket and produced a handful of tangled wires which he had ripped from his shackles. It would be the work of moments to short-circuit the electronic lock. As he set about his task, he tried not to think about the many other people for whom he wouldn't have time to do this. He was jeopardizing himself by even freeing one of them. Was a life any more important just because he had spoken to its owner? Because he would be crushed if the boy was to die? He should leave, instead of wasting time fighting to keep one more face out of his gallery of guilt. But no. That, he told himself, was the logic of the Cybermen. His feelings were part of what made him better than they were.

With a click, the locking bar disengaged. The Doctor pushed the door open and stepped into the tiny cubicle beyond. It was empty, and the yawning gap in the back wall told him why. He emerged into another passageway. It extended a short way to his right and much further to his left, before making a right-angled turn in each direction. The opposite, inner wall was a convex curve, which presumably met itself on the far side. A circle inside a square, connecting every cell on this level. Certainly, there were a number of access points along this length, all similar to the doorway in which he stood.

As the Doctor thought about his next move, six men appeared at the right-hand corner. They were silent and their heads were bowed as they shuffled towards him. They weren't moving by choice. The Doctor caught a glimpse of reflective silver as he ducked back into the cell and flattened himself against the wall. When he judged that the group had passed, he peered into the passageway and saw the back of a Cyberman, driving the despondent Agorans before it. Its design was familiar: he had encountered representatives of this particular offshoot in his fourth incarnation, on Nerva Beacon. He had defeated them only with luck and with the help of the Vogans. He certainly wasn't prepared to take them on with neither weapons nor assistance.

He waited until the monster had disappeared around the far corner, then he hurried after it as stealthily as he could manage on the metal surface. He needed to learn more without being detected. He turned the corner to find that the Cyberman and its prisoners were no longer in sight. The cells backing onto this corridor had not yet been opened. Presumably, the conversion candidates were being collected a few at a time, to be taken . . . where?

The answer to that was obvious. A single arch punctured the right-hand, curved wall. A white light spilled from it, dispelling the gloom in an oblong pool. The Doctor sidled closer and listened for activity. He heard only the low-level rumbling of machines a short distance away. The Cyberman could be on the far side of the room by now, its back to him. Or it could be waiting behind the doorway.

He ventured a quick glance, then a longer one as he saw that it was safe. He stepped out onto a narrow balcony, through which a ladder descended. He immediately realized that he was on the Cybermen's ship, and in some sort of conversion chamber. He could see another two balconies above him and two below, presumably venting onto basement levels. Five floors, one hundred cells on each. Five hundred Agorans to be herded to unenviable fates.

The railed balconies circled the room and were lined by glass-fronted compartments, each large enough to hold an upright human body. The Cyberman was on the same level as the Doctor, manhandling its last acquisition into one of these. Watching it warily, he lowered himself to the next balcony, where it couldn't see him. Here, he took the opportunity for a closer look at one of the compartments, scowling at the machinery which was visible through its transparent door.

Another, wider, ladder in the room's centre led up to the cockpit of the ship. If he could reach that, he could sabotage or even commandeer it. First, he had to cross the base of the chamber.

The Doctor was halfway down the final ladder when he saw it. Another Cyberman, all but concealed by the consoles from which the conversion process would be controlled. He froze, one foot in the air, and began to reverse the direction of his climb. But it had seen him.

'Stop!'

He redoubled his efforts. From what he remembered, these Cybermen had head-mounted weapons; lethal but with limited range. If he could get out before it closed the gap between them, he would be safe.

Wrong again! It produced a gun and blasted a chunk of ladder out from beneath him. The Doctor grabbed at the first balcony and hauled himself up onto it. He flattened himself as he heard another shot and he felt a blast of heat in which molten rivulets dripped from the railing. He tentatively raised his head and saw that the Cyberman was marching towards him with frightening speed. No doubt its colleague above would be doing likewise. He scrambled up and dived through this level's doorway, narrowly avoiding a third shot. He was in a corridor identical to the one above, but as he sprinted down it, he was dismayed to see that the exits from this one were closed. Worse still, as he rounded a corner, he glimpsed another Cyberman at the corridor's far end, collecting a group of prisoners together. It had heard his footsteps and it whirled to face him.

'Stop!' it ordered. The Cybermen were nothing if not imaginative, the Doctor thought. He turned to see that his trigger-happy friend from the chamber was emerging into the passageway. No escape that way. He ducked back around the corner. The Cyberman in this corridor at least had no gun – but it was approaching at an alarming rate. The Doctor's hands groped across the flat outer wall in search of the invisible seam which had to be there. He found it and forced his fingernails beneath it, flipping it open to reveal a control pad. He stabbed at it and stumbled gratefully through the revealed aperture before it was half-formed. The cell into which he emerged was occupied and a middle-aged Agoran man leapt to his feet and stared in terror.

'Do pardon my intrusion,' the Doctor muttered. He grabbed the wires from his pocket as he raced across to the main door. Short-circuiting the system would be difficult from this side. He pushed two bared ends into the gap between door and wall and wriggled them blindly. A tingling in his scalp alerted him to the fact that his pursuers had arrived.

The prisoner cowered in a corner as the Cybermen took one step in unison and halted inside the room. The armed one brought up its weapon, although at such close quarters it wouldn't need it. The Doctor turned to face them, his eyes drawn – as the Cybermen's designers had intended – to the clusters of barrels which peered from their helmets. His hands were still behind his back, working frantically.

'You are our prisoner.'

'Yes, it appears so. I suppose you're going to lock that door, then, and leave me trapped here in this nasty old dungeon?'

'No. We are going to kill you –'

'Oh.'

'– if you do not cease your interference with the security mechanism and raise your hands.'

The Doctor smiled bashfully and slowly brought his right hand around and up.

'Both hands!' the Cyberman ordered.

The door slid open, thankfully, and the Doctor, forcing himself to act on instinct alone, pushed backwards and fell, face-up, into the corridor. Two blasts passed over him and blew a hole into the far wall. He scrambled up and threw himself towards the nearest junction. As on the level above, he had a choice of four directions. He chose one to take him away from the cell block. There was no time to make a more considered decision: despite having sacrificed speed for endurance, the Cybermen were far from slow – and they were persistent, above all. He had to lose them, fast.

A narrow staircase offered a return to ground-floor level. He took it three steps at a time, but descended considerably faster at the sight of three Overseers at its head. They hadn't seen him, but the diversion had wasted time. As he bounced off the bottom step, the first

Cyberman appeared in the connecting corridor and fired. Another wave of heat swept across the Doctor's face and he knew that the guards above would have heard the explosion. He reached a crossroads and propelled himself in a random direction before any of his foes could get him back into sight. The passage twisted around a number of outcropping rooms and the Doctor made himself slow down so that his footsteps wouldn't ring out so prominently.

Minutes passed with no sign of pursuit. Then, to his alarm, the corridor ended. His own distorted reflection greeted him mockingly from a blank silver wall and he remembered the exterior layout of Population Control, seen as he was marched towards it three weeks ago. He recalled its sprawling wings, the legs of the great mechanical spider, and he realized with horror that he had blundered straight into one. All the Cybermen had to do now was station a sentry at the junction and search each corridor in turn. They would find him.

A klaxon alarm began to sound and the lighting panels in the ceiling dimmed, taking on a blood-red hue. News of the Doctor's escape had been relayed to the control centre. He now had every Overseer in the building to contend with – as well as the Cybermen. A scout ship of the type he had seen would normally have a crew of eight. He had encountered three. The other five could be anywhere.

The Doctor hurried back along the passageway, trying each door as he passed it. Maybe one of the rooms would provide access to a different level. At least he might find somewhere to hide from the inevitable patrols. The first door was locked; the second opened onto a small storage area, piled high with circuit boards and fuse wire. The third took the Doctor into a darkened room which, as his eyes adjusted, he saw was some sort of medical laboratory. Three beds were covered in crisp white sheets and surrounded by complex equipment, primarily scanning devices. Clearly, this was where Overseer surgeons

102

investigated the sex and genetic purity of the unborn, tampering with either if necessary. Where the child-to-be was deemed unsalvageable and of no ultimate use, the machines provided a further option. The Doctor was repelled, but hardly surprised.

He closed the door, muffling the wails of the alarm, and crossed to one of the scanners. Booting it up was a simple operation – as was programming it to give him what he wanted. Another flaw of Cyber thinking, he thought with grim satisfaction. Population Control's systems were efficiently designed and fully integrated, which made it easy to access one from another. Once he was inside the medical computer, he could leapfrog into the defensive and architectural datapools and call up full schematics of the complex. If there was a way out of this, he could find it in short order.

If there was a way out of this.

The emergency alarm had been sounding for almost five minutes. Madrox's immediate reaction, prompted by an electric jolt of terror, had been to spring across the control centre to check the status of the defences. He had had nightmare visions of Henneker leading an army across the grounds. Although they had been unfounded, the truth was not much more palatable.

'Patrol 3B reports that the Doctor has escaped from his cell, sir,' one of the Overseers had told him. Madrox had not even listened to the details. He had ordered all patrols to be recalled to duty, to track the alien down. He had tried to sound as efficient and in control as possible, although he had known it was too late to impress the Cybermen. He had presided over one problem too many.

It had come as a surprise, then, when the Cyberleader had not only failed to reprimand him, but had also countermanded his instructions. 'My troops will deal with the Doctor,' it had said. Since then, it had not spoken. Madrox sweated, even under the cold red light, and wished it would just put him out of his misery.

He retracted that wish when, finally, it swung around to face him. Madrox clenched his fists and gritted his teeth and wondered what it would feel like to die. Its words were unexpected. 'You have done well. Census records show an increase in Agora's population during each of the last three periods.' Madrox didn't know what to say. He wanted to ask why he was not to be punished for the Doctor's escape – but why tempt fate?

The Leader took four measured steps towards him. 'Our race is in need of organic resources. We will convert the current prisoners and return for more in precisely 1.5 years. You will ensure that each holding cell is filled as normal.'

Madrox was aghast. One and a half years? Eighteen months before he had to face them again? Five hundred more Agorans to die at the Cyberleader's whim? 'I–I beg your pardon, Leader, but I don't think we can do it. The population of the colony –'

'Population levels will be maintained.' The Cyberleader loomed over him, adopting an exaggerated posture which suggested anger at the questioning of its edict. It could have felt no such emotion, of course, but the simulation was clearly affected for the sake of intimidation. It was successful. 'Your own computers show that it is possible. You will oversee. If you cannot serve in that capacity, then you will be just as useful to us as the first of Population Control's new intake.'

Madrox nodded hurriedly, realizing that shock had made him push too far. At least his own life wasn't in danger. At least he was still in command. Any time was better than none. Far better than lingering death.

'Leader,' said the Cyberman at the console. 'There is a problem.'

If those words had had physical form, they would have been shards of ice sliding down Chief Overseer Madrox's back. The Cyberleader seemed to glare at him for a moment, then it strode to its deputy's side. 'I have received a report from a unit at the conversion chamber,' the Cyberman said. 'One holding cell is empty. The quota for this period has not been met. Our human agents have failed.'

Madrox took an involuntary step backwards as the Leader rounded on him. 'What do you know of this?'

'Nothing, I swear.'

The monster crossed the distance between them far more quickly this time. It bore down on him like an unstoppable tank and Madrox lost all composure. He cringed, threw up his hands and babbled, 'The cells were full, I swear. It must have been one of the Overseers. It must have been Taggart. He betrayed me before you arrived. I didn't think it was worth bothering you with details. I was going to sort him out myself, but he hasn't been detained yet and he must have freed the prisoner.' He ran dry, but thankfully the Cyberleader had checked its approach. It was well within reach, but it hadn't moved to strike. Could he have been so lucky again? He cautiously lowered his hands, aware that he had been humiliated before Patrol Two. He hated such undermining of his authority.

'Overseer Taggart is known to us. He is recorded as a former dissident in our history computer.'

'That's right,' said Madrox, nodding eagerly. 'He helped out in the rebellion, but you gave him a chance because he surrendered.'

'He will be dealt with.'

Madrox was beginning to relax, the immediate danger averted. 'Taggart is still young enough to be good conversion material,' he offered. 'He could replace the missing prisoner.'

'As could you.'

Before the significance of those words could sink in, the Cyberleader's hand was around Madrox's throat. His breathing was stifled and he felt his cheeks turn crimson, his eyes bulging out of his head. Hydraulic muscles flexed and he was lifted clear of the floor. His feet pedalled uselessly; his hands lashed out, but only bruised themselves. The

Cyberleader's words were dulled by a sound in his ears like rushing water. 'However, if, as you say, Taggart can be converted, then you are dispensable. You can pay the price for your failure and become an example to those who will follow you.'

The pressure increased and, in the seconds remaining to him, vivid memories flashed through Madrox's mind: the gamble with which he had become a slave; his predecessor, reeling from a fatal blast; himself returning the Cyberleader's gaze steadily as his colleagues recoiled. Above all, Madrox thought of his child. His first one, unborn. He would not see him now.

The Doctor dropped into a crouch as the lift doors opened. If there was a Cyberman waiting for him, he wouldn't be able to hide – but at least he could surprise it by attacking from beneath gun level.

He needn't have worried. The service elevator opened into another unoccupied laboratory. This one held a dozen huge containers, in which the Cybermen's plastic-metal compound seethed, prevented from solidifying by an electrical current. Thoughts of sabotage crossed the Doctor's mind, but he had no time. His use of the lift would have been reported to the control centre. He had programmed it to visit every level – and, hopefully, the ground floor with its exits would be seen as a better prospect than this upper sub-basement – but still, he should move on quickly.

A short walk brought him to the cell block, which he circumvented. He recalled the plans of the complex, mentally superimposing them over the reality. He knew where he wanted to be.

The door to the chamber was locked, but not so efficiently as to resist the Doctor's well-practised abilities. The room beyond was enormous and dark, but in the dim red light from the corridor, he could just make out a familiar shape. The TARDIS. The Doctor smiled. The main computer's inventory file had been correct. He greeted the deceptively small blue box like an old friend, running his hand along its pitted surface. But something was wrong. His key – which the Overseers had confiscated – was in the lock. Not that they would have been able to use it. It would only respond to the Doctor's unique molecular structure. But then, why had they left it here?

Part of him wanted desperately not to worry about it. He had pinned his hopes on being able to somehow force the TARDIS's emergency exit door, combining his lockpicking skills with his telepathic link to the ship. It wouldn't have been easy and it might not have been possible. Now fate had handed him a quicker, more sure way. Hadn't it?

The Doctor reached out and grasped the key. Then paused. The darkness closed in around him and he felt the skin of his neck begin to prickle with a familiar premonition of danger. He twisted to look back over his shoulder. He stared intently into the deep shadows, and frowned.

Something glimmered.

The Doctor sighed, removed the key and turned his back to the TARDIS. 'I'm sorry. No entry.'

The Cyberman emerged from the dark recesses. Two more closed in from equidistant points around the chamber, cutting him off from the door. Hegelia had been quite right. The Doctor's so-called escape had been controlled from the start, from afar, with the intention of bringing him here. The Cybermen had wanted him to open the TARDIS door. Once he had, they would no doubt have shot him on the threshold.

'I hate to disappoint you,' said the Doctor, straining to put a brave face on his defeat.

'There is no disappointment. That would be an illogical reaction.'

'Oh, yes. I was forgetting.'

'You merely force us to put an alternative plan into effect.'

The Doctor had a quarter of a second to consider

107

ducking as fire flashed in the Cyberman's head-mounted weapon. Not long enough. A sharp, hot sensation built in his chest, circled to encompass his torso and erupted into a roiling ball of electric pain. He gasped and fell to his knees.

The Cyberman fired again and the Doctor lost control of his muscles. He felt himself pitching helplessly forward, but lost consciousness before he hit the floor.

Hegelia had seen enough. She marched into the control centre and halted, arms folded, her eyes burning holes into the Cyberleader's helmet. 'Leave him alone!'

The Cyberleader turned to face her. Hegelia prayed that she had engaged its interest rather than its wrath. That seemed to be the case. It loosened its grip on Madrox and lowered him. His face was purple, his breathing forced.

'The Chief Overseer has not failed you,' she said.

'Explain.'

'He was instructed to provide five hundred humans. He has done so.'

'He has not. One cell was empty.'

'I know. And, meanwhile, I have been waiting an intolerable length of time for your attendance. Had you been more efficient, I could have informed you long ago that I am your final candidate.'

The Cyberleader didn't answer. Hegelia imagined its logical mind ticking over, trying to work out the rationale behind her statement. She allowed a smile to play about her lips as she clarified her intent with the pronouncement she had waited a lifetime to make.

'You heard me correctly, Cyberleader. I wish to be converted. I want to be a Cyberman.'

7

Adapt or Die!

Taggart's half-waking dreams were worse than ever. Their livid colours exploded across his mind's eye each time sleep beckoned. The imaginary smells of carnage made his nostrils twitch. His pulse rate quickened with terrors long past.

The year was 2178 and Benjamin Michael Taggart was twenty-six and already living on borrowed time. The image of the ship was obscured in his mind by a mist born of panic, but Taggart remembered the children, bundled into its cockpit, barely comprehending what was happening. Only Grant Markham, the eldest, appreciated that they were about to leave their planet. Youthful excitement lit his face and widened his eyes. He was too young to understand everything.

It had taken three weeks of furtive trips to the landing site to work out the unfamiliar ignition and navigation controls. Three weeks during which the Overseers of Taggart's patrol had debated what to do with their find over and over again. This was their eventual decision: to give at least the children some hope of a normal existence. They christened the mysterious vessel *Lifeline* and prayed it would live up to that name. They couldn't even watch its automated launch. They had to be on the far side of the colony. Once the children had gone, life would continue, and they couldn't afford to be found when the radar reading was investigated.

2191 again. Taggart opened his eyes and stared up at the dull metal ceiling of his meagre quarters. The clock revealed the cruel truth of how little time he had lost to dozing. It was always this way when they were here.

Waiting for his crimes to be discovered; for the Cybermen to march through the door and take him. Wondering how much longer his execution could be postponed.

On the playback screen of thirteen years before, Taggart saw Overseer Madrox sneering threats. He saw Tim Roylance, his old Patrol Leader, pinning the young upstart against the wall and outlining in detail what would happen if he dared to go to the Cybermen with his discovery. Their next visit – the first since the rebellion – had been more fraught than most, but Madrox had chosen the path of self-preservation and looked for other ways to further his career. Amendments to census records had gone unquestioned and the children had not been missed by most.

Patrol Leader Roylance was dead now, as were most of Taggart's few friends from that distant time. Madrox had been quick to exercise his powers, when he got them, to rid the Overseers of all those he deemed to be corrupting influences. Those he had not disposed of himself had been reported for behavioural lapses, real or imagined. Madrox had taken no chances and he had forgotten nothing. Somehow, Ben Taggart had been spared. He had lived with the fear for a decade and a half. Five visits. This time, as always, time crawled by reluctantly. The walls leaned over him with the physical impossibility of claustrophobic delirium, and Taggart wondered how much longer it could be before his turn came to die.

The ArcHivist's unexpected pronouncement was greeted by silence. Madrox knelt on the floor of the control centre, hand to his throat, and stared as if he couldn't believe that salvation had come from such a quarter. The Cyberleader showed no such expression, of course, but Hegelia's words had given it pause. It would need more information to interpret this superficially illogical occurrence.

'Why do you desire conversion?'

'Is that so hard to understand?' she countered.

'The feelings of organic animals are irrational and therefore unpredictable.'

'You need not look to the future, Cyberleader. Look instead to your own past. Remember the "animals" that you once were. The proud people of Mondas wanted to be converted, didn't they? You made the choice to become Cybermen. Why do you assume that nobody else can share your lofty ideals?'

'Not all Mondans welcomed our proliferation. It is a matter of record that emotions blind organics to its benefits.'

Hegelia took a step forward, resisting the urge to take the Leader's arms and stare into its eyes in an attempt to communicate her passion. 'I am not blind! I have devoted my life to researching the history of your race. I have studied the Cybermen from afar for so many decades.' She paused. She wanted to talk about her devotion to her field; her joy at the uncovering of each piece of the puzzle, each fragment which brought her closer to total knowledge. It wouldn't understand. 'I have learnt what it is to be a Cyberman,' she said instead. 'I know that it is a . . . logical path to take.' She struggled to fight down her emotions, speaking in as calm and detached a voice as she could muster. 'I am yours.'

'Do not listen to the human.' This came from the other Cyberman, which had stood and was approaching them. 'Emotional creatures lie – and this one is a companion of the Doctor. His deceit is well known.'

'Why should I lie?' demanded Hegelia.

'You fear conversion and will resort to illogical means to avoid it. This is a trick.'

'I do not fear conversion, I embrace it.' Hegelia turned back to the Leader. 'Why should I fear? You can see that I am old. I am nearing the end of my lifespan. Conversion would enable me to overcome that weakness of my organic form.'

'Your age makes you imperfect.'

'What nonsense! Where I come from, medical science

111

is more advanced than you can imagine. I am fit for your purpose – and, willing as I am to undergo this operation, the chance of its success is improved. I will not resist the brain alterations as some do.'

Clearly, the Cyberleader hadn't yet reached a decision. Hegelia decided to play her trump card. 'You may not realize this, Leader, but I have travelled to this colony from the far future.'

She didn't even know if it had heard her. The pregnant atmosphere was suddenly dispelled by the arrival of three more Cybermen, the foremost of which had the Doctor's unconscious body slung easily across its shoulders. It dropped its prisoner into an untidy heap and made its report. 'Our attempt to capture the Doctor's TARDIS failed. He would not operate the locking system.'

The Cyberleader greeted the news with a curt nod. 'Remove him to the ship. He will accompany us when we return to the main warcraft. I will extract his secrets from him there. Also, locate Overseer 4/3 and bring him to me.'

The Doctor was lifted again and two Cybermen left the control centre obediently. The third awaited instructions. Hegelia, somewhat put out by their inattention to her, cleared her throat and addressed the Cyberleader in commanding tones. 'As I was saying, I have travelled here from your future.'

'I am aware of your previous statement.'

'Then you should consider what it means for your race. If you were to accept me for conversion, my memories would enter your history computer. Memories, Leader, of future battles; of Cyber defeats. With that information, you could avert your destined extinction.'

'The Cybermen will not die!' The weight of determination given to that statement belied the Cyberleader's claims to impartiality. It was, naturally, the result of a programmed imperative.

'With the knowledge I possess, you will not have to. What is your decision?'

'No.'

'I . . . beg your pardon?' Hegelia felt her mouth go dry and she couldn't believe the evidence of her ears.

'You will not be accepted for conversion. As the Doctor's other companion is not available, your presence will be required to ensure his co-operation.'

'But my knowledge –'

'With the Doctor's TARDIS, we can reverse all setbacks both in the future and in the past. It is the greater prize.'

For one of the few times in her life, Hegelia didn't know what to say. She felt her aspirations slipping away like sand through her fingers and she could do nothing to stop it. She had gone over her argument a thousand times in her head. It had been perfectly logical. She had not foreseen its inadequacy and had therefore not made contingency plans. But the Doctor's presence had thrown several metaphorical spanners into everyone's works. She should have anticipated that. She hadn't.

The Cyberleader turned away dismissively and ordered that Hegelia should be taken to join the Doctor. The last of the Cybermen which had brought in the Time Lord jerked to life and seized her arm in a threateningly strong grip. She didn't struggle as it led her away. Her mind was in turmoil, still trying to cope with the stupefying impact of her failure.

Her escort halted at the sound of the Leader's voice as they reached the door. 'Should your companion refuse to divulge his secrets,' it said to Hegelia, 'it will prove necessary to maim or destroy you. However, in the event of your outliving such a use, you may be converted.'

Somehow, Hegelia didn't find the promise very comforting.

Jolarr pushed his way through the scrub and located the hatch where Taggart had said it would be. He knocked on it tentatively, but received no answer. He was uncomfortable being so close to Population Control, and the noises occasioned by a gentle breeze planted paranoid thoughts in his mind. His gaze flicked from one direction to another, expecting enemies to rise from the darkness created by an overcast sky. The dangers of being outside had been evinced by the desertion of the villages, even before the curfew. Jolarr was frightened.

A particularly cough-like gust of wind galvanized him into action. He jerked the trapdoor open and, without pause, swung his legs over the parapet and dropped through. He cried out as he collided with something soft and irregularly shaped, the object tangling itself around his body as they hit the rough dirt floor together. Focusing through the darkness and his own panic, he saw that he had landed atop Grant Markham, who had evidently been making his way up the entrance ladder to greet the visitor. Jolarr got to his feet and mumbled an embarrassed apology as he brushed down his dishevelled green suit. Only then did he register the bunker's other occupants.

'What's going on?' he asked in a small voice, backing away from the five armour-plated hulks which confronted him. 'What are they?'

'Bronze Knights – our secret weapon against the Cybermen.' The speaker was the blond man alongside whom Jolarr and Grant had made their unsuccessful flight earlier. He proffered his hand to his guest, who took it hesitantly. 'Well, one of our weapons anyway. You're the second. I'm Henneker, by the way.'

'What do you mean? What do you want?'

Henneker gave him a smile which was slightly more sinister than it was reassuring. He clapped a firm hand onto Jolarr's shoulder and guided him towards and into a seat. He leant on the wooden chair back and loomed over him, making Jolarr feel as intimidated as he had been by Madrox. 'You can help us to win this war,' he said with studied earnestness. 'Where is your ship? What weapons do you have?'

'Just a minute,' Jolarr protested. 'I can't answer that!'

114

'You have a friend in prison, don't you?'

'Yes, but –'

'How else do you think we can rescue her?' Henneker's voice was stressed. He was on the edge, and Jolarr's rejection could topple him over. Jolarr hadn't expected this. He had hoped to be given a chance to rest and some reassurance that Hegelia could be freed. He threw a pleading look towards Grant, but his fellow teenager only shrugged in a gesture of helpless sympathy.

'What about your bronze things?' Jolarr asked. The creatures – if they were truly alive – had gathered into a crescent formation at Henneker's back. Their coppery hides absorbed the feeble electric light and their rigid eye slits seemed to be narrowed in threat.

'You've seen what's going on,' said Henneker, 'what the Overseers and the Cybermen are doing to our people. We need every advantage we can muster.'

'I know, but I can't do anything for you.'

'You mean you're on their side?'

'I'm not!'

'Then help us!' Henneker turned and tore at his hair, then buried his face in his hands as if to calm himself down. Jolarr could empathize, to some extent, with his frustration. Since his own arrival on Agora, he had felt alternately terrified, alone and unbearably impotent. Nothing he had watched or read had prepared him for a dreadful reality like this. A life of dedicated research had done little to teach him the practicalities of survival in the sort of situations he had been learning about. It was tempting just to reveal his knowledge and to let Henneker make the tough decisions – but if one thing had been drummed into him at Arc University, it was the importance of leaving history unchanged. To surrender a ship – worse still, a time ship – would be to violate that edict and to court unthinkable consequences.

He couldn't explain, of course, that he was from the future. That would only increase the rebel leader's desire for his technology. 'I really am sorry,' he offered instead.

115

'I'd like to help you, but there are good reasons why I can't, believe me. I have to free my colleague and get both of us away from this planet as soon as possible.'

'We all want to get away from here. It's just that some of us aren't lucky enough to have the option.'

'I'm sorry,' said Jolarr again.

Henneker punched him in the face. Jolarr winced, more with surprise than with pain.

'What do you think you're doing?'

At first, Jolarr didn't know where the strident female voice had come from. Then he blinked away the tears drawn by Henneker's blow and saw that a woman had entered through a red curtain at the far end of the bunker. She was on the young side of middle age; short and pretty, in a hard sort of way, and in the advanced stages of pregnancy. She stood with her arms folded, glaring.

'This is nothing to do with you, Max.'

'Oh no? I'm helping you to overthrow the rulers of this colony, remember? If I thought you were going to be as bad as they are, I'd withdraw my support.' Henneker rounded on her, but the woman called Max didn't give him time to speak. 'Now if you've quite finished bullying that poor boy, I'm ready for the next two volunteers.'

The curtain billowed out beside her as two more Bronze Knights pushed through it. The bunker extended further beyond the partition than Jolarr would have guessed, and he realized that the creatures were being manufactured in the additional space. Was 'manufactured' the right word? he wondered. From Max's comment, he guessed that the Knights were cyborgs – created, like the Cybermen, from organic stock. It was some consolation to him that Grant shifted to avoid the new arrivals. He too had qualms.

Max raised an eyebrow. 'So? I've got one subject through here. I believe I'm looking at the other.'

'You're having the operation yourself?' Grant asked Henneker, clearly surprised.

'It's called "leading by example".'

116

'It's called "wanting body armour and a big gun",' Max contradicted him scathingly. Henneker shot her a dirty look and she beckoned him towards the curtain. 'I suggest you lead on.'

Henneker hesitated, glancing towards Jolarr with an expression of regret. One of the Knights reacted to his indecision. 'We could extract the alien's secrets from him,' it said, its part-human voice sending a trickle of dread down Jolarr's back.

'You'll do nothing of the sort!' Max ordered.

Reluctantly, Henneker conceded. 'Okay, forget the boy. But don't let him leave here before I get back. I might still be able to use him.' Max rolled her eyes and pulled the curtain around both of them.

Jolarr rubbed his smarting cheek and looked up at the unnerving array of cybernetic warriors, gathered around him and staring balefully as if willing him to dare risk a movement. He was almost alone with them now. Grant stood in the background, but he was watching and not acting.

Jolarr sat very still and tried not to think about what Henneker might do to him once he too had become one of these powerful, inhuman monsters.

Taggart knew what the sound portended as soon as he heard it. The unnaturally regular rhythm of metal on metal, its volume increasing, could only have meant one thing. It was his turn, finally.

He greeted the Cyberman in a standing position, waiting in front of the door as it softly swished open. A part of his mind marvelled at how calmly he was accepting this. His overwhelming emotion was not fear, but rather an abiding sadness. He had expected to be dragged to his death, when it came, with tears and screams. Instead, he thought of Lakesmith and Henneker and Roylance.

He thought of Grant and that image lingered longest.

'You are required.' The Cyberman took Taggart's arm

and propelled him down the familiar stark corridors. He hung his head and avoided the sympathetic looks of the occasional Overseers who shrank against the walls to allow them clear passage.

The journey seemed to be over in seconds, although paradoxically it felt like for ever since Taggart's fate had been sealed. He was pushed into the control centre, which was already occupied by another Cyberman and by the black-liveried Leader. The Overseers of Patrol Two pretended to be busy at their work. Madrox was present, but uncharacteristically, he didn't look at Taggart either. He cowered in the background as if afraid to draw attention to himself.

The Cyberman let Taggart go, and only then did he realize how weak his legs felt. He struggled to stop himself from collapsing as the Cyberleader confronted him. 'You have betrayed our race.' It was not a question.

'Yes.' Taggart's vocal chords didn't engage and his confession came out as a husky rattle. Get it over with, he thought. Kill me!

'You have been working to ferment rebellion against us.'

He almost answered in the affirmative again, but caught himself in time. He still couldn't speak so he shook his head instead. He knew that his autonomic responses had given his guilt away, though. He made a belated attempt to control his facial expression – but, at an inaudible signal from its Leader, the Cyberman behind him dug the fingers of both hands into his shoulders. Taggart squealed and the precarious support of his legs gave way. His knees struck the floor with a painful clang. The Cyberman bent forward and increased the pressure so that he felt as if it might drive him into the ground.

'You have been working to ferment rebellion against us.'

'Yes!' he cried, and his captor relented but didn't release its hold.

'Many components of the human body are not needed

during conversion,' the Cyberleader warned. 'Should you attempt a further deception, we will break a redundant part of your bone structure. I believe the pain for you would be –' It paused, as if searching its vocabulary for the correct words. '– quite exquisite!' Taggart remembered Lakesmith's blood-freezing cries and didn't doubt the truth of that. In a public show of power, the Cybermen had torn the old rebel leader's arm from its socket, snapped his spine and even pulled a rib through the walls of his stomach. All with their bare hands. Lakesmith's survival had been a miracle. Scant wonder that he had volunteered for Max's operations. What had he to lose?

'I'm not controlling the rebels,' Taggart insisted pathetically, as if it might save him. That provoked no reaction, so he stumbled on: 'Henneker is. Ted Henneker. He's using Arthur Lakesmith – you remember Lakesmith? – but he's the one who's running things.' Despite the slackening of the Cyberman's grip, his muscles ached. A dull throbbing sent sharp knife blades slicing down his sides. His eyes were watering and his vision was misted as he looked up at the Leader to see if he had said enough.

'Continue.'

Taggart's stomach somersaulted and he felt the sick fear of a terrible moment fifteen years ago, returning with unbearable force. He had already repeated everything that Madrox knew. To say more would be to doom Agora's second rebellion as surely as he had helped to doom its first.

'I don't know anything else,' he said, and the pressure on his shoulders increased without warning. He gasped and crumpled further, seeing black spots as something gyrated inside his head. He prayed that he might find safety in unconsciousness; perhaps he would wake up somewhere better. But such release was not to be. He was freed unexpectedly, and he pitched forward onto the unyielding floor, whimpering. The Cyberleader poked at him with its toe, then gave the dispassionate order: 'Break him.'

119

'No!' Taggart rolled onto his back and put up his arms in a futile warding-off gesture. The Cyberman simply snatched one of the limbs with both hands and snapped his left forearm without effort. Taggart yelped at the poker-hot pain and felt bile rising in his oesophagus.

'Where are the rebels based?'

Taggart dearly wanted to deny that he knew the answer (a few hours ago, it would have been true, too – damn his curiosity!). His lips moved accordingly, but he couldn't bring himself to speak the lie. The price of discovery was too great.

But, equally, the silence of his indecision tempted retribution. 'We will continue to damage you until you speak,' said the Cyberleader, nodding towards its subordinate. The grip was shifted to Taggart's wrist. He felt his bladder let go.

'I'll tell you what you want to know, I swear, just don't hurt me again, I'll tell you . . .' His voice petered out into a croak as his captor took his other arm, hauled him to his feet and let go. Taggart's face was flushed and uncomfortably hot and wet. He wiped his sleeve across it, but it did no good. He blinked away tears and looked to the Cyberleader, shaking as a cold wave broke across his body.

'I'll tell you what you want to know,' he whispered, knowing that he was signing the death warrants of dozens.

Hegelia was sitting uncomfortably on the floor of the Cyber ship's rear chamber, back to back with the unconscious Doctor, their wrists tied by wire. She was trying to persuade herself that, despite her setback, she had gained something. Cyber troops were herding Agorans into the compartments on the highest level. The conversion process would begin soon and she would become one of the privileged few to have seen it.

She felt the wire which bound her twisting and pulling against her skin. The Doctor was awake, but feigning slumber and working on escape. 'I have been told to inform you,' she said in a loud enough voice, 'that if you slip your bonds, the Cybermen will shoot us both.' He ceased his struggles and she felt his shoulders slump. 'Accept defeat. Enjoy the spectacle. We are quite honoured to be witnessing this procedure.'

'I find nothing honourable in the perpetration of casual slaughter!' snapped the Doctor.

'Why employ such perjorative language? All we are seeing is the use by one race of another for the purpose of their continuance. The Cybermen are acting no more cruelly than do carnivorous species.'

'Except that most carnivores aren't blessed with such willing victims,' said the Doctor with heavy disapproval.

'There is no point in fighting them. One may as well stop the caterpillar from attaining its imago form; to deny it increased brain power and defensive abilities. It could be argued that the Cybermen are pushing humankind beyond the confines of its evolutionary cul-de-sac. They can be seen as a natural force.'

'The Cybermen have nothing to do with nature,' the Doctor retorted. 'They are an abhorrence! You could see that if you only had a heart.'

'I do have a heart,' she said stiffly.

'Oh, but don't you wish you didn't!'

Hegelia was not surprised that he knew. She was disappointed, however, that he didn't understand. 'I am the foremost authority of my time on the Cybermen, Doctor. I have dredged up every last document which exists about them, every text file written. I have studied fragments of their buildings, the burnt-out shells of their vessels and even the remnants of their corpses. But all that is nothing compared to the experience which I am now earning.'

'I'm pleased for you – but some things aren't worth experiencing.'

'I think they are. How do you imagine I feel, Doctor, having spent my life in the pursuit of total knowledge, to

121

be unable to discover the one most basic fact of the Cybermen's existence? I need to know what happens to the mind once it has been operated upon. Does the personality of the individual endure somehow, subverted or altered? Would I be conscious of my actions? Could I disapprove or would I willingly serve the Cyber cause? What would it feel like?'

'I do understand,' said the Doctor, 'but you're asking the same questions which sentient lifeforms have asked about death since the beginning of time – and the problem is the same. However it feels, whatever you find there, you can't tell anyone about it.'

'That does not matter,' said Hegelia. 'I would know. At last, I would know all.'

'And once your emotions had been neutered and your heart and soul ripped out, you wouldn't care in the slightest.'

'You talk about soul – but my transition, my glorious synthesis, could only bring me one step closer to communing with the world-soul, to which we are all connected.'

The Doctor fell silent, but Hegelia could hear him sighing and she felt his head shake. Let him think what he would. She had adjusted to her disappointment now, and her mind was ticking over with new ideas. She would get what she wanted.

She craned her neck to see what was happening on the topmost balcony. Most of the compartments seemed full. She could discern the silhouettes of human forms, immobile behind glass doors. Beside her, the Cyberman stationed at the chamber's base had finished its preparatory work. The consoles stood ready for the last human to arrive, whereupon the conversion machinery could be put into action.

Hegelia ached with the bittersweet anticipation of that moment.

Scenes from Ben Taggart's latest nightmare:
'Where are the rebels located?'

'What are they planning?'

'When will they act?'

He sat on the floor of the tiny metal cell, knees up against his forehead, arms wrapped about them, fingers laced together. His eyes were tightly closed and he wished with all his soul that he could open them to discover that the last thirty minutes had not happened.

Why had he said so much?

That question didn't need to be asked. Ben Taggart was a coward and always had been. In the face of torture, he had reverted to type and given in. He had told the Cyberleader what it wanted to know.

Taggart bit back a sob and contracted his muscles, as if hoping to wrap himself into a ball which reality couldn't pierce. A searing pain shot up his broken left arm. He almost welcomed this punishment for his sins. It was nothing compared to what he had let his so-called friends in for with his weakness.

'Where are the rebels located?'

'They have an underground hideout. It's right outside Population Control, on the outskirts of Sector Two. The access hatch is hidden under foliage.'

'What are they planning?'

He had lost all sense of time. He didn't know how long he had spent here, wallowing in the misery of his memories. In those few, isolated moments when Taggart was able to suppress recriminations, he found that there was more than enough self-pity to occupy his mind instead. His own position was hardly enviable. He was cold and alone, abandoned in a claustrophobic holding cell with conversion the only future he had to look forward to. He wondered what it would feel like and imagined that it would be like dying. Which might well be for the best, he supposed.

The worst part of it was the waiting. He felt a sudden empathy with the poor souls who had sat in cells like this for days, weeks, sometimes years. He wondered how many of those people he had brought to Population

Control himself. The faces of some of them flashed across the backs of his eyelids – faces Taggart had hoped and believed he had forgotten. He opened his eyes to banish the spectres and tried to focus on the room's bare walls instead.

He remembered the Leader, announcing that it would send out a contingent of Cybermen to locate the rebels' bunker and to destroy all those within. 'The organics require a further demonstration of our superiority. They will have one.'

A series of clangs cut through his reverie. For the second time that day, Taggart was to be collected. He used his good arm to lever himself to his feet. The seam of the cell's back door was invisible, but he knew where it was. He waited for it to open.

In an unexpected and unwanted contrast to the calm resignation of earlier, Taggart started to cry. His attempts to compose himself were only partially successful and he greeted his latest Cyberman escort with a crumpled face and streaming eyes. At the creature's wordless bidding, he stepped through into the corridor which he knew would take him to the Cyber ship, joining a straggling group of fellow sacrifices. They shuffled on in silence, Taggart's arm throbbing and hanging like a dead weight, slowing him down. They halted three times, waiting as the Cyberman ushered three more frightened men out of their cramped cells to join them.

As the funereal procession continued, Taggart tried his best to be optimistic. He did have one small hope, he consoled himself.

He didn't know quite how it had happened. Perhaps, somewhere in his subconscious, he had possessed one small, untapped reserve of courage. Perhaps he had been motivated by Henneker's stinging criticism or by Max's trust and had wanted to prove himself. Or maybe he had just been more scared of Lakesmith, the lumbering Bronze Knight, than of the Cyberleader. Whatever. Taggart had been surprised to find a lie tripping easily off his tongue. He had told his interrogator that the rebels had constructed a surface-to-air missile, with which they intended to shoot down the Cyber ship as it departed. He had insisted that only Henneker and two or three friends were involved in the plan; that he had discovered it by accident and had merely committed the crime of silence. Then, when he had expected only more pain, the Cyberleader had sent him away. It had believed him.

The rebels had a chance. Their position had been compromised, but their weaponry had not. The Cyber-men had no idea what they were marching into. That might make a difference.

As Ben Taggart emerged into the conversion chamber, he realized with a depressing sense of futility that he would never know whether it had done or not.

8

How Does It Feel?

Grant and Jolarr had been left alone with seven Bronze Knights for over two hours, and in that time, not a word had been spoken. After twenty minutes, Grant had built up the courage to slip through the semi-circle of cyborgs and to take a seat beside their alien captive. Jolarr had rewarded his attempt to give moral support with a faint appreciative smile.

At last, Max reappeared at the curtain. Looming behind her were the shadows of two more Knights. Grant rose and stared at them as they tottered, unsteady on their new legs, into the already overcrowded area. He was fascinated by the thought that one of them had been his close acquaintance of the past few weeks. The creatures were identical, though; he couldn't make out which was Henneker. Jolarr stood too and edged behind Grant for what little shielding he could offer. His expression was stiff with apprehension. Grant hoped that Max would protect him.

'Where are the next two volunteers?' the foremost of the new Knights asked.

'Nobody has entered the bunker,' a predecessor reported.

'They have failed us. I will collect them.'

Max reacted with astonishment. She darted to block the Knight's path to the exit ladder. 'Are you mad? You can't show yourself out there, you'll terrify people!'

'That is unimportant.'

'And what if the Cybermen learn about you? We'll lose our element of surprise.'

'We need organic stock. If the humans will not honour

126

their promises to provide it, they must be made to do so.'

'Henneker?'

Grant didn't know what had made him call the name, apart from the recognition of something familiar beneath the artificial tones which all Bronze Knights shared. He was terrified of what the rebel leader had become, but at the same time, he felt himself compulsively drawn to this awesome fusion of biology and technology. The Knight pivoted to face him and Grant stepped forward tentatively and reached out. His fingers brushed against the coarse, grainy texture of its – his? – armour. He recoiled, one whispered, impassioned question leaping to his tongue. *'How does it feel?'*

'I do not understand.'

Gesticulating hopelessly, Grant tried to put thoughts into words. 'The brain alterations. What have they done to you?'

'I am unchanged.'

'How can you be? You're acting so differently. You were talking about "the humans". You seem more . . .' Grant stopped before he said something that the new Henneker might not like.

'All very interesting, I'm sure,' Max cut in, 'but do you think we can get on with the business of defeating Cybermen?'

Henneker thought for a moment. Then, without a trace of emotion, he said, 'It will take more time to find volunteers for the Project. We are behind schedule. We already outnumber our enemies.'

'You're saying we should attack now?'

There was a sudden flurry of movement. Two Bronze Knights lurched towards Grant, who instinctively shied away. Henneker swung around to see what was happening, lost his delicate balance and collided with one of his fellows. Three Knights went crashing to the floor, their armours impacting with hard dirt.

Grant saw the cause of the disturbance. Jolarr had taken his chance to flee. He had sidled to the foot of the ladder

127

and was halfway up it before he was observed. Grant could see the desperation in his milk-white face and he found himself willing the alien to succeed. But, even as Jolarr reached the top rung, the first of the Bronze Knights closed the distance and grabbed at him. Jolarr kicked out and its hand was deflected. The trapdoor flew open and sunlight silhouetted Jolarr's head and shoulders. Then he cried out. The cyborg had managed to get a grip on his ankle.

'For heaven's sake,' cried Max, 'just let him go!'

Jolarr kicked again with his free leg. His soft-shoed foot couldn't have harmed his captor, but still it reacted with a familiar human reflex. It flinched, let go, and Jolarr scrambled to freedom. The Knight climbed onto the ladder, but Max was close enough now to lay a restraining hand on its arm.

'We don't need him,' she said firmly. 'We've made our plans – and Henneker is right. The Cybermen have been here too long already. If we're to stand a chance of saving the people in Population Control, you have to attack now.'

Grant felt something in his stomach turn over. It was not planned that he should have much involvement in the upcoming battle, but even so, he faced the prospect of it with trepidation. After all this time, there would be an outcome, one way or another. He looked around the bunker at the nine Bronze Knights and wondered if they could be enough to rescue the Doctor and liberate his world.

Jolarr emerged into the fresh, post-rainfall atmosphere with a mixture of relief and panic. He imagined the Bronze Knights clambering up the ladder to recapture him, and as soon as he had dragged himself clear of clinging vegetation, he pushed his legs into a frantic sprint. It didn't last long.

He came up short at the sight of three figures, poking in the undergrowth just metres ahead. Cybermen! And they had seen him. The silver giants turned as one and Jolarr back-pedalled, almost slipping on the wet grass, turned and pelted towards the nearest village. His thoughts took seconds to catch up with his actions. The Cybermen knew of the bunker. They had been attempting to locate it – and the most logical explanation for his appearance nearby was that he was one of the rebels they had come to find. Somehow, Jolarr didn't feel like stopping to explain the truth.

He shot a quick look over his shoulder and saw that two of the monsters had resumed their search. The third was pursuing him. It had no gun, but that was small consolation. He dived across the village boundary and put a building between them. His heart felt like it was about to explode, but he had to keep going. He had to lose the creature before he tired.

If Jolarr had learned only one thing from his research, it was that the Cybermen never gave up.

'Not such an interesting sight after all, is it?' said the Doctor.

Two Cybermen remained in the conversion chamber. They had taken a console each and were operating controls with perfect synchronicity. Nothing else moved, except that Hegelia fancied she could see an occasional flicker inside the now fully occupied compartments.

'It will be worth the wait,' she said, 'when those majestic creatures emerge.'

'They won't. I had a closer look, very briefly, at their cubicles earlier. They double as freezer compartments. Once they've been converted, the new Cybermen will be held in suspended animation until their bodies and minds can adjust to the changes forced upon them. By the time they awake, this ship will be light-years away from here and we'll be either free or dead.'

Hegelia scowled at this further bad luck. 'Why do they need to be frozen? They should not have to "adjust", as you put it.'

The Doctor tutted with mock disapproval. 'Remember your history, ArcHivist. These Cybermen have suffered a heavy defeat. Their forces are scattered, resources depleted. This chamber is set up to add to their numbers as quickly, and with as little material, as possible. The equipment is actually quite crude. If you've ever attempted brain surgery with a hammer and chisel, you'll know why the patient needs a few days' bed rest afterwards.'

'I hardly think the analogy is appropriate. We are talking about a race far more advanced than humanity.'

The Doctor answered with a sardonic laugh. 'I don't know why you need machinery to turn you into a Cyberman. You're halfway there already.'

Hegelia hardened herself to his flippancy. She had better things to become upset about. She had been mentally running over her options and it now seemed that there was only one feasible one. She sighed. 'All right then, Doctor.'

'What?'

'If you must break free, I will do what I can to help.'

She couldn't see her fellow captive's face, but she could almost hear the broad grin stretching across it. 'That's very kind,' said the Doctor, 'but the only help I need is for you not to alert the Cybermen to what I'm doing.'

Hegelia could already feel him working at their bonds. She only hoped that she was doing the right thing.

Jolarr had paused but for a few seconds to get back his breath and to assess his position. The Cyberman had appeared almost instantly from behind a nearby building. Whilst its prey had twisted and turned, attempting to frustrate pursuit, it had predicted his erratic path and moved to block it.

Jolarr coaxed his unwilling body into motion, desperately reaching for the nearest corner. The Cyberman fired and he felt a hot, prickly sensation washing over his back. He kept on going, expecting to be laid low by the fatal afterkick. It didn't occur. He had been just out of range of the head-mounted weapon, he realized with delirious relief as he left the Cyberman's line of fire. But he wasn't out of danger yet. It would still be following relentlessly.

The best way to outmanoeuvre it would be to do something completely illogical – and that meant dangerous! Jolarr raced around three sides of the two-storey house which was sheltering him. He didn't have time to worry about what would happen if the Cyberman was still waiting, back in the street where he had left it.

He peered around the final corner and saw it, stopped at the next junction, its back to him, clearly considering which way to head. His gamble had paid off. As soon as it was out of sight, he could sprint away in the opposite direction.

Then it turned and headed towards him, its stiff gait bringing it closer with numbing speed. Jolarr ducked back around the house and ran, something catching in his throat as he realized the futility of his situation. How could he – the young, inexperienced academic – ever hope to elude this unstoppable dreadnought?

He was still dwelling on such pessimistic thoughts, still looking over his shoulder, when he ran full tilt into somebody. He tried to push the villager aside, but the young, bearded man was deliberately holding him. Jolarr's arms were pinned and the Cyberman was behind him again.

'I've got him for you,' the man called in a reedy voice. 'Sir!' he added as the Cyberman drew closer. Jolarr guessed that he had not come face to face with one of his masters before. A panic-driven adrenalin surge gave him the strength to take advantage of his captor's moment of paralysis. He wriggled and broke free, pushing the man towards the Cyberman as it manipulated the controls on its chest unit and the echoing *chung!* of its gun rang out. The unintentional victim let out a howl and fell backwards, into the arms of the startled Jolarr. Repulsed, he hurled the corpse away from him. A belated nervous reflex caused it to cling to the Cyberman and, whilst it was shaking itself free, Jolarr fled.

His narrow escape had forced him to make a decision. He couldn't outrun his pursuer, but he could outfly it. It meant leaving Hegelia behind on this planet, but he had no choice. She was probably dead in any case, he tried to convince himself.

With renewed determination, Jolarr changed course and headed towards the field in which the time ship had landed. His one priority now was to locate it and escape.

The atmosphere in the bunker was tense, despite the fact that only two of its occupants were still capable of expressing apprehension. The nine Bronze Knights were flexing their muscles, getting used to their new casings before they embarked upon the mission for which they had been created. Max watched on with a mixture of emotions. She was proud of her accomplishment, but sad at what she had had to do to nine human beings – and worried at what those beings might, in turn, do with the powers she had given them.

She had to accept that it was all out of her hands. She had done her part. She was becoming aware of a dull ache behind her eyes which reminded her how hard she had worked and for how long. Suppressing a yawn, she headed for the ladder.

'Where are you going?' asked Grant. She realized that he was wary of being left with the cyborgs.

'Home,' she said. 'I'm tired and I want to sleep. I suggest you do the same.'

'But we're about to attack!'

'No, the Knights are about to do that. You and me are going to sit here, twiddling our thumbs and worrying. Well, no thanks. If I can't do any more for the effort, I might as well do something for my own health.' She gave him a wry smile as she took the first rung. 'I'm sure I'll hear the result as it comes in.' Then she turned to

Henneker and wished him good luck, the words seeming inadequate. He nodded an acknowledgement.

Max hauled herself up the ladder, then realized that fatigue had made her forget to check if the way was clear. For a moment, she considered taking the risk. As always, though, common-sense prevailed. Ignoring the protests of her muscles, she lowered herself again and glanced towards the monitor.

The picture flickered and rolled – and, for a second, Max convinced herself that she was seeing phantom images; that two huge figures weren't standing outside and that one of them wasn't kneeling to pull open the hatch. Another sliver of time passed by as she stood, staring, her brain and mouth seized up with the indecision of unexpected danger. It was fortunate for everyone that Grant looked over to see what was happening, and yelled in terror as he too saw the approaching Cybermen.

Henneker and the other Bronze Knights moved swiftly towards the ladder – no fear in them, Max noticed. They pushed her behind them and Max felt strangely touched by the protective gesture. Grant needed no such encouragement to leave the firing line. He was already heading towards the curtain, behind which he might find concealment.

The last thing Max saw, before she decided that her wisest course of action was to join him, was the trapdoor splintering open to reveal two silver faces, four tear-pulled eyes, framed against the square of light which filtered into her once-safe haven.

Then all hell broke loose.

The Cyberleader had stalked into the conversion chamber – and, to Hegelia's consternation, the Doctor seemed intent upon baiting it.

'How long are you planning to keep us here?' he protested, when it finally responded to his persistent shouts of 'Hey, you!' and approached the captives.

'Your fate has been explained to the woman. To

reiterate the details would be an inefficient use of my time.'

The Cyberleader moved to return to its fellows, but the Doctor wasn't so easily brushed off. 'My colleague here is interested in you. She wants to know how it feels to become a Cyberman.'

'We do not have feelings.'

'That's what I told her. The funny thing is, she doesn't understand what a drawback that is. Perhaps you could tell her; get these silly ideas out of her head once and for all?' Hegelia twisted to glare at him. The Doctor ignored her. He was staring up at the Cyberleader with a childlike grin.

'Emotions are unnecessary. They hamper the course of logical thought.'

'So you wouldn't claim to enjoy life at all?'

'Of course not.'

'There you are then, ArcHivist. Do you really want to become an emotionally stunted, mindless automaton? You wouldn't enjoy it!'

'I would thank you to leave me out of this discussion, Doctor.'

'We are the purest form of life in the cosmos!' the Leader roared, with ironically more feeling than Hegelia had displayed.

The Doctor tutted. 'Dear oh dear. A blatant exhibition of pride – an organic emotion and one of the Deadly Sins to boot. You're undermining your own argument, Leader. And, whilst we're on the subject, I wish you wouldn't keep doing that.'

'To what do you refer?'

'The way you put your hands on your hips. I know it's meant to make you look fierce, but it does nothing for you, believe me.'

Almost self-consciously, the Cyberleader shifted its stance. 'You must see some value in emotional responses then,' the Doctor pressed on, 'to simulate them as you do. Pride, arrogance, scorn, anger . . .'

'The intimidatory effect upon organic beings can be useful.'

'And what about the rest of the range? Compassion? Love? Fear? What if I was to say that I'm holding a handful of gold dust behind my back? Would that not worry you at all?'

'I am not programmed to mimic fear.'

'I know.'

Without Hegelia realizing it, the Doctor had worked his hands free. He brought one around now in a whiplash motion, opening his fist so that, for one second, she thought he had thrown something into the Cyberleader's chest unit.

The hand was empty. The Leader didn't move.

The Doctor smiled again. 'An autonomic fear response could have saved your life then, if I really had been carrying gold.'

'You were not. I scanned you and found no trace of the element. Your demonstration was worthless.'

The Doctor's face fell. 'Tin-plated spoilsport!' he muttered.

'Resorting to insults will be of no benefit. They will not affect me.'

'Perhaps. But they make me feel better.' The Doctor sighed. 'I don't expect you to understand that either.'

Grant and Max had withdrawn to relative safety behind the curtain – but, although Max had hidden behind the depleted vat of reddish-brown compound, Grant had been unable to sacrifice his viewpoint on the scene in the main part of the bunker.

His first coherent observation was that the Bronze Knights outnumbered the Cybermen nine to two. His second was that the latter were much stronger, more experienced and had surprise on their side. Tension stole his breath as the first of the silver monsters clambered into the cellar. But the Knights' position gave them an advantage. Two of them yanked the Cyberman clear off the ladder. It resisted, its strong hands snapping free two rungs. It emitted a mechanical, keening wail and lashed out blindly. Its fists caught one of its captors. The Knight relinquished its grip and staggered into the wall. Its fellows shifted to avoid its uncontrolled lurch and, still unsteady on their feet, two collided and fought to keep each other upright. The confined space was working against them. The Cyberman had already managed to wrench itself free and its in-built gun blazed furiously. Electricity coruscated around the bulky armour of a Bronze Knight. The Cyberman fired again and Grant felt a tingle of hopeful excitement as its victim managed to remain upright. It reached for its attacker and struggled forward. Then, to Grant's dismay, it pitched into an uncontrolled dive and, aided by a chop to the neck, crashed helplessly to the ground at the Cyberman's feet.

Its colleagues were closing in now, and the foremost three brought up their arm-mounted blasters. Grant had not seen them operate before and he was impressed, in an awful sort of way. Accompanied by the sound of a gunpowder blast, they shot out jets of blue flame which seemed almost liquid. The bursts converged on the intruder's chest. It reeled, but didn't fall. Suddenly, the second Cyberman appeared in the midst of the mêlée and Grant realized, in a heart-stopping moment of horror, that it had leapt from the top of the ladder and taken its enemies by surprise. It brought its powerful fists down on two bronze heads and followed through with equally devastating blows to the abdomens of the same Knights. In one case, it was lucky. Its fist penetrated to the complex circuitry beneath the armour. An electrical fire broke out in the Bronze Knight's stomach. Its scream grated even more than that of the Cyberman before. It flung its hands to its face – a typically human reaction – and went backwards head over heels, bringing down one of its allies with it. Something exploded inside its casing and Grant knew this cyborg would not be getting up again. He had lost track of which Bronze Knight was which – had he just witnessed the death of Henneker? Or Lakesmith?

The rest of the Knights, unused to combat, were having trouble coping with a two-pronged attack. They couldn't use their weapons without risking harm to each other, and the Cybermen more than matched them for strength. The battle had descended into a confused mass of heaving armoured bodies. Grant found the sight repellent and yet compulsive.

One of the Cybermen was in trouble. Four Knights had managed to co-ordinate their efforts. One held each of its arms, preventing it from operating its weaponry. A third whipped its legs out from under it and the fourth achieved a headlock. It still didn't give up. It heaved and strained and managed to free its left arm, knocking over a Bronze Knight in the process. But it was too late for it to build on that success. Grant watched with wide-eyed fascination as the Cyberman's head was pulled inexorably from its body. It thrashed its free arm and gave out a nerve-jangling distress rattle. Its colleague was hemmed in and could do nothing to prevent the inevitable.

The Cyberman's head was held high like a trophy, its winner giving an electronic whoop of triumph. The decapitated creature jerked and finally toppled. The broken ends of wires sparked in its neck and a viscous, dark liquid seeped into the dirt. It might have been oil; it might equally have been blood. Grant flinched from the gruesome sight, either way.

The other Cyberman, surrounded by enemies now, began to fire indiscriminately. At least three Knights were hit, and one went down as a thin haze of smoke drifted across the battlefield and clawed at Grant's throat and tear ducts. Through a watery veil, he saw the Cyberman breaking through the living barrier which had kept it from its colleague. It made a belated attack upon the slayer and floored it with three crippling blows. Grant blinked, reacted too late to the near-spherical, shiny projectile which span through the air, and screamed as the first Cyberman's disembodied head landed squarely in his hands, its mouth disgorging a small quantity of clear liquid onto his shirt.

Max heard him and yelled, 'For God's sake, get over here!'

Grant pushed the head away from him; by the time he had forced himself to avert his gaze from its upturned, lifeless face, the fight had moved closer. Another Bronze Knight fell and grasped at the curtain but only succeeded in bringing it down. Suddenly exposed, Grant tried to join Max behind the vat, but a retreating ally cut off his path and he could do nothing but cower against the wall and pray that the invading monster could be kept at bay.

The battle had become concentrated in what had been Max's work area. The Cyberman hefted one of the tables on which her operations had been carried out, and hurled it. But the Knights were more co-ordinated now and making use of their heightened awareness and improved reactions. Two of them moved to catch the makeshift weapon and proceeded to use it to drive the Cyberman across the bunker's width. It was staggered for a moment, but then fired twice more. One of its foes fell. The Cyberman matched its strength against the other and managed to fling both Knight and table away from it. Another Knight closed in and leapt on its back, one arm snaking around the Cyberman's throat in an attempt to do to it what had been done to its colleague.

Grant had no hope of reaching Max, but he did now have a clear run at the exit. He looked from ladder to Cyberman, paralysed by indecision. He reasoned that he could hardly put himself in any more danger, and made the break.

Halfway, he froze at the sound of the Cyberman's death-throes. It was still held fast and another Bronze Knight had moved in and fired its blaster, at close range, into its chest unit. It fired again and something exploded. Grant knew he should continue his flight, but he was rooted to the floor. His skin still crept at the sight of friends and foes alike, but somehow, he couldn't bring himself to tear his eyes away from the spectacle.

When the dying Cyberman's last, misdirected blast struck him, Grant's first reaction was one of utmost surprise. He gaped at his own chest and saw no sign of an entry wound — but he felt that something had broken inside. For the smallest part of a second, he thought he might have sustained a minor injury. He could stand and talk and ask Max for medical help, once the dust of battle had settled.

But then something burst in his stomach and Grant felt a trickle of blood welling over his lower teeth and onto his chin. The Knights — those which remained standing — had clustered around the fallen Cyberman and were making sure of their victory by gleefully dismembering its corpse. He tried to shout to them, but couldn't even manage a croak as he felt his legs give way and his immediate surroundings suddenly seemed much further than they were.

The last thing Grant Markham saw was the ground rushing up to meet his open eyes. He couldn't even put out a hand to arrest his fall.

Jolarr had long since stopped measuring time's passage. He only knew that it seemed he had been running across Agora's barren land for ever. His formerly pristine graduation suit was soaked with sweat and his chest felt like a circular saw had been let loose inside it. He couldn't even think about the monster which was following him any more, nor about the blessed escape which lay at the end of his ordeal. He just had to concentrate on his feet, to make sure that the hard, lumpy ground didn't steal them from under him — and with them, his life.

He finally reached the spot where he and Hegelia had hidden the time ship, an eternity ago. As he fumbled in his pockets for the recall unit, he looked behind him for the first time in minutes. The Cyberman had lost ground, but not nearly enough. And it was still coming. He panicked as he couldn't find the device, then felt a cold wash of relief as his fingers closed around it. The white box's keypad blurred and he cursed and forced himself to concentrate. It was harder than it should have been; he kept expecting to be bathed in the lethal fire of the Cyberman's gun. But then, as fear sharpened his senses, it all became clear and Jolarr stabbed out the combination which would bring him salvation.

Nothing happened.

A prickly feeling crept up his spine. He operated the unit again, but with the same alarming results. He cast about for some evidence that he had come to the wrong place, but saw none. He tried again and again, knowing that such efforts were useless. Somehow, the time ship had gone. He was trapped here. And doomed.

The Cyberman approached.

Jolarr gave up. He knew that the only thing he could expect now was death. He dropped the recall unit and surrendered to fatigue. He greeted the Grim Reaper on his knees, waiting in miserable submission for the Cyberman to enter killing range.

He had heard that, at times like this, one's life was reputed to flash before one's eyes. All Jolarr saw was the four walls of his room at home, the computer screen and a pile of academic texts. He felt regret at having used his time to do nothing more than study the writings of others, and at never having had the chance to make his own discoveries or to put his knowledge to good use.

But then, if he had stayed within those walls and continued to experience life at a distance, he might have lived a lot longer.

The Cyberman stopped and, for a moment, Jolarr thought it was deliberately attempting to prolong his agony. That wasn't logical, he told himself. It seemed to be making some sort of decision, and Jolarr suddenly felt hope once more. What if he could slip past the monster whilst it was distracted? He could return to the village and make a further attempt to shake it off amongst the buildings.

Sharp pains stabbed through his knotted leg muscles as he tried to rise, and Jolarr realized that his optimism had been premature. Even if he could overcome his physical limitations, he would have to take a wide arc to circumvent the Cyberman without getting too close – and it would move to cut him off. At his peak, it would have been difficult to escape. At the moment, it was impossible.

As Jolarr accepted his bleak destiny a second time, the Cyberman turned and marched away in the direction from which it had come. He stared, hardly daring to believe the evidence of his sight – but, as its back diminished further into the distance, Jolarr had no option but to believe.

It must have received a signal, said one thought amongst a whirlwind. It must have been told of something more important than his destruction. Fate had spared him.

And, for a long time, all Jolarr could do was sit with his face in his hands and weep.

When Max was sure it was safe to do so, she emerged from her hiding place and surveyed the smoke-obscured, emotion-wrenching aftermath of the brief but hard-fought battle. Her Bronze Knights had won, but at a cost. At least four were damaged and two would not be fighting again.

'The Cybermen know of our location,' said one of the survivors, 'but we have proved we can defeat them. We must attack now, before they can surprise us again.' The speaker had to be Henneker; as dispassionate as ever. More so. Perhaps it was best.

'Be careful,' warned Max in a dead voice. 'You still outnumber them, but they've proved it won't be easy. The score is two all.' She indicated the fallen.

'They have killed three,' a Knight corrected her,

matter-of-factly. She thought that this one had Lake-smith's voice.

At first, Max didn't know what he meant. But then, as she stepped gingerly over the bodies of the dead, she felt an ice-cold hand reach into her guts and turn them upside-down.

She hadn't seen Grant fall – but his body lay, all the same, twisted painfully, his face frozen into an open-mouthed expression of shock. She knelt beside him and tested for a pulse, but Lakesmith confirmed what Max already knew she would find.

'His heart no longer beats,' the Bronze Knight said. The information clearly meant little to him, and Max cursed herself for dampening that particular emotional response. 'He is dead.'

9

Desperation

Madrox had not said a word since his death sentence had been rescinded. He still half expected the Cyberleader to march in and deal with its 'unfinished business', and he wasn't about to remind it – or its troops – that he was here and alive. He hovered at the periphery of the circular control centre, ready to respond with staged efficiency to any request made. He watched as the four men of Patrol Two carried out their monitoring duties, supervised by two Cybermen – and he studiously fixed his mind on the time, a few short hours hence, when this would be over. Once the conversions were complete, the masters of Agora would leave for another three years.

No – for a mere eighteen months, this time. He couldn't let that matter, though. So long as he survived, he would have reason enough to be grateful.

Madrox was then almost overcome by a miserable sense of impending doom when he realized that yet one more thing had gone wrong. The Cybermen didn't communicate verbally at first, but they turned to face each other in a way which, had they been human, might have denoted concern. One strode towards a console, ignoring the Overseer who darted out of its path. 'I will request instructions,' it said – and, as it operated the controls, Madrox shrank into the shadows and prayed that the unspecified problem wouldn't be the death of him.

For too long, nothing happened. Then, just as he was beginning to think that the uncertainty, the silence and the tension would break him, a siren squealed. The perimeter breach alarm had activated.

The Overseers leapt to emergency stations, knowing what the price of hesitation would be. The Cybermen moved as one to the main screens and watched as a nervous operator punched in a section code relayed by one of his fellows. 'There they are – they're trying to break in!'

Madrox edged around the room until he too could see. He suppressed a gasp at the sight of half a dozen or so figures clustered around Population Control's fence. The night was drawing in and the camera didn't function well in the dark, but Madrox saw that the would-be invaders were like nothing he knew. They were squat but imposing – and, although they were humanoid, there was a non-human quality about them. They seemed to absorb what little light there was, but Madrox thought he detected a glimmer of red. His first notion was that these were alien enemies of the Cybermen, mounting a surprise attack. His second was that they were automatons, devised by Henneker and his rebels. Either way, he would be considered responsible.

The foremost of the figures had already managed to damage the fence. Now, with a tremendous effort, it tore the chain links apart and created a hole just big enough to pass through. Even over the piercing shriek of the alarm, Chief Overseer Madrox fancied that he could hear the sound of one more nail entering his metaphorical coffin.

'Things not going well, I take it?'

Hegelia couldn't believe that her fellow captive was taunting their jailer again. 'Do not draw his attention,' she whispered. She could feel that he had almost slipped his bonds. Did he want to have to go through the process a third time?

' "He"?' the Doctor repeated with loud indignation. ' "He"? I think even our Cyber friend over there would agree that "it" is a more appropriate pronoun for such a creature.' He raised his voice further, directing his remark towards the Cyberleader. 'Despite its occasional pretence at humanity!'

Still he was ignored. The Leader had not so much as glanced at its prisoners in the last few minutes. In mid-response to one of the Doctor's insults, it had frozen, then cocked its head to one side as if listening. It had now positioned itself behind a console, where it worked in silence. 'What do you think has happened?' asked Hegelia.

The Doctor shrugged. 'Who knows? Technical failure? Armed uprising? Perhaps my assistant has finally got his act together.' His hands were still working behind their backs. He stopped suddenly as the Cyberleader swung to face them. It crossed the chamber and stood, towering over them, legs astride. It placed its hands on its hips, then seemed to think better of the gesture and removed them.

'I have to attend to other matters.'

'Ah, well. Goodbye then,' the Doctor responded cheerfully.

'You will not attempt to escape in my absence.'

'If you say so.'

'My Cybermen have orders to damage you should you ignore that instruction.'

'I rather thought they might have.'

The Cyberleader turned and left via the ladder to the cockpit. The Doctor immediately slipped his hands free from the wire. 'What are you doing?' Hegelia hissed.

'Risking crippling injury and possible death to save a large number of lives. It's my job.'

'But you heard the Leader. You are not being logical!'

'Thank you,' said the Doctor. 'I think that's the nicest thing you've said to me. Now, when I move into action, I suggest you take cover. I don't want those Cybermen to see you. They might decide to stop me by using you as a hostage.'

Hegelia's skin felt cold and prickly, as if goosebumps were breaking out across her face. She flexed her wrists experimentally and the wire fell from them. The Doctor had freed her too. She looked at the two remaining

145

sentries, nervously. Both were working at their consoles. 'One of them has a gun.'

'I had noticed actually, but thank you.'

'Are you positive that you are not going to place us in peril?'

'Of course not. But I am sure that, if I do nothing, five hundred people not a million miles from here will suffer the consequences.'

Hegelia swallowed and fell silent. She wondered if a prayer might be in order at this juncture.

The fence was down in three places and the robots – or whatever they were – were in the grounds. Madrox felt drained, as if he had simply run out of fear. The only emotion he could feel was awe at the sight of the monstrosities; seven of them, marching in formation. Whilst they were only pictures on the monitor, they seemed unreal. He had to remind himself that only a short distance separated them from him.

A short distance and a devastatingly potent defensive system.

'Orders, sir?' The request had to be repeated before Madrox realized that it was meant for him. He snapped out of his reverie, turning cold as he saw that he was being stared at by four Overseers and two Cybermen. 'I thought –' he began, giving his masters an apologetic look. No, never mind what he had thought! They didn't want to hear excuses. They were waiting for their Chief Overseer to do his job.

'Erm – switch from random defence to manual. Bring the concussors on line. No, belay that.' His mind was beginning to work. 'Prepare the grids. Let's give them a shock to their systems.' He moved in closer to the screen, pushing between both Cybermen in the process and only registering that he had done so when it was too late to be nervous about it. This wasn't a problem, he told himself. This was going to be his salvation. One last chance to demonstrate his effectiveness.

The Overseer at the console punched up a status report. The lines of a circuit diagram flickered and changed. As Madrox had ordered, all power could now be routed into the metal plates which lay, scattered across the grounds, an inch beneath the soil. Another display juxtaposed their positions with the radar images of the attackers. 'That's good. Now power up, on my mark. Not yet – no point in wasting it, and we don't know what detection equipment they have. We'll do this on the last second.' He glanced back at the alien onlookers. They had to be impressed by this. He concentrated on the screens, breath held, until the optimum moment arrived.

'Mark!' he snapped. A scarlet coloration swept across the diagram, illuminating the routes to the plates as they became live. He grinned. He had got four of them. He switched his gaze to the video screen, on which those afflicted were thrashing in pain as electricity crackled across their casings. He noted with glee that one had grabbed hold of a colleague, conducting the lethal flow. These were no robots, he saw now – merely weak men in armour. Henneker and his cronies, no doubt. They would learn the cost of challenging him before they died.

Madrox's celebrations were premature. He hadn't seen the guns welded onto the forearms of each creature. One went into action, powerful blasts churning the ground beneath its allies. Another followed its lead. Madrox scowled as the lights representing two plates blinked out. A third attacker was dragged free by the very comrade it had inadvertently stricken – whilst a fourth accomplished the impossible itself, shooting its own plate into fragments once it was clear.

'We've damaged them,' said Madrox. He wasn't sure if that was true, but it was important to maintain morale. 'Now, while they're reeling, prime the mines – everything in B Quadrant. That should finish them.'

A sudden explosion and a deathly scream distracted him. He looked up in alarm and saw an Overseer tumbling from his chair, smoke rising from his collar, face set into a ghastly rictus. Behind him stood the Cyberleader. Although its normal weaponry would most probably have proved fatal, it had chosen to use its more powerful handheld gun to announce its presence. 'He was not working efficiently,' it said. Madrox gaped as a second Cyberman brushed the dead Overseer aside and took his seat, keying the relevant information into the console. He tore his gaze from the macabre scene, knowing that this was not the time to let fear freeze him. The display showed that his orders had been obeyed with greater speed than he had expected. The example of Overseer 2/4 had not been lost upon his erstwhile teammates.

Madrox studied the video monitor, feeling pinpricks of sweat breaking out on his cheeks. The creatures blundered across the minefield, heedless of danger. At last, one made a mis-step and a cloud of mud and smoke blossomed around it. As the disturbed earth settled, another mine exploded and Madrox's vision was obscured once more. He waited impatiently to see how much damage had been done.

The answer seemed to be very little. The casings of the attackers had been tarnished and smoke-blackened. The torso of one was even chipped and distorted. But still, all seven marched on.

'Ready the concussors! And release the gas – they can only be human inside that armour!'

'No.' The Cyberleader had decided to intercede. 'Divert all power to the laser blaster.' Madrox was speechless, but didn't dare to object, as the Overseers followed their new instructions. 'Now, aim for the foremost of the targets – and fire!'

The screen flickered, losing its picture momentarily as the most powerful of Population Control's weapons blazed into action. Madrox had a fleeting impression of flying shards of metal – and by the time the image was restored, one monster was finally down. Its armour had burst open and Madrox could see the wiring within. He also thought he could discern human organs, but he averted his eyes. He didn't want to know too much.

Another of the attackers had been caught in the periphery of the tremendous blast. It had lost an arm and it swayed but remained upright. The remaining six creatures drew inexorably closer. 'There's nothing I can do now,' Madrox protested. This wasn't his fault. 'You've drained all power. By the time the defensive systems are back on line, they'll be here!'

'That is correct,' said the Leader, 'but all other measures would have been ineffective. I have killed one of the intruders.' With chilling indifference, it added: 'We will deal with the remainder at close quarters.'

The Doctor waited until both Cybermen were facing away from him. Then he leapt to his feet and rushed for the controls. Hegelia quickly did as he had advised, hitching up her robe and scurrying to take cover.

The Doctor launched himself at the machinery, but managed to grasp only one lever before its owners reacted. The nearest Cyberman took one step and knocked him away with a sweep of its arm. He hurtled into a graceless arc, hit the floor and slid on his back. Both Cybermen bore down on him and Hegelia shivered as she remembered the Leader's threats. But the Doctor, far from being winded, was scrambling to his feet. He ducked past the slow-moving Cybermen, put the master console between him and them and dived for the ladder which led to the compartments. He hauled himself onto the first balcony and halted breathlessly in front of the first glass door. The unarmed Cyberman followed; the other brought up its gun to cover him.

'Not logical!' the Doctor crowed, pointing towards the levelled weapon. 'If you fire that, you're more likely to hit the person behind me. You'll kill one of your own kind and wreck your precious equipment into the bargain!' It hesitated and, with a clenched-tooth smile of insane determination, the Doctor turned, pulled open a small hatch in the wall and ripped out a handful of wires.

'That's one man spared from your manipulation!'

The other Cyberman was on the ladder now. Despite herself, Hegelia called out a warning. 'Doctor!'

He had seen it. As it dismounted, he hurtled along the balcony, putting himself out of its range. It made an attempt to bring him down anyway. Fire spat from its head and the Doctor fell, but picked himself up, apparently unharmed, and continued to run. The Cyberman followed. Its comrade below pivoted, keeping the Doctor in its sights. Hegelia shrank behind her console and resolved not to draw attention to herself again.

The Doctor stopped to perform a further act of sabotage. 'Four hundred and ninety-eight to go,' he boasted, brandishing the disconnected wiring before moving on.

'Desist, or be destroyed!' warned the ground-level Cyberman.

'Not a convincing threat. You see, I've saved two lives. I can save a lot more before you kill me. Logically, I should continue.'

'There is no logic in perpetuating the existence of organics.'

'Of course not!' bellowed the Doctor in a mocking tone. He turned, flipped open another maintenance hatch and wrenched out its innards.

The Cyberman fired. Through luck or judgement – Hegelia couldn't tell – the Doctor avoided the blast. The door of the disabled compartment exploded into a shower of boiling fragments and Hegelia's nose wrinkled at the smell of burnt flesh. 'Oh, that was clever, wasn't it?' the Doctor shouted, scornful and bitter.

'You yourself intimated that the human within was of no use to us.'

'Perhaps – but do you want to render this whole chamber inoperational?' The other Cyberman was still coming. The Doctor hurried along, keeping a measured distance ahead. For now, he left the compartments alone. Hegelia guessed that he was waiting for his foes to consider the merits of his argument before risking more lives.

150

The Cyberman below seemed to have done just that. As the Doctor came full circle and reached the ladder again, it lowered its gun and marched towards him. He hurried up four more levels and raced along the topmost tier, Hegelia craning her neck to follow his progress. When he was halfway around, he set to work on the compartments again. One – two – three. But time was running out. Both Cybermen had reached the ladder and, as they emerged onto the Doctor's level, they separated and approached him from each side. There was no other way down. He was cornered.

Hegelia watched on breathlessly as the Doctor continued to work, displaying an almost casual disregard towards his impending fate. Then, as his pursuers closed in, he looked up, glanced at each of them in turn, gripped the balcony rail and vaulted over it.

For a moment, his legs dangled in mid-air, a single arm holding his weight. Then his questing hand found the balcony's edge and he lowered himself, straining with the effort, until his feet could touch the rail below. He swung over it and landed unsteadily on the metal surface, even as the Cybermen met above his head. They halted in unison and the unarmed one pivoted and returned to the ladder. The other straddled the railing and began to climb down after its prey.

The Doctor was using his momentary advantage. Conversion became an impossibility for four more subjects. Then he took flight before the armed Cyberman could get too close. Its comrade had almost reached the ladder and Hegelia was put in mind of a macabre, live session of . . . what was the name of that classical board game again?

The Doctor was surrounded once more, the approach of one Cyberman forcing him towards the other, which stepped off the ladder and remained still beside it. Even the Doctor wasn't agile enough to climb to a higher tier unaided. The only way he could go now was down – and down again, until he was back at ground floor level and could be killed without risk. The game would take some time to run its course, but the ending was certain. The Doctor, however, did not bow to the inevitable. He waited for the last second before swinging, more easily this time, down onto the third, central, balcony. As Hegelia had predicted, the unarmed Cyberman retook the ladder, lowered itself to his level and stood sentry once more. The other clambered immediately, if awkwardly, onto the railing. But this time, the Doctor's plan was different. Remaining beneath his pursuer, he set to work behind the nearest hatch, conducting an operation of far more complexity than the wanton destruction of earlier.

As the Cyberman's lower half dropped into his view, the Doctor swung to face it with a gleam in his eye and a wire in each hand. He thrust the stripped ends into the creature's stomach and it gave a shriek as an electric halo fizzed about its armour. Still, it clung – and fought to continue its downward climb until it finally attained the Doctor's level. Hegelia saw determination in the Time Lord's face as his reeling victim nevertheless gained ground across the balcony's painfully narrow width. As the Doctor's back hit the wall, he cast the wires aside, cutting off the lethal current an instant before a steely hand took his forearm. The Cyberman held him and raised its gun, preparing a point-blank blast which would kill even a Time Lord.

But the Doctor kicked out and, to Hegelia's astonishment, the Cyberman staggered. Its grip was loosened and it teetered over the balcony rail, more weakened than it had seemed to be. The Doctor leapt after it and pushed its head down to shift its centre of gravity. Despite its flailings, it toppled – and fell to the ground with a final-sounding crash, limbs splayed at impossible angles.

Only then did the ArcHivist see that its comrade had abandoned its post. As the Doctor turned to check on its position, it closed in and clamped its hands onto his shoulders. He squealed and fought to remain upright. The pair were locked in combat for an unbearably long moment, but the Doctor's legs were starting to buckle. He stood no chance against the might of a fully functional Cyberman.

Hegelia acted on instinct – a truly unfamiliar experience to her. She sped across the room until she reached the blackened remains of the fallen Cyberman and prised its gun from lifeless hands. She steadied the butt against her shoulder, backing up until she could see the scene above her clearly. The combatants had twisted so that the back of her target's head was presented. The Doctor was on his knees, his expression a pained grimace. As Hegelia fumbled for the trigger, the Cyberman began to turn, as if sensing her actions. Maybe it did – or maybe an automatic signal from its dead comrade had alerted it to the loss of its weapon.

She fired. The shot went wild, sizzling over the Doctor's head and blowing a hole into the wall between compartments. The Cyberman was facing her now and Hegelia realized that she was close enough for it to kill. It reached for the controls on its chest. She closed her eyes and fired again. When next she looked, it was reeling, smoke pouring from its joints. She had hit it. But it wasn't dead yet. It steadied itself and took aim once more. The gun dropped from Hegelia's fingers; her feet were rooted to the spot. She expected to die.

But then the Doctor, temporarily forgotten, directed all of his remaining strength into one last desperate shoulder charge and the Cyberman lost its balance and followed its predecessor into a downward spiral, flames exploding from it like a brilliant orange firework.

When it was all over, Hegelia stared at the mangled, interlocked remains of the creatures and waited for her ears to stop ringing and her heartbeat to resume its normal pace. The Doctor was leaning over the balcony rail, his face flushed with success. 'You see?' he shouted. 'Logic *can* breed inefficiency. A human foe would have shot me dead in the first place, without thinking!'

* * *

The cyborg creatures were in the building. Madrox could hear their ponderous footsteps reverberating through the metal corridors as they drew closer. His hands were sweating, his shoulders ached and the blaster almost slipped through his fingers, seeming to grow heavier. The control centre doors had been propped open; he and the remaining three men of Patrol Two had a clear view down the access corridor. Behind them, the Cybermen waited outside the line of fire. The humans were merely cannon fodder – but any objections would have made their deaths more certain and instant.

They came into sight, then, at last – all six of them, lumbering steadily up the passageway with no pretence at caution. Madrox boggled through his sights. In person, they seemed larger, even more imposing, more deadly. For a moment, he didn't have the strength to pull the trigger. But then he remembered the fate of Overseer 2/4 and he obeyed the Cyberleader's instructions. As did his colleagues. As always.

The intruders shook but didn't fall beneath the concentrated onslaught. Madrox was reminded of tales he had heard of the first rebellion; of how the Cybermen had proved resistant to the same weapons. The strength of their casings had been only one factor. The microwave emissions of the guns had been useless against inorganic matter. Madrox's current targets had to have almost as many artificial components as did the Cybermen themselves. He wondered how far Henneker's fanaticism had made him go.

The answering fire, conversely, was instantly fatal. Two Overseers fell, their body armour useless against the blue spears of flame which impaled them. The intruders were almost upon them and Madrox's nerve gave way. He rolled beneath the next volley and scrambled for cover within the control centre. A Cyberman tried to take a bearing on him, but he was too fast – and, within seconds, the cyborgs had arrived and it had more urgent business to contend with.

154

The Cybermen reacted with their customary efficiency. The Leader's gun was ready; it fired three times into the nearest intruder, which buckled and fell. But others were already retaliating. The Cybermen were obviously affected – if not felled – as jets of fire ripped through them. One of the silver creatures staggered forward, closing the distance until it could use its head-mounted weapon. It fired repeatedly, but its targets were unharmed. It found itself surrounded by three cyborgs and, as Madrox watched, its limbs were torn from it like wings from a fly. The odds were five to two now and he was beginning to realize that the Cybermen may be defeated. Not that it mattered either way. Both sides had reason to kill him. He glanced to where the only other surviving human cowered beneath a console, tears staining his cheeks. They exchanged a brief helpless look.

The Cyberleader had pressed its gun into service again. The already damaged, one-armed attacker fell, giving out a horrendous rattling wail. But two more copper-coloured cyborgs had managed to close in and seize the deadly weapon, fighting to wrench it from its owner's hands. The Cyberleader held on and attempted to bring down one of them with its less powerful, in-built gun. The cyborg was beginning to visibly weaken. The other two attackers had concentrated their efforts on the remaining Cyberman. Caught at the intersection of four searing blasts, it held up well for a few seconds before it finally crumpled. White fluid spilled out of its mouth and seeped from its eyes. Madrox found the pitiful display quite painful to watch. He looked away and caught sight of the external monitor – on which he saw another Cyberman approaching.

It was visible for only a moment before passing out of the camera's range as it moved into the building proper. Madrox wondered where the creature had come from and concluded that it had to be one of those which had been sent to the rebels' bunker. It would be approaching the control centre, where it would take the invaders unawares.

The Cyberleader's persistence had paid off. Another of its enemies was falling – but the odds were three to one now and the outcome was not in doubt. The sight of Madrox's long-feared paymaster struggling to avoid its inevitable death seemed bizarre. But things were changing on Agora, and Madrox had just one chance to curry favour with the main beneficiaries.

The one-man Cyber cavalry would have the advantage of surprise, but not of numbers. It might inflict some damage, but it surely couldn't overturn its race's defeat. If Madrox was to shout a warning to its foes, he would only be hastening the inevitable, whilst improving his own outlook. Then he had a better idea. The attackers were occupied by their savage dismemberment of the shrieking Cyberleader. The last Cyberman stepped into view at the far end of the approach corridor. Madrox hefted his Overseer-issue gun and took aim. It was too far away to harm him; he had plenty of time to let off two or three short blasts. They wouldn't damage it much, of course – but his actions would show willing. They might even save his life.

He fired – and the Cyberman staggered. It seemed to be in pain. Madrox was confused, but he was committed now and his target was moving closer with terrifying speed. He didn't have time to think. He shot it again.

And, to his utter astonishment, the Cyberman fell.

'We've got problems,' said the Doctor.

'The other Cybermen?'

He shook his head, without looking at Hegelia, and continued to tinker with the controls on the main console. 'The people in this chamber,' he said. 'They've already been damaged by the first stage of conversion. They couldn't survive outside their compartments.'

'I see.'

'And I'm afraid there's no way of stopping the process

without shutting down life support systems.'

'Then you have two options,' said Hegelia practically. 'You can terminate the lives of almost five hundred people or you can allow as many Cybermen to be born onto this world.'

The Doctor gave her a scathing look. 'I do realize that.'

With the imminent danger having passed, Hegelia found her detached interest returning. 'I would be fascinated to hear what your choice is. Do you really believe conversion to be a worse fate than death? And are you prepared to kill on the basis of that belief?'

A look of anger crossed the Doctor's face and he pounded a fist into the console. He glared at it murderously for a moment, then flicked a few switches, crossed the chamber and began to climb back up onto the balconies.

'What are you doing?' Hegelia asked.

'I've slowed the rate of the process as far as I can,' he said without stopping. 'For now, there's something else to attend to.' He disappeared through the first-level entrance into Population Control.

Left alone, Hegelia surveyed the rows of compartments with a barely suppressed thrill of excitement. Her plan was working.

Madrox was standing, stunned, in the aftermath of battle; in the debris of familiarity. The control centre looked like a mannequin store in a riot. Its floor was strewn with dismembered limbs and twisted artificial bodies. It took some effort to remember that living beings had once inhabited these shells. A low-level haze hid some of the gory details and gunpowder and blood assailed Madrox's nostrils.

The attackers stood victorious, albeit with only three of their number remaining. Madrox felt his heart flutter as one stomped towards him. He shuffled away nervously and almost yelped when it spoke in a horrible, clipped –

but somehow familiar – tone. 'Time to pay for your war crimes, Madrox!'

'H-Henneker?'

'No longer. I have the power to punish you for every injustice you have heaped upon our people.'

This time, Madrox did let out a strangulated cry. He tried to retreat further, but was already up against an instrument bank. 'They forced me to do it. I helped you, didn't you see? I shot the last Cyberman. It would have surprised you. It would have –'

The creature which was Henneker started towards him again. Madrox flung up his arms in an instinctive gesture, only to have both caught, just below the wrists. He stared imploringly into the implacable face of his captor, but felt the pressure of the restraining fists increase all the same. 'Please, don't . . .' he begged tearfully, but choked back further entreaties as a shooting pain precluded speech. Blood welled between metal fingers, muscles screamed and a bone was dislodged. Madrox's legs gave way and he would have sunk to his knees but for the cyborg's strength which kept him hoisted. He was going to black out.

Then, for the second time that day, his life was saved by alien intervention. 'If you've quite finished brutalizing a fellow human,' boomed the strident tones of the Doctor, 'perhaps you would be interested to know that this is all extremely far from over!'

Madrox felt light-headed as Henneker released his grip and allowed the former Chief Overseer to collapse. Through pain-blurred vision, he was aware that the Doctor was scrabbling through the remains of the fallen, until he located the Cyberleader's detached head. Forcing his fingernails into the gap between its face and its earmuff-like antennae, he tore its frontage away. 'I'm too late,' he grumbled, ripping out a component which pulsed with yellow light. He dropped it, ground it into the floor with his shoe, then turned to Henneker with an urgent expression. 'I don't know what's happened here,' he said, 'but somebody had better explain to me quickly.

158

We have a lot of work to do. We've bested a token force of Cybermen, but their Leader has transmitted details back to base. Within the next few days – or hours, or minutes – we're going to have to deal with reinforcements!'

Madrox sobbed and tried to bury his head in the floor.

10

Change of Life

News travelled swiftly, in the way that momentous news will. Not many believed it at first – but the hopeful few gathered outside Population Control, where the damage caused by the Bronze Knights was discovered. The bravest of them picked her way through the shattered defences, leading a ragged cheer as she announced that the complex had been laid open. Within an hour, the grounds and immediate environs were thronged with colonists, checking for themselves before believing. Talk of the Bronze Knights, the world's alleged saviours, was rife; stories varied from the cautious to the implausible. But the spreading mood of optimism was tempered as rumours of Cyber reinforcements circulated.

Dawn's first light had begun to caress the grass when a Bronze Knight finally emerged from the building, eliciting an appreciative – if somewhat fearful – gasp. Under one arm it carried a box speaker, from which wires ran to its casing. Its voice was amplified by the apparatus, carrying to all.

'You need not fear me. I am the man whom some of you once knew as Ted Henneker. I am also the leader of the Bronze Knights, a newly created cyborg race. We have utilized our enemies' own technology against them – and we have won.'

Max Carter threaded her way through the onlookers, to where the main entrance doors gaped open. Grant leaned heavily against her, out of danger but not yet fully recovered. As Lakesmith had observed, his heart had stopped – but, after tense, breathless moments, Max's

CPR had proved successful. Her perseverance set her apart from Cybermen and Knights alike. That worried her. Her own creations would have left Grant for dead, analysing his condition in strictly clinical terms.

'We have won a spectacular victory,' Henneker was announcing as she passed. Max nodded towards him, but he didn't return the acknowledgement. His voice drifted after her as she hauled Grant into Population Control. 'We have defeated our oppressors, but there has been a price. Several of our number fell in battle – including Arthur Lakesmith, a hero to whom we owe an incalculable debt.'

Max heard the tidings, but her emotional centre was too weary to react. She trudged on, the sparse corridors pricking at mental blisters to release a succession of shielded memories. She tried to ignore them, to forget the horrors of her last visit here.

The route to the control centre was signposted by a trickle of curiosity seekers. Max followed, to find a room packed with the rebels' allies – and only two surviving Bronze Knights, amidst the remnants of their fellows. Of course, there had to have been deaths, she told her sinking stomach. For that matter, she hadn't seen any sign of the conversion subjects. Had the attack come too late?

'Doctor!' Grant left Max's side and moved unsteadily towards a tall, fair-haired man with a confident bearing and atrocious dress sense. Despite his dishevelled appearance and the bruises on his face, he brimmed with vitality. So this was Grant's alien friend, Max thought.

'Oh, it's you,' the Doctor observed dismissively. 'What kept you?'

Grant was visibly taken aback by his abruptness. 'I was injured. I've been unconscious for most of the night.'

'Really? What about the three weeks before that?' He gestured distastefully towards the Bronze Knights. 'Or have you been too busy playing Doctor Frankenstein to spare a thought for my plight?'

'How dare you!' Max exploded, her fury demanding

161

the Doctor's attention. She marched up to him and, to his evident surprise, slapped his face. Her pent-up bitterness, frustration and loss had found a target for release. 'Your friend has been working night and day to help you,' she raged. 'If it weren't for his input, the Bronze Knights would never have been built, the Cybermen would still be in occupation and you would probably be converted or dead!'

The Doctor recovered his wits and squared up to her, swelling with indignation. 'And you think your Bronze Knights are such an achievement, do you? I call them an abomination!'

'And you would have found a better solution, I suppose?'

'Well, since you ask –'

'You are needed.' Max jumped at Henneker's filtered voice by her ear. He had approached unheard and interrupted without leave. The Doctor had given way, but he regarded the newcomer through hooded eyes, clearly disliking what he saw. Grant had backed off instinctively. 'Our people have been ransacking the complex for raw materials and preparing the Cybermen's laboratories for our purpose. You will be required to manufacture as many Bronze Knights as you are able. We will provide volunteers.'

'They're sending reinforcements, aren't they?' said Max gloomily. She had heard the rumour outside and had known it almost immediately to be true. 'How long before they arrive?'

'We do not know. Begin your task.'

He made to turn, but Max stopped him. 'Wait! What about the prisoners?'

'Irrelevant. You have important things to consider.' Henneker walked away, moving amongst the others and dispensing orders. Max gaped after him. Then, at a loss, she turned to the Doctor, who greeted her with an eyebrow-raised *I-told-you-so* expression.

'Just tell me what's happened to them, can't you?' she

snapped impatiently, taking Henneker's rudeness as a personal embarrassment. 'My brother was brought in here!'

His attitude changed at a stroke. His face fell and he looked at her with sympathy. Max had thought herself prepared for the worst – but now, a hitherto unsuspected reserve of misery flowed into her heart. She felt tears pricking at her eyes.

'What's happened?'

Hegelia sat in a comfortable plastic chair, chin supported on steepled fingers. She had retired to this rest area to update her audio notes and to await the right moment to execute the next stage of her plan. At first, then, she was none too pleased to be disturbed by an unexpected visitor. On reflection, though, it would be useful to say a few words to young Jolarr.

'I've been looking for you everywhere,' said the boy, relief apparent. 'When we were separated, I thought . . .'

Hegelia was almost touched by his concern, but she couldn't allow it to divert her from the matter at hand. 'I hope you have taken careful note of all that has happened.'

A slight frown creased his white forehead. 'I could hardly forget it, ArcHivist. I was chased by a Cyberman. It nearly killed me.'

Hegelia clapped her hands together. 'Excellent! You have an advantage which I was never afforded, Graduand: early contact with your subject matter. Cherish the memory. No amount of research can ever equal what you have learned on this expedition.'

Jolarr was bewildered. 'You're saying I should study the Cybermen – like you have?'

Hegelia stood now and looked him in the eye. 'Why do you think I brought you here? I am growing old, Graduand; I will not see the Arc Hives again. But my research must proceed. The Cybermen are important, both historically and strategically. Nobody knows where or when they will rise again – and I believe whole-heartedly that, one day, they will. I need a successor, and I have chosen him: a boy with the intelligence, the ambition and now the experience to continue my work as I would wish it to be continued. I hope you will not do me the dishonour of refusing my request.'

'I . . . no, ArcHivist. I mean, I would be delighted.' He didn't look very happy. His features cycled through an array of expressions, not knowing where to settle. Still, the promise had been elicited. Hegelia was satisfied.

She resumed her usual brisk manner and imparted her final instructions. 'I want you to observe as much as you can, whilst avoiding inordinate danger.' She reached into her cloak and handed him a micro-cassette. 'When you return, download this into the Cyber Hive and add your own impressions to create a full document. You may not see me again, but if you do – and if you can do so without harm – take my recorder from me. It should contain more useful information. Questions?'

'You make it sound as if you aren't coming back.'

'Dismissed!' Hegelia made to turn her back on him.

'The time ship,' Jolarr blurted out. 'It's gone!'

She pouted. 'I feared that might happen. I must apologize. It seems my tampering with the navigational circuits has caused the vessel to experience temporal drift. Still, a solution presents itself. You will travel home with the Doctor.' Jolarr nodded dumbly. 'That is all, Graduand.'

He looked as if he wanted to say something, but then he thought better of it. He turned and scuttled out of the room. Hegelia watched him go, then settled back into her seat with a deep sigh.

She had now made provision for her departure. That just left one more person to brief.

The Doctor and Max mounted the final flight of steps to the building's roof, disappearing from Grant's view. He sighed and followed at his own pace, still weak from his close encounter with death. Life wasn't fair. The Bronze Knights had triumphed and the Doctor was free. He had waited three weeks for that. But the threat wasn't over yet and his travelling partner was all but ignoring him. Grant was reminded that he had known the Doctor for only a few days before his capture. His one trip in the TARDIS seemed a long time ago now.

He attained the flat metal roof and saw the spherical cockpit of the ship rising up from its centre. Its door lay level with the surface. The Doctor had to be in there. Grant approached, and wondered if the Time Lord had brought him to Agora deliberately to leave him. He prayed not. He felt like a stranger on his own world.

The cockpit's interior was almost as dull, grey and functional as that of Population Control. The Cyber ship's vertical orientation caused the viewscreen to be positioned in the concave wall above them, with most of the flight controls. A hatch below vented onto a ladder, which stretched into the ship's rear chamber. The Doctor was standing on the threshold of this, looking into the darkness.

'Is Max down there?' asked Grant, to break the ice.

He nodded. 'The conversion chamber. I sealed off the other entrances. It's safer that way.'

'I hope she finds her brother.'

'Maybe.' The Doctor wrenched his gaze from the gloomy pit. 'Most of the people down there are dead or unconscious, I'm afraid.' He turned to a computer terminal, situated along what would, in flight, have been the ceiling.

'Can I do anything?' asked Grant, as the Doctor began to tap in a series of instructions at lightning speed.

'Make the tea, if you can find any.'

'That's what you said on the Network.'

'You still haven't made any!'

'Look, Doctor . . . I'm sorry it took me so long to do something. I tried my best.'

The Doctor looked at him with genuine affection. 'I

165

know. Don't worry. I'm used to companions performing last-second saves. It's just that the last second isn't usually so long in coming.'

He returned to his work and Grant, more cheerful now, asked, 'What are you trying to do?'

'Solve a problem. I can't halt the conversion without shutting down the system and to shut down the system would kill everyone in it. Their lungs have been removed, you see. They rely on the machinery to survive.'

'Can you freeze them or something? Stop them from becoming Cybermen till we can work out how to put them back together?'

'That's what I'm doing,' said the Doctor, his tone suggesting surprise that someone else should have thought of it. 'The subjects would have been cryogenically stored once conversion was complete. I've rewired the compartments and reset the controls downstairs; now I can fool the main computer into thinking it's time to pump in the freon. A lot of the subjects won't have the strength to endure revival, but I can at least save some. It's a better solution than that proffered by your friends.'

'What friends?'

'The Bronze Knights. I think Henneker would rather I didn't "waste my time" on work irrelevant to the war effort. He'd happily shut down the whole chamber and sacrifice everyone. Well . . . perhaps not "happily". That implies a human emotional response.' He shot Grant an accusatory look, which the teenager automatically resented. He was about to say something in his defence, but the Doctor jumped to his feet, announcing, 'A work of pure genius!' and made for the door.

'What about Max?' Grant asked, as they re-emerged onto the roof.

'The hibernation circuits will kick in by stages. She has about half an hour to say what she needs to. I think we'd best leave her to it, don't you?' They were approaching the steps back into the building, but the Doctor groaned and came to a halt as an arched forehead of coppery-red metal hove into view above the parapet. 'Which one are you, then – Happy, Sleepy or Grumpy?'

'I have been searching for you,' said the Bronze Knight, in Henneker's voice. 'Your aid is required. You will help us to improve our design in advance of the Cybermen's attack.'

The Doctor snorted, his response addressed to Grant. 'You see? His one concern is the advancement of his own kind. Who does that bring to mind, offhand?'

'If you can think of a better way of winning this war,' said Henneker, with a hint of annoyance, 'I suggest you offer it.'

'In case you hadn't noticed, I've just finished saving a great many lives. I'm on my way to the control centre now to work on our next most pressing problem.'

'No. You have had time, Doctor. Now you will follow instructions. If you do not help, you will be considered hostile to our cause.'

'Oh, of course!' the Doctor scoffed. 'Because your word is law now, isn't it, Mr Henneker? By what right do you claim to be better than the Cybermen anyway? You've bullied your people, you've brutalized your captured foes –'

'We have saved Agora from the Cybermen's clutches.'

'And gathered it into your own. I want you to try something for me, Henneker. I want you to show me what the difference really is between you and the Cybermen. I want to see how you react to certain death!' The Doctor's hand had snaked its way into his pocket. As Grant watched speechlessly, he withdrew it and made to hurl something at Henneker's face. The cyborg reacted with blurring speed. It grabbed his wrist and twisted until the Doctor cried in pain and fell to his knees, his fingers spasming open to reveal an empty palm.

'What was the purpose of your demonstration?' asked Henneker.

'To prove a point,' the Doctor grunted through gritted teeth. 'Admittedly, it backfired somewhat.'

Henneker let him go, and the Doctor rubbed his sore wrist gratefully. 'A work space is being made ready on the first basement level,' the Bronze Knight said. 'I will expect both of you, plus Maxine Carter, to report there in twenty minutes.' He turned and lumbered back down the steps. The Doctor glared after him as he got to his feet. Grant could see red finger-marks on his skin.

'Is that what you've allied yourself with?' the Doctor spat. 'Is that your proud creation?' Grant couldn't answer.

Max had reappeared in the ship's hatchway. One look at her face told Grant that her news wasn't good. Both men fell silent as she approached, arms wrapped about herself, quivering slightly. Her face was smudged, as if she had been crying but had tried to hide the evidence. 'I found Martin,' she said sniffily. 'He's unconscious. I can't wake him.'

'It was to be expected,' said the Doctor gently.

Then Max turned to Grant and, despite her own sadness, he saw compassion in her eyes. 'But some of them are still awake in there,' she said. 'And ... somebody's asking for you.'

Hegelia walked sedately towards the cell block, unchallenged by either the frenetically active followers of Henneker or by the single Bronze Knight which clanked past her as she circumvented the control centre. She turned to watch the creature as it receded into the distance. It was but a pallid reflection of a Cyberman, but still it interested her. If she was given the opportunity later, she might congratulate its builders. For now, her sights were set on the main prize.

The defeated Overseers had been herded into the top-floor cells, well out of the way. Hegelia found one on her first try. The black-uniformed man stared out from the tiny room, eyes red, hair wild. 'Are they going to kill me?' She ignored the bleated question. She closed and locked the viewing hatch. He was not the one she wanted.

She moved down the row, glancing into each cell, until she found him. Madrox had folded himself into a blubbering heap, the sight of which disgusted her. 'Get on your feet, man!' she ordered. His shaking stopped and he cautiously peered out from under his arms. 'I said, get on your feet! Do you intend to surrender so easily?'

'Can – can you get me out of here?' Madrox's tone was imploring. He tried to stand, but collapsed onto his backside and fell against the wall, where he stayed. Hegelia saw that his face was bruised, his uniform torn and his lower left leg was twisted at a painful angle. The Bronze Knights had not been merciful.

'Not yet,' she answered, 'but I believe that, once again, we can work to each other's advantage. You do realize that Cyber reinforcements are heading towards this planet?'

'No good,' he said, voice straining with the effort of keeping his pain in check. 'I failed them. They'll kill me.'

'Not if you achieve what their own troops could not. Not if you can get into their ship and restart the conversion process. Not if you can unleash five hundred new Cybermen upon the colonists. Their victory would be inevitable then – and you would be the man to thank. Your life, and your position as Chief Overseer, would be safe.'

Hegelia saw the merest glimmer of Madrox's old obsessional light returning to his eyes. That was what she needed. But he was clearly recovering his analytical skills as well and a shadow of suspicion clouded his face. 'What do you want out of this?' he asked.

She told him.

The conversion chamber was cold, its lighting subdued. Grant stepped off the main entrance ladder and headed for the room's edge, head down, taking shallow breaths through his mouth to avoid the stench of putrefaction. As per Max's instructions, he climbed to the highest balcony and counted to the tenth compartment clockwise. He eased open the glass door, on which a thin layer of frost had formed. He half expected the arms of a Cyberman to spring out and encircle him. Instead, there was just a man, nestled within a mechanical cocoon. A metal skullcap had slipped askew on his head, internal needles drawing blood. Grant was glad that so much of the ravaged body was concealed.

For a second, he thought the man was dead. Then Ben Taggart's eyes flickered open and a half-smile twisted his face.

'I'm glad ... you could make it,' he croaked with obvious effort. He allowed his eyelids to fall. 'So much to tell you. Don't know where ... to begin.'

The compartment was radiating deep cold, matched by the chill within Grant's body. 'You're my father, aren't you?' he blurted out, the words almost painful as they passed through the lump in his throat.

Taggart's eyes opened again, in surprise this time. 'How ... did you know?'

'I just did – almost from the time we met. Then, when you asked to see me ...' He let the uncompleted sentence hang in the air. He was feeling something inside, but he wasn't sure what it was – nor what it should be. Ben Taggart was his father. The man he had not seen for thirteen years, and rarely before that. And his father was almost certainly dying. How was he supposed to feel?

'You don't ... remember?'

'Very little,' said Grant honestly. 'My mother's face, sometimes – but not always the same. The Cybermen, in nightmares.'

'Your mother. She was a good woman ... Jean Markham.' Grant had already observed that, on Agora, the mother's surname was passed to her offspring. Taggart, after all, would have fathered more children by other women, keeping up conception rates. Grant wondered how many half-brothers and sisters he had; how many the Cybermen had killed. 'She didn't ... deserve what ... happened,' said Taggart. A tear seeped onto his cheek.

170

Grant was fascinated, yet at the same time frightened. He wanted to ask more, but couldn't. But Taggart was keen to unburden himself and Grant had no choice but to listen. He was rooted by the lure of a secret past life, terrified of what he might find there.

'2175,' whispered Taggart. He was more lucid now, more in control of his vocal chords. 'You were . . . how old?'

'Three.'

Recollection brought a faint smile to his lips. 'Three, that's right . . . and we were plotting to depose the Cybermen. Arthur Lakesmith was going to save the world. We could do anything then. We . . . beat the Overseers and waited. We waited for a year. But the Cybermen . . . were too much. The guns didn't harm them.' The smile had gone, replaced by an expression of tortured anguish.

'I've been told about the rebellion,' said Grant, attempting to speed the tale past this uncomfortable chapter.

Instead, Taggart seemed to remember something. His eyes widened in alarm. 'I betrayed them. I betrayed them again. I sent the Cybermen to the rebels' bunker.'

Grant took that information in and made a quick deduction. 'But you couldn't have told them about the Bronze Knights.' He tried to sound enthusiastic. 'You sent the Cybermen into an ambush. They were torn to pieces!'

'That's . . . good to know.' Taggart settled back into his memories, adopting a haunted, far-away look. 'It didn't work out so well last time. They . . . wanted revenge for the uprising, you see. They swept across the colony, killed anyone they found. Jean . . . Jean . . . went into the street. She thought it was over. They shot her. She died.'

Grant stared. His mind was racing, filled with thoughts he could barely comprehend. They resolved themselves into recollections, crystal clear, as if they had been there all along. He had known his mother's fate. The images of that day had been stored in his subconscious; he had just needed someone to point them out. And now Grant

171

Markham was four years old and playing with a wooden abacus on bare, but homely, floorboards; giving up his calculations as a premonition of danger hit, communicated silently by Mummy's fretting. Four-year-old Grant burst into tears. Mummy tried to bring comfort, but it was only a token effort. Her face was lined, her body tense. Grant was inconsolable. And then she was leaving, with a promise not to be gone too long. She wanted to know what was happening; if the home team had won. She hurried outside and little Grant suddenly felt more alone than ever before or since. A tow line of fear yanked him through the door, crying out for her as he hurtled down the dirt track of the road, arms outstretched. She was still in sight and she turned at his cries. He doubled his speed and fell, bawling as he scraped his elbows and knees. When he looked up, there were robots in the street. Two silver giants, bearing down upon Mummy, who saw them and screamed and backed away. But the robots advanced like the evil mechanoids of fairy tale; childhood bogeymen made solid.

Grant closed his eyes and stifled a sob at the memory of his mother, twisting and burning in the fire and smoke of the robots' weapons. The body had not so much fallen as melted, the force of the blasts disintegrating bone and frying tissue. The monsters had swept on towards him. Grant had lain face-down, fists pounding, tears blocking his vision so that all he could see were the silver poles of their legs as they stalked closer, preparing to send him to join Mummy in the pits of Hell.

The robots – the Cybermen – had spared him that day. They had left him with the nightmares, the instinctive fear and the memories which he had kept locked away for over a decade. Others had not been so fortunate.

There was more. Strapped into the cockpit of a spaceship, looking up at a ring of faces bidding him farewell. Grant thought he recognized Ben Taggart amongst them. Then the fleeting image was gone. He was looking at an older, paler Taggart, eyes closed and breathing shallow as if sleeping. Grant reached for the cubicle door and was about to close it, leaving his father to his final rest.

He couldn't.

'What happened next?' he asked in a hoarse whisper. 'How did I come to leave Agora?'

For a moment, he thought Taggart hadn't heard. Then his eyelids fluttered and his cracked lips moved to resume his muttered tale. 'Two years passed. I became an Overseer. I . . . sold out the rebellion to save my life. But things weren't as bad for us in those days. Madrox hadn't taken over. Security . . . not quite so tight. My patrol found a ship . . . one day, in the Outlands. We thought that at least a few could flee. The Old Earth Organization had left, years before the Cybermen . . . with the colony ship. They'd established New Earth. We thought we could save . . . the children, and send a message with them. There were four of us in Roylance's patrol, four spaces in the cockpit. We filled one each. You weren't my only child, but you were the last . . . you were the one without a mother to look after you. I thought . . . at least you didn't have to grow up with the fear.' His eyes closed again then. Just as Grant thought they weren't going to re-open, Taggart thrust his hand out of the compartment, trailing wires behind it, and clamped his freezing fingers onto his son's wrist. 'Why . . . did you come back?'

'I didn't mean to – but what does it matter? We defeated the Cybermen. We made Agora safe – and it was partly thanks to you.' Grant didn't have the heart to mention the imminent reinforcements.

Taggart smiled. 'And you . . . your Bronze Knights. We made a good team in the end, didn't we?'

'Of course we did.'

'We . . . did.' And then Taggart's grip went limp and his arm fell back to his side. The cold emanating from his compartment was intense now and Grant realized that he would have to close the door to give him a chance of being frozen like the others. Not that it mattered, a voice inside told him. Ben Taggart was already dead.

'Goodbye,' Grant whispered. It seemed inadequate. He waited a moment longer, not wanting to bring this to an end. But Taggart didn't move. Grant closed the door and watched as its inside surface frosted over in a second, obscuring Taggart's peaceful face.

He stood then, surrounded by emptiness, lonely in the knowledge that he had gained a father only to lose him for ever.

It was a long time before Grant Markham summoned up the will to leave the chamber.

The Doctor put out a hand to halt Max outside her newly outfitted surgery. 'You can't do this,' he insisted. 'Take a look at what you're creating. The Bronze Knights have had their emotions stunted and their powers increased beyond your ability to control them. They've become single-minded and ruthless. You must stop this insane experiment!'

'And do what?' Max countered hotly. 'Allow the Cybermen to dominate us again?'

'Give me time. I can prepare a surprise for them.'

'Like what? You've been here for weeks, but all you've done is wait to be rescued! It took my Bronze Knights to get the Cybermen off Agora — and they're still the surest way of keeping them off!'

'Can you live with their actions on your conscience?'

Max boiled over. 'Don't you dare preach your sanctimonious clichés to me!' she thundered. She stabbed a finger in the vague direction of the conversion chamber. 'My brother is lying dead in their ship. And you – you haven't had to live through Cyber occupation. You've never had a part of yourself ripped out because it didn't live up to expectations!' She placed a hand on her bloated stomach, feeling her body shake as her protective armour cracked and the force of her lifelong hurt finally flooded out. It felt masochistically good. 'They killed my baby in the womb, Doctor – don't pretend you can imagine a fraction of that pain! And then, when I couldn't keep

174

up their breeding quotas, when I felt incomplete and I couldn't let any man come near me . . . then they came for me in the night and dragged me into their godforsaken complex. They made sure I met their quotas then, all right.'

The Doctor looked crestfallen and sympathetic, but his lower lip still protruded stubbornly. Max clenched her fists and gritted her teeth, fighting down the dangerous tide. 'Don't tell me my methods are wrong,' she threatened in a low, husky voice, 'and don't get in my way. I want the Cybermen off this planet, out of my life – and I'll do anything to achieve that. Anything!'

As Hegelia reached the steps to the roof, she was startled to see the young human boy – Grant Markham, she recalled, the Doctor's current companion – descending them. 'Where have you been?' she snapped.

Grant looked as if he hadn't been aware of her presence. 'The conversion chamber,' he answered in miserable, leaden tones, confirming Hegelia's suspicions.

She softened her words with effort. 'Did you leave anybody in there?'

Grant shook his head. 'It's empty. The subjects have been frozen over.'

'Good!'

Hegelia was about to start forward when Grant stopped her with a plaintive question. 'You're a researcher, aren't you? You've been studying the Cybermen?' She nodded, keen to get on. 'What do you think it feels like?' Grant asked. 'To be converted, I mean?'

The ArcHivist's impatience dissipated. She felt a smile tugging at her mouth. 'I do not know. It is impossible to tell.'

'To have your brain operated on,' mused Grant, 'your personality altered. You wouldn't have to know fear or sadness again – but would you still be in control?'

'Your thought processes would be clearer.'

'And the body much more reliable.' Grant looked

down at his own hands as if considering their weaknesses. 'Things wouldn't hurt as much, would they?' Hegelia was no longer sure if he was talking physically or emotionally.

'That is certainly true.'

Grant nodded. Then, as if in a daze, he walked on past her, resuming his journey, lost in thought. Hegelia watched him for a moment, her own mission almost forgotten. He was in the process of making a decision; perhaps the most important one of his young life. His next stop would no doubt be Max Carter's surgery. Hegelia approved, and she hoped that the boy would find what he was searching for.

But she had needs of her own – and she was not planning to settle for second best.

11

Ultimatum

Night had fallen and almost lifted again. The excitement and the frenzied activity which had greeted the last sunrise had been replaced by muted apprehension and seething impatience. People were beginning to remember the last ambush laid for the Cybermen and to realize that victory was not yet certain.

Grant dozed in a chair in Max's surgery, conscious enough to recognize his dreams of killer robots as precisely that and to resent their continued intrusion upon his psyche. He opened his eyes and stretched, accepting that true sleep was a long way off despite his weariness.

Max laboured over half a dozen gestating Bronze Knights; the day's third batch. Population Control's medical computer had speeded up the process exponentially. Four colonists had recently staggered into the room under the weight of yet another vat of reddish-brown compound, brewed in a chemical laboratory nearby.

The Doctor had steadfastly refused to help out. Confined to the surgery by Henneker, he had spent the first hour at the computer terminal, reprogramming it so that he had access to the building's long-range scanners. Since then, he had placed himself on unstinting watch. It comforted Grant to know that so long as the Doctor was quiet, the Cybermen were far away.

He wondered how long that state of affairs could last.

Madrox had managed to compose himself. Hegelia's visit had given him fresh hope, and sheer will power had helped him to cope with the throbbing pain of his injuries. One foot was useless and he was sure that a muscle had been torn in his left arm. He struggled to stand anyway, using one wall of his cell as a support.

He thought of his unborn baby. A year ago, the idea of procreation wouldn't have occurred to him. It was something that he, alone in the colony, didn't have to do. Paternal feelings, then, had crept up and hit him when they were least expected. Driven by inexplicable urges, he had taken the next opportunity to provide himself with a sire. Now the prospect of the birth was half of what kept him from giving in. He needed to regain the Chief Overseer's position. He had to be able to provide the best for his boy; to keep him safe. Then, once she had seen his love for the child, Max Carter would accept that he had only done what he had to. Perhaps she could even begin to love him.

The invisible hatch in the cell's back wall slid open, revealing the passage to the Cyber ship's conversion chamber. Framed by the aperture was ArcHivist Hegelia. Madrox greeted her with a nod and a confident smile. 'I'm ready.'

'Then let us not delay,' she said. She hung Madrox's arm around her shoulders and supported him as he hobbled out into the corridor.

Jolarr sat and fidgeted in the control centre, wishing he knew where Hegelia was and what she was planning. Failing that, a conversation with the Doctor (or better still, with Grant, who was altogether more approachable) would have been acceptable – but Henneker had forbidden anyone from disturbing work on the new Bronze Knights. So Jolarr was trapped here, feeling useless, waiting for something to happen. When it finally did, he cursed himself for his impatience, longing for the comfort of inactivity. But it was too late for that.

'The Cybermen are here,' announced Henneker. He turned from the controls and marched towards a mushroom-shaped console in the centre of the room. In his wake, three human colleagues crowded around the information displays, straining to discern what Henneker had seen already. It took them a few seconds longer, but their worried expressions attested to the fact that they had corroborated their leader's observation.

Henneker batted a metal chair from in front of the communications console. He glared down into the blank viewscreen and waited to be contacted.

'Oh, no!'

Grant was sorting through and priming a stack of newly constructed blasters when the Doctor's whispered explanation froze him. 'What is it?' he asked, dreading the answer. But the Doctor was already on his feet and heading for the door.

'Get out of here, both of you!' he shouted over his shoulder.

Grant and Max exchanged a concerned look, then Grant hurried out after his companion. 'Is it the Cybermen? Are they back?'

The Doctor didn't break his stride and Grant had difficulty keeping up as they mounted the stairs to the ground-floor level. 'They're back – and they're using what, from the radar image, seems to be a Selachian warcraft.'

'Is that bad?'

The Doctor rounded on him, bringing Grant to an abrupt halt. He reached out, seized the boy's arms, swung him round and gave him a hefty push towards the exit. 'Bad enough for you to die if you don't get out of this building now!' he thundered. Then he was off again, heading towards the control centre.

Grant stared after him for a second, before fear and common sense combined to send him racing for the door.

The screen burst into life and Jolarr, part of the curious arc which had formed behind Henneker, flinched at the image of a Cyberman's head and shoulders. It was identical to its fallen fellows; it could have been any of them, resurrected. Jolarr wondered how many of the creatures had been maufactured.

'Your people have committed crimes against the Cyber race,' it stated. 'If you surrender, the punishment will be minimal.'

'We defeated your first party,' said Henneker arrogantly, 'and we can defeat you too. Leave our world alone. If you dare to land, we will tear you apart!' His words were accompanied by a cheer from only some of his allies. Others joined in belatedly, half-heartedly. Jolarr shared their fear that this wasn't anywhere near over yet.

And then the alien known as the Doctor raced madcap into the room and skidded to a halt, his arms gesticulating wildly. 'It's a trick – get out of here!' Without waiting for a response, he hurled himself at a console and opened a channel to the public address system. 'Evacuate the building – I repeat, evacuate the building. Utmost priority. Your lives are in peril!'

The screen went blank. A few people made for the door, but Henneker confronted the Doctor instead, flanked by two of his newest cyborg recruits. 'You should be working in the surgery.'

The Doctor's temper flared. 'Instead of which, I'm trying to save your misbegotten life. There isn't time to discuss it, just get out!' Jolarr was convinced. He made for the door, as did the Doctor himself. But Henneker moved to bar the Time Lord's way and Jolarr hesitated, afraid for the life of the one man who could get him off this planet.

'Tell me what is happening first.'

The Doctor's eyes flashed with fury and he seemed about to argue. Instead, he accepted that it would be more expeditious to explain. 'The Cybermen have captured a Selachian warcraft. The weaponry of those things is phenomenal. They can punch a plasma beam straight through this planet from orbit and atomize anyone who happens to be in its path. Now, they want revenge for the killing of eight of their kind. The dead Cyberleader's message to them was broadcast from this room. They've just established, via the communications link, that it is still occupied by their enemies. What do you think their next move will logically be?'

Henneker held his stare for a moment longer, then turned and lurched towards the door, gesturing to his comrades to do the same. 'Thank you,' said the Doctor, with heavy irony. He ducked past them, reaching the exit first and propelling Jolarr — who still stood, slack-jawed — outside into the labyrinth of grey passages.

They hurried on, joined by colonists and Bronze Knights alike as they neared the main entrance doors. The panicked exodus was in full flow. The Doctor kept a grip on Jolarr's upper arm, dragging him onward at breakneck speed. Then, suddenly, he stiffened, his eyes widened — and, a half-second later, Jolarr heard a terrible, screeching, crackling sound from above.

'Down!' the Doctor screamed, flinging himself to the floor, bearing Jolarr down beneath him. Reactions sharpened by fear, most people followed his lead. But Henneker and four Bronze Knights scrambled instead to create a living barrier between their vulnerable colleagues and the control centre. Jolarr had but a moment to feel the beginnings of a new respect for them; then he was deafened by a tremendous explosion and showered with metal shreds as a furious blast of hot smoke stabbed at his throat and eyes and, dulled by the ringing in his ears, he registered the shrieks of the would-be evacuees.

The dust hadn't even settled when the Doctor rose again. 'They've destroyed the control centre,' he reported, voice raised above the clamour. 'We have about a minute before their weapon recycles. We should get well clear of the building. We'll be safe outside.'

Jolarr picked himself up and made an attempt to brush debris from his tunic. It was pointless. The expensive garment, already damaged, was now ruined. Anyway, he had his own life to preserve. He wished he hadn't caught the Doctor's muttered addition to his rallying call: 'Well, relatively safe . . .'

The next few minutes were a smoke-filled blur. Jolarr, unable to see two metres ahead, kept close on the Doctor's confident heels. At least that multi-coloured coat was hard to lose. He was coughing and spluttering by the time they emerged from the building and joined the crowd which congregated outside in the sharp, almost painful light of the morning. He looked up, expecting to be greeted by the sight of the Cybermen's warcraft. But it was invisible; too far to see, though near enough to inflict its devastating damage. The outer shell of Population Control, so far as Jolarr could make out, was intact – but thick smoke blossomed from its centre as if carrying a message of surrender to the heavens.

Jolarr was transfixed by the black plume. When he regained awareness of his surroundings, he realized that the Doctor had left his side. He was back at the doors, chivvying people away from the building and offering encouragement to those who ran, staggered or were carried out into the fresh air. Jolarr recognized few of the evacuees, although he did glimpse the surgeon, Maxine Carter, amongst them.

Last out were the Bronze Knights – more than a dozen of them, marching in formation and taking up positions in a line parallel to the complex's front wall, keeping their charges safely at bay. Surrounded but alone, Jolarr cast about for ArcHivist Hegelia, but couldn't see her. He remembered, with a shiver, the finality of her parting words. 'I will not see the Arc Hives again.' Had she been expecting to die? If so, how could she have anticipated this turn of events? Perhaps she was not inside, he thought. Perhaps she was elsewhere, pursuing other plans.

The crowd shifted and Jolarr welcomed the sight of Grant Markham, a familiar face amongst strangers. They exchanged no words as they drew together, only wan smiles – but both were pleased to have found some form of companionship amidst the terror and uncertainty. They stared up into the sky, awaiting the Cybermen's next move. Like everyone else, they reacted with the shock of the unexpected when it came.

There was no sense of the plasma beam approaching. Suddenly, it was just there; a streak of jet black from above, purple fire licking at its edges. Another hole was punched through the metal roof as if it were paper. The sound came next, that terrible high-pitched static noise, like someone screaming at the end of a faulty communications link. The beam moved sideways, slicing through Population Control with startling ease. Its rending cry mingled with the colonists' frantic shouts as they scrambled to get further from the targeted area. More smoke rose, and this time the damage was clearly visible from Jolarr's position. One whole wing of the complex had been boiled away, reduced to pitiful scraps of steaming metal and a scattering of white ash. He couldn't help wondering, with a clinical distance that was almost repellent to him, what this astounding weapon might do to living tissue.

It occurred to him that he might soon find out.

The ship rocked for a second time. In the conversion chamber, Madrox clung to a console and fought to keep his balance despite his useless leg. Hegelia seemed less affected by the activity, and she managed to continue her work by his side. He found her calmness inexplicable. 'They're going to destroy the whole complex!'

'Of course they are not,' she said disdainfully. 'It would be illogical for the Cybermen to sacrifice their own vessel, let alone this chamber with so much precious machinery and five hundred semi-converts to their race. The bombardment will end soon. They are simply demonstrating their strength.'

'So long as they still think it's worth bothering with Agora,' Madrox added. The frenetic motion ceased and he gingerly removed his weight from the *ad hoc* support,

183

expecting to be felled by a third blast. It didn't come. Not yet.

Hegelia stepped back with a broad but tight-lipped smile of triumph. 'They will,' she said confidently. 'Now, we can ensure it.'

The crowd outside Population Control had been in the process of dispersing. Many of its constituents were heading homeward, to be with loved ones or simply to cower in comforting, but ineffectual, hiding places. Instead, they found themselves frozen, incapable to a man of lifting their feet, their gazes riveted by the ghastly black object which had appeared overhead and which now dropped from the sky, as if uncontrolled, to halt with impossible abruptness only a few hundred metres above the crippled and smouldering building.

The Cybermen's ship – a Selachian warcraft, the Doctor had called it – was a hundred times larger than the eight-man shuttle which Jolarr had seen landing two nights and a day since. Its portal-less hull was a sleek, glossy black. Three gravity discs formed a centre line down its flat underside; these too were black and were therefore barely visible. The only colour on the monstrous vessel was provided by the gleaming white rows of serrated teeth which were painted across the snub nose, giving a psychologically advantageous impression of the ship as a ferocious creature ready to strike. As a possession of the emotionless Cyber race, it was quite incongruous – but it was here, and it had already proved itself effective.

Without changing orientation, the warcraft described a large, slow circle, as if uncertain of which way to go, of who to slaughter. The people beneath were likewise confused. As mobility was restored to each in turn, they began to separate and to run this way and that, some falling, some keeping their heads down and screaming as they fled for their lives, even though there could be no hope of escape. Jolarr and Grant remained still, side by side, in mute, numb acceptance of the fact that their lives were all hanging by threads, subject to the Cybermen's whims.

And then the warcraft chose its direction at last and the gravity discs propelled it silently, swiftly, like the carnivorous great fish it resembled, until it was hovering above one of the villages.

And silence fell upon the land.

When Jolarr thought about it later, he found it difficult to recall the incident with any degree of continuity, any sense of having actually witnessed the terrible scene. His memory consisted of a vague sense of the screeching static sound and a series of flash frames, frozen images of destruction. And the smell – the unbearable, pungent, cloying odour of burnt wood and burnt flesh, mingled with the heady scent of absolute fear. The black and purple beam struck out once, twice, three times, the space between its onslaughts stretching into eternity. Each time, it swept through the village which Jolarr later learned was called Redemption, unyielding as it carved up and vaporized the settlement in a brutally efficient pattern, until there was nothing left but debris and the ashes of the lives and hopes it had stolen with its searing, concentrated radioactive flame.

There were people sobbing and howling at the unfairness of it all. It felt unreal. Jolarr kept expecting to wake up, to be spared from the merciless reality of a horror too great to be allowed to occur beyond nightmares. Beside him, Grant was shaking and staring and muttering something over and over, too softly to be heard. The Doctor moved to his side, appearing as if from nowhere, and gave his hand a comforting squeeze although his face was blank, wiped clean by the enormity of the crime just perpetrated.

And then the warcraft was moving back towards them and retaking its position above Population Control, as if readying itself to choose a new target and to strike again. 'Don't panic,' the Doctor shouted, his advice lost to the

185

sound of colonists doing precisely that. 'They've made their point. They'll want to talk next.'

He was almost instantly proved right. An amplified Cyber voice boomed from the warcraft, cutting across and all but silencing the din of the onlookers. 'You have witnessed a demonstration of our unparalleled might. You will now surrender or we will proceed to destroy your colony. We require that you reactivate the conversion chamber in our scout ship, replacing any organics therein which have perished. Once conversion is complete, you will launch the ship – containing the five hundred new Cybermen, our enemy the Doctor, his two companions and his space-time vessel – and program it to dock with this craft. You may then be spared. Your surrender will be unconditional. Its terms are not negotiable. You have two hours to communicate your acceptance.'

A cyclone of thoughts and emotions laid waste Grant's mind and heart. He was staring at the warcraft, but without truly seeing, so that he was barely aware of its rapid ascent and its disappearance into the unfathomable sky. To all his hurts and misfortunes, he could now add his reluctant observation of a massacre which would haunt him for the rest of his days. He had not known any of those caught up in the carnage, but in a sense that made things worse. As with the revelation and probable death of his father, his expectations of what he would feel wrestled with haphazard ideas of what he *should* feel, leaving Grant with an empty stomach and a clamour of nagging, contradictory voices in his head which agreed only on one thing: that he fervently, desperately, wanted this to stop. He had had enough.

And then there was that other voice: the new one, with its persuasive, insidious, unrelenting suggestion that there was but one way to leave all this behind . . . *One way to cast off the pain, the emotional suffering, and to make sure that it can never penetrate your skin again.*

186

It made sense, much as a part of Grant wished it didn't. Metal was, after all, far stronger than mere flesh. It would protect him from harm, from upset, from a cruel and uncaring life. It wouldn't be like dying, he told himself. He would just be able to see things more clearly, to be unhampered by emotions; to be capable of turning them off – not forgetting, but not allowing unpleasant memories to cause unnecessary, pointless pain. He flinched from the thought of being encased, of becoming what he had feared for so long – but, at the same time, he felt a strong attraction to the idea. The operation would take the fear from him, but the knowledge would remain to satiate his scientific and emotional thirst. Grant had always been fascinated by a technology denied to Agorans and developed only so far on New Earth. Why should a senseless phobia prevent him from experiencing its ultimate application? He could even serve his planet, doing some good instead of being always in the background, scared and useless.

Oh yes, it made sense. Far too much sense. And Grant knew, in the sudden unnerving certainty of that fateful second, that the biggest decision of his life had finally been made.

The instruments in the conversion chamber had been primed and the subjects thawed. Hegelia had waited a few minutes longer, until she could be sure that the Cybermen's attack had ceased. Then she had calmly, coolly, climbed up to the first balcony. Madrox watched, his throat dry, as she checked compartment after compartment, eventually finding one in which the occupant was quite definitely dead. Without a modicum of respect, she hefted the body from its supported standing position and disengaged the wiring which attached it to the machinery. Not without effort, she manoeuvred the cadaver from its niche until she could let it drop like a discarded doll. Then, with a care that was almost reverential, she eased her own body into the vacant berth.

Madrox tried not to watch as the ArcHivist slid thin needles into her own arms and legs. He concentrated instead upon the console: the ship's computer believed that over three hundred subjects could still be successfully converted, despite the inclement conditions suffered by their organic components. He would be the saviour of the Cyber race, and he was sure that he would be rewarded.

'I will leave the door of my compartment open for the present,' Hegelia called. 'It will not affect the process until the cryogenic circuits engage. When that happens, I want you to take my micro-recorder from me, to be conveyed to my young assistant, Jolarr. You can then seal me in.'

'Okay,' said Madrox, wondering if he would be able to climb the ladder with his injured leg. It didn't matter. By that time, his survival would have been ensured. Hegelia's wishes were unimportant.

The ArcHivist had briefed him on the workings of the machinery. She had programmed the console anyway, so that all Madrox had to do was operate half a dozen controls in a pre-arranged sequence. As he did so, he glanced up at her and felt a tremor of revulsion. She was donning a silver helmet, pressing it down to flatten her hair. Blood trickled onto her forehead as internal spikes sunk into her brain. She brought her right hand up to speak into a small black box, her voice betraying her controlled pain.

'I am making this record in the hope that it will find its way to the Arc Hives. My name is Hegelia, I have spent my life as an ArcHivist researching the Cyber race, and I am about to make my ultimate discovery. I am to undergo conversion, to become a Cyberman myself. I do not know how much of the process I will be able to relate before my mind is changed or controlled, or before the pain becomes too much for me to bear. I hope that I can add something to your understanding. At least I know that I will be fulfilled.'

She paused then and Madrox twisted the last dial.

* * *

'I'm not going back in there!' the colonist protested. 'What if the Cybermen start blasting the place again?' He was bolstered by a murmur of assent, but no more. His supporters hovered, watching the dispute and tacitly praying for the success of their own interests. Grant threaded his way through them until he could see clearly; observing, assimilating and waiting.

'They won't,' said the creature which had once been Henneker. 'They have given us an ultimatum. It is not in their interests to cause more damage until we have answered.'

'And what's the answer going to be?' the man challenged, his red-bearded jaw set defiantly.

'We will not surrender.'

'You'd rather we all died?'

'It will not come to that. We are prepared to fight. Return to the complex. We will continue the Bronze Knight Project.'

Henneker turned away and the Knights proceeded to usher people into Population Control. Some went willingly, others less so but frightened to object. Grant saw that Jolarr was amongst the latter, casting a forlorn look back at his closest friend on this world. But, to the relief of those so inclined, their red-haired representative hadn't yet had his say. He interposed himself between Henneker and the building. 'What good are your Bronze Knights if the Cybermen can kill us without landing?'

'Good point,' interjected a female voice. It was Max. 'I think you should answer that, Henneker.'

'We will not be defeated.' Grant detected a trace of anger in Henneker's reply. 'Follow orders. Return to work. Be ready to fight.'

'You haven't answered the question,' said Max pointedly.

Grant became aware of the Doctor's presence at his shoulder. 'Can't you do something?' he whispered to him.

'It's better that the Agorans see the truth of their so-called heroes without my involvement.'

189

Grant responded indignantly. 'And you think we should surrender too, do you? Well, why not? After all, you're free now — let's welcome the Cybermen back, slope off in the TARDIS and let them kill another few thousand people!'

The Doctor looked at him with a mixture of hurt and surprise. Grant averted his gaze, determined not to be cowed. He realized that similar muttered discussions were being conducted throughout the crowd.

In front of the building, temperatures were rising. 'Nobody asked you to do this,' the red-haired colonist stormed. 'We all know what happened in the last rebellion — the ringleaders became Overseers and the civilians suffered! Who gave you the right to risk our lives again with your games? You've caused the deaths of everyone in Redemption and you're doing your damn best to make sure the rest of us follow!'

Max tried to intercede. 'Okay, let's calm this down . . .'

But Henneker had brought up one arm, his fist was nuzzling his detractor's chin so that a blaster was aimed at his face, and his fury could not now have been more evident. 'I am working for the good of our world. You can help me or you can get out of my way!'

'Henneker, stop this!'

The colonist was sweating, but his eyes still burnt. 'You're going to kill me, is that it? Well, go ahead.'

So Henneker fired. The sudden blast blew half of the man's head away, eradicating his momentary expression of surprise. He was dead before his body realized the fact and hit the ground. The crowd swept back, repulsed, and Grant felt as if he was going to be sick.

Max launched herself at Henneker and pounded on his casing, yelling: 'You stupid bastard! You stupid, stupid bastard!' With no more than a shrug of the shoulders, he dislodged her and pivoted, gun raised, to greet the Doctor, even before Grant had realized that his companion had left his side. The Time Lord halted his forward flight and gritted his teeth, controlling his righteous rage. He stared down the muzzle of Henneker's gun.

'Is this how you serve Agora's "good"?'

'My world will be best served by the Cybermen's destruction. You can help us to achieve that.'

'That's what I've been trying to tell you.'

'No. You will do this on my terms. You have not been truthful with us.' The Doctor raised an eyebrow and Henneker clarified: 'The Cybermen mentioned a "space-time vessel".'

'You have proved that you're not responsible enough to use it!'

'Once our army of Bronze Knights has been completed, Doctor, you will take us back in time to defeat the Cybermen before they ever attacked. We will save the lives of everybody.'

'I won't do it! It would break every Law of Time, cause chaos in –' The Doctor wasn't allowed to complete the sentence. Henneker swung a metal hand to deliver a blow which sent him reeling. Somebody caught him and he was helped to regain his balance, a hand pressed to his forehead. Grant started forward but thought better of the action.

'What the hell do you think you're doing?' shouted Max, only to find herself ignored. The Doctor had recovered his wits and seemed about to speak again, but Henneker plunged a fist into his stomach and the Time Lord went down with a gasp.

'You have the means to save our world,' said Henneker. 'If you will not do so, you must be considered hostile. You will be imprisoned, like the Overseers, to be dealt with when the war is over.'

The Doctor dragged himself up onto his knees and made one last attempt to force Henneker to see sense. 'I can't take you to the past. You think it would save lives, but you don't know the carnage it would cause. You can't just alter history and expect the timestream to stand up to such abuse. Your world would collapse and take a good portion of the universe with it!'

191

Henneker considered. Then, to the Doctor's evident relief, he said: 'I accept your explanation. However, you can use your ship to transport us undetected to the Cybermen's warcraft, where we can engage them in combat.'

That seemed quite reasonable to Grant – but the Doctor didn't give his answer immediately. He looked at Henneker in silence for an interminable moment, then a profoundly sad expression darkened his face and he shook his head. 'I'm sorry. I don't trust you.'

Henneker's patience was exhausted. He turned and beckoned to two Knights. They lumbered forward, took positions beside the kneeling Time Lord and hefted an arm each. 'Imprison him,' their leader rapped. 'Tie him securely.' The Doctor was dragged to his feet and guided, unprotestingly, into Population Control. He didn't look back.

In the aftermath of his departure, a frightened hush fell over the spectators. Then Henneker addressed them, repeating his instruction that they should return to the complex and continue their preparations. This time, there was no argument. The colonists began to file back into the building, watched over by the cyborg saviours who had suddenly become their subjugators.

Grant picked out a path towards Max, who was standing and hugging herself, eyes big with misery and shock. 'What have we created?' she whispered as he drew level with her.

'Things will get better once the Cybermen have gone,' he said. 'The Bronze Knights' motives are good. They're trying to save lives, not take them.' He forced himself not to look at the grisly corpse of the man slain by Henneker's gun. 'Perhaps they just think more clearly than we do. That's what they're supposed to do, isn't it? They're trying to win, the only way they can. They can't let emotions get in the way of that. They can't afford to feel compassion – or hurt, or emptiness. At least they're doing something.'

Max looked at him as if she knew what was coming and didn't like it. 'What are you trying to talk yourself into?' she asked.

'I want to help,' said Grant. 'I want to know what to do. I want to be protected.' He took a deep breath and released the words which demanded to be freed.

'I'm volunteering to become a Bronze Knight.'

12

You've Got to Have Soul

Hegelia knew that conversion had begun when she felt an intense, numbing coldness creeping across her. It reached her brain and threatened to shut down her mind, coaxing her into an ethereal world of hallucinatory comfort. She fought it, concentrating on the micro-recorder, solid in her hand. She forced coherence into her thoughts and directed it towards her vocal chords. 'I am being anaesthetized,' she dictated, aware that the words were sluggish and distant. 'I doubt that is because the Cybermen feel compassion for their subjects. Rather, I suspect they recognize the possibility of the brain's expiring if the body's pain becomes too great. I will attempt to retain lucidity and continue this record for as long as I am able.'

There was nothing more to say for the moment. Despite herself, Hegelia felt her thoughts drifting off at a tangent. She thought about the Cyber army that she was unleashing and she felt a pang of guilt. She denied it. The people and the places around her might seem real, but they were no more than pages in an ancient history text. By her time, the situation on Agora would be utterly insignificant but for what researchers could learn of the Cyber legend from it. In any case, she had changed the outcome already, by being here and by killing a Cyberman herself. She was only correcting things.

She couldn't let such doubts sway her. Hegelia had travelled to Agora for just one reason, and this was it. She should feel only pride at her significant accomplishment. She had reached the long-awaited zenith of a lifetime's toil and was documenting, for the first time, an experience which few people could even hope to know.

If this was history, then ArcHivist Hegelia's name was about to go down in it.

'It's no use arguing with me,' said Max. 'I'm in charge of this surgery and I'm not going to operate on you!' She pushed past Grant and settled at the computer terminal, checking the heating system which kept her customized plastic-metal compound in its semi-liquid state. Grant followed and protested to her stubbornly turned back.

'Why not? What's wrong with me?'

'You've made the wrong choice, that's what. You're upset about Taggart and the Doctor and everything else, you've been reminded of your mortality and you think you've found a quick fix – for both body and emotions. Well, tough!'

'I'll go to Henneker,' threatened Grant. 'He won't let you turn me down.'

'No, I don't suppose he will. After all, if I stand up to him, he can just blow my head off, can't he?' Grant winced and Max rammed home her point. 'Not that you'd care. No, you're taking the easy way out. You want to be like that yourself.'

'No, I don't – that's the point! I'd have some power. I could stop the things they're doing, make sure they act for the good of everyone. They wouldn't ignore me if I was one of them.'

Max gave up trying to work – and trying to ignore him. She turned to face Grant and, seeing that she was calming herself down, about to try reasonable discussion, he sat and waited to hear her out.

'Remember what we talked about,' said Max. 'We don't know what happens to the human mind once the brain has been altered. It's all very well to decide now what you'd do as a Bronze Knight – but afterwards, you'd think differently.'

Grant knew that she was making sense, but he desperately wanted her not to. He had taken long enough to come to a decision. He couldn't bear the thought of its logic crumbling, leaving him unsupported and uncertain all over again. 'I'd think more clearly, that's all,' he protested. 'I wouldn't be hampered by . . . regrets and sorrow.' He thought of Taggart and blinked back tears.

'No, Grant, that's just what we'd like to think. We all want to feel there's something inside of us, some indefinable, unassailable core containing the essence of our beings. A soul, if you like. We hope that, whatever is done to our bodies, up to and including death, that core will remain intact — because we can't imagine what it would feel like if it didn't. But look at Henneker. Is he the same person who gathered us together and set us to work on the Project? He's changed — and, yes, perhaps his soul, his identity, is intact somewhere, but can you really believe it's in the head of that creature which committed murder outside?'

The only answer Grant could give was a mute shake of the head. 'Worse still,' said Max, more gently now, 'what if we've destroyed the person that Henneker was? What if, by tampering with his brain, we've caused more damage than death could ever have done? What then?'

At first, Madrox watched the process in fascination.

A hundred surgical implements seemed to grow from the walls of Hegelia's compartment, poking, prodding and inserting themselves into her body. It looked as if a silver web was being spun about her, obscured by the wispy vapours of whatever was making the room feel so cold. But Hegelia was obviously not in pain; at least, not so much that she couldn't keep up her record. 'I am now clamped into position,' she reported. 'I cannot see what is happening, as I am unable to turn or lower my head. My vision is also blurred, a side-effect no doubt of the cold which numbs my neural pathways. I do feel, however, that the Cybermen's instruments are moving into place and are almost poised to begin conversion proper.'

The spectacle was gruesomely compulsive. Madrox

waited for the web's mechanical elements to mesh, to resolve themselves into familiar Cyber armour which would clamp itself about its subject. In fact, the next stage was far more horrible than his naïve expectations had led him to prepare for. He felt bile rising in his throat as the compartment's instruments jerked into action and Hegelia's torso was savagely ripped open. He tore his gaze from the ragged flaps of skin, the exposed tissue, the welling blood which a vacuum pump removed before it could cause inconvenience. He doubled up, his empty stomach heaving, thinking of the hundreds of other people, their similar fates hidden behind frosted glass.

For the first time, Madrox began to wish that he had never been persuaded to start this.

The atmosphere in Max's surgery was subdued. For a long time, the only sounds came from the bubbling contents of the vats and the odd minor stirring of the latest six would-be Knights in their mouldings.

'How can you do it?' asked Grant finally. 'If that's the way you feel about the Bronze Knights, how can you keep building them? How can you accept more volunteers?'

'With difficulty,' Max said drily, 'but what choice do we have? The Cybermen must be beaten. We can worry about the consequences later.'

'Why them and not me?' The question came automatically. Grant wasn't sure what he would say if Max couldn't answer. He no longer knew his own mind as he thought he had done.

'You never really spoke to Arthur Lakesmith, did you?'

Grant shrugged. 'A few times, before the operation.'

'I was eighteen when he led the first rebellion,' said Max, with the distance of faded recollection. 'Everyone said this was it; that the Cybermen were going to be overthrown. When it didn't happen, things felt even worse than before. The world was depressed. A lot of people committed suicide. That's one reason for not converting you. You haven't lived through it like the rest of us. You don't have the same reasons for making the sacrifice.'

'And Mr Lakesmith?' Grant prompted.

'You don't want to know what the Cybermen did to him.'

'Did they take his arm?'

'They took his spirit. They allowed him to live, but crippled and obsessed by his defeat. It was four years before he would even come outside again. Once he did, he just used to shamble about the market-place, looking sorry for himself and jumping out of his skin if anyone spoke. He was the best advertisement for obedience that the Cybermen could have had.'

'He didn't seem so bad when I met him,' said Grant. 'A bit withdrawn, perhaps.'

'Henneker gave him something to look forward to. As a Bronze Knight, he thought he could be whole again and strong enough to make up for his failure. That's why I let him be the first one, the guinea-pig. He didn't have much to lose.' Max's eyes misted over. 'Whatever he did have, he lost it. I hope he's happier now.'

'And the others?'

'They're harder to justify, but they don't really have a life to go back to when this is over. You do. Apart from which, I know you better than most of them. I don't want to see you harmed. I know that's not a very logical reason, but I don't want it to be. I'd rather it was human.'

Grant nodded, feeling as if he had just been allowed to put down a crippling weight. His mind was clear again – at least, relatively so.

'I think I'd rather be human too,' he confessed.

Hegelia collected her thoughts and began to speak, although she felt as if a lump of ice had formed in her throat. 'The numbness has spread, so I can no longer be sure if I am even holding my recorder. If it has fallen, I

198

hope it can still pick up my voice.'

An image of childhood was conjured up unbidden: Hegelia, sitting in bed, peering over the tops of sheets drawn up to protect her. Her father was reading from the book of tales. A special one tonight. A real one. No fictional monsters impressed young Hegelia, nor worried her. From an early age, she had learned to distinguish between fantasy and reality, to dismiss crazy notions of dragons and bogeymen. But the Cybermen were different. Confined to mythical status though they had been, they were undeniably real. It wasn't beyond possibility that one might have survived; might have travelled to her homeworld and secreted itself beneath her bed. Hegelia had had bad dreams that night, but had found them strangely stimulating too.

She struggled to return herself to the present, dully alarmed at the effort it took. She had been trying to describe something.

Something . . .

She remembered.

'I can no longer measure time. Hours might have passed, or minutes. I once felt something tearing and believed my robes to have been stripped from me. I now recognize that, in fact, my skin was ripped apart.' Dimly, it registered that she should be more distressed about such an occurrence. 'I have been split open like a rotten fruit,' she said in a vain attempt to provoke an emotional response. 'I know this is true as I can feel the stirrings of instruments within me. No doubt, redundant organs are being removed.'

Hegelia held on to that notion for a moment and tried to deduce more precisely what was being done. It dismayed her that, having reached this moment, she could not be fully cognizant of all that was happening to her. Still, her responsibility was to record the experience from the inside. Others could study the mechanics from without.

Then, suddenly, she felt as if a cloud had parted,

allowing her to receive sensory information which previously had been obscured. She became aware of a hollow sensation, as if a cavity had been drilled out of her chest, and she was certain that she no longer had a pulse. 'My heart has been taken,' she said, her voice lowered until it was almost reverential in tone. 'I am existing on a life support system. I have passed the point of no return.'

Then Peter was very frightened, because the lever he had pulled had opened the Cyberman's frozen tomb. He had woken the sleeping beast and it was coming out to get him.

'My head is supporting additional weight. Something hard and flat is being pressed against each ear. I can, however, still feel cold air. The faceplate has not been attached.'

'Are you going to keep me a prisoner?' asked Peter.

'No,' said the Cyberman.

'Are you going to turn me to stone? Will you eat me up?'

'None of those things,' said the Cyberman. *'You have set a monster free. Your punishment is to be turned into a monster yourself.'*

'The helmet seems to be feeding information to me. I was already aware of Cyber history, of course, but I am relearning it from a fresh perspective. I view each incident as an entirely necessary task, performed with tactical genius. I take no discomfort in failure, but see instead how remaining resources can be redirected into future efforts. Regrettably, I cannot grasp every fact which enters my mind. It feels as if . . . yes, as if the data is merely passing through to a computer storage and retrieval system. Or to . . . or to . . . *another mind?*' The idea was appalling. For the first time, Hegelia was scared. Then a calming presence insinuated itself upon her thoughts and, although the situation was still as terrifying, the fear was lessened. 'Could this be it?' she asked herself wonderingly. 'Could my self be destroyed and replaced by a manufactured personality? I am aware of it now: a heavy presence in my mind, crowding out my identity. Could this be another aspect of me? A part of my brain unlocked by conversion? I do not know.'

It occurred to her to question the reason for her monologue. By accessing her memories, she was able to learn that she was attempting to make a spoken record of her apotheosis. Hegelia couldn't see any logical reason for continuing to do so. She fell silent.

She was starting to hurt. It didn't matter. In moments, the pains of the flesh would be gone for ever. Her legs had been removed. Superior, prosthetic limbs were being attached to the stumps. Her hands would be next. Her brain sent signals to the muscles in her fingers, telling them to relax, to drop the recorder before it was destroyed. She wasn't sure if the message got through. She couldn't explain why it was important that it should. Why did she want to keep talking?

'My brain is fully connected to the Cyber computer,' she said in a voice which seemed indefinably different. 'My eyes have been scooped out and the sockets filled with ruby ocular crystals, the inputs from which are to be routed to my cognitive processors. I will be fitted with a chest unit, after which final cranial operations will take place. I have been born into the Cyber race and my duty is clear.

'We will conquer. We will proliferate. We will be supreme.'

Grant opened the door to the special cell and was rendered momentarily speechless by the sight of the Doctor, held by stocks and manacles, his face seeming even more battered and painful in the half-light.

'How did you get in here?' the Time Lord asked suspiciously. Grant waved a bunch of keys in answer. 'Ah. Your friends have sent you to interrogate me. Well, fire away! Hit me first if you like. I'm helpless, after all.'

'Doctor!'

'Are you still happy with your creations?' the Doctor snapped. 'Are you proud now they've ended somebody's life? Look at me! I was held like this for over three weeks whilst you were playing real-life Meccano. I was hoping you might come to the rescue; instead, I end up back here, plus a few extra bruises! Do you really think you've made things better? From where I'm forced to kneel, you haven't had the slightest effect!'

He paused for breath and Grant took the opportunity to interject. 'Henneker let me come here because I said I could persuade you to help him.'

'Never!' the Doctor bellowed theatrically.

'But I asked him,' Grant continued patiently, 'because I thought I could free you.'

'Oh.' The Doctor's angry expression softened to an almost (but not quite) apologetic one. 'You can't. The locking mechanism is computer controlled and activated by a random sequence of –'

'I know.' Grant reached into the pocket of his tunic to produce a perspex cube containing a tangle of multi-coloured wires. 'I've brought a remote connector to the base's main computer. Once it's wired in, it'll run a program of mine to anticipate the next combination.' He crouched and began to run his hands over the stocks.

'Control panel. Just to my right.' Grant found and opened it, seething but trying to hide his irritation at the abrupt directions. The Doctor was quick enough to criticize; might an expression of gratitude be too much to hope for under the circumstances?

He hesitated, the cube poised in his hand. 'Did they hurt you? The Bronze Knights, I mean.'

'A little. They saved the main event for later. They don't want to damage me too much; not while there's a chance I'll help them.'

'Why don't you? Whatever you think of the Knights, the Cybermen are worse – and they're the biggest threat at the moment. If we can't stop them, they'll commit genocide!'

'I'm not letting those creatures into my TARDIS,' said the Doctor firmly.

'Why?' Grant challenged. 'Because you don't like them?'

'Partly,' he admitted. 'And because I don't trust them to leave it once they're in.'

'But if it's the only way –'

'It isn't!'

'So what are you going to do?'

The Doctor scowled. 'I don't recall your promise of freedom being conditional upon my agreeing with you.' He glared pointedly at the cube and, feeling a surge of annoyance, Grant thrust it into place with more force than necessary. A second passed and the Doctor was released. He let out an exaggerated sigh of pent-up frustration and struggled to his feet.

'So? What now?' asked Grant.

The Doctor thought for a moment, then seemed to regain his characteristic confidence. 'Now,' he said, 'we beat the Cybermen! Their deadline's nearly up, so I want you to get Henneker to broadcast a surrender. So long as they think he's converting the subjects as ordered, they'll leave you alone. That buys me a few hours.'

'Won't they be able to tell? If they can find out about the Cyberleader's death across light-years, surely they can patch into the scout ship's computer systems?'

'That's your second job. Get into the ship and make the computer tell a false story. Can you do that?'

'I'm not sure.'

'Splendid! Tell Henneker that, instead of sending the ship up with five hundred Cybermen when the time comes, he can fill it with Bronze Knights. It wouldn't work, of course – the Cybermen will be wary of such a predictable ruse – but it should keep him quiet and happy and out of your hair, for a while at least. All clear?'

Grant nodded and the Doctor made for the door. 'Wait a minute,' the boy called after him. 'What about you? What are you going to do?'

His companion paused on the threshold, looking as if an explanation would be a monumental imposition upon his time. 'I'm taking the TARDIS to the warcraft, of course,' he said, 'without passengers.'

'On your own? But how many Cybermen are on that thing?'

The Doctor shrugged as if he didn't care. 'Anything from two to two million. Somewhere at the lower end of the scale, I should think, if they're making their threats from afar.'

'Then surely you'd stand more chance –'

'*Without* passengers!' the Doctor reiterated adamantly. Before Grant could object further, he seemed to suddenly think of something and added: 'Oh, and by the way, thanks for releasing me. It's just a shame you were partly responsible for my capture in the first place.' Then he disappeared, leaving Grant uncertain as to whether he'd just been handed new hope or merely the recipe for a fresh course of disaster.

Madrox leant against the console, shivering and holding back tears as the pain in his leg sharpened and spread upwards. Hegelia had stopped talking again; her conversion had to be almost complete. He should be making his way up the ladder, to seal her cubicle and to rescue the recorder which lay before it. He couldn't. The thought of what had happened up there revolted him. At this moment, Madrox would have more gladly surrendered himself to the Bronze Knights than ever have to look at a Cyberman again.

'What is it doing to me?'

The plea was uttered in the deep, artificial tone which Madrox knew too well. Its plaintive, human bleat added a note of unnerving incongruity. Despite himself, he looked to its source.

Hegelia's legs and torso were encased, although her arms were bare. Two mechanical appendages worked to weave exoskeletal piping into the rapidly solidifying substance of her armour. The familiar chest unit had been attached and the ArcHivist's suddenly white and emaciated face peered blindly from between the striated blocks of a Cyberman's headpiece.

'I confess that I am beginning to worry. I expected to record full details of the conversion as it transpired; however, I find my senses limited. I do not fully understand what is happening – and what I do feel, I lack the vocabulary to describe.' Hegelia's tone fluctuated between restrained panic and detachment. 'A moment ago, my tongue reported my connection to the Cyber computer. I am not sure if I composed that message myself or if it was the responsibility of another presence. Perhaps that presence will overwhelm me. Will my personality endure, but submerged or controlled? Will only part of me survive, to be merged with an Artificial Intelligence? Or will I be erased? I had thought myself prepared for such an eventuality, but now that I am standing on the brink of the abyss, I feel –'

Hegelia stopped talking. It was as if she could no longer see the point. Her arms were being sheathed in plastic-metal compound. New pipes had been attached to the fluid reservoir at her back and were being threaded along the newly reinforced limbs. Madrox realized with a start that Hegelia's hands were gone. They had been sheared off, so fast that he hadn't noticed. A plate swung in front of her face, hiding the ArcHivist's fear behind its blankness. Madrox saw too late the spinning drill bits on its inner surface. They were pressed hard against flesh. Blood seeped through the mouth slit and round the faceplate's edges as useless organic material was broken down and scooped out, clearing space for efficient electronics. He retched again, and this time he managed to bring up stomach lining.

The creature which had once been Hegelia didn't flinch.

The Cyberman's existence began. It was ready to receive orders. It knew itself to be a recent convert to the never-ending cause and saw that to be good. It possessed memories from the time before the Change, but saw no reason to access them. One day, it would sort through the data, keeping any which might prove useful, relinquishing the remainder. For now, it had to rest. Its organic components needed time to adapt to the rigours of birthing. It cycled its computer mind into downtime, registering the status information relayed to it by the compartment in which it found itself. It knew that cryogenic systems had engaged, activating a control device within its own circuitry and sending it into hibernation. It knew that a sheen of frost was forming across its impenetrable casing.

And, suddenly, it knew that it couldn't let itself be frozen.

This unit had information which its fellow newborns didn't. It was contained within the memories of the human which had contributed to its creation, but an autonomic scan had picked it up and flagged it as important. A rebel movement on the planet had achieved a partial success, destroying a small contingent of its masters. The main warcraft was in orbit around the world and the situation was precarious. No Cybermen remained on Agora, but for those in the conversion chamber. The Doctor was involved.

It might prove advantageous, the Cyberman considered, to mobilize all newborns, despite the risk involved to them. It couldn't just sleep; it had to obtain instructions on the matter. It overrode the hibernation circuits and forced its new muscles and hydraulic systems to activate. Its audio detectors came on-line in time to hear the cracking of ice as it forced its way from the womb and stepped out onto the balcony, pausing as it adjusted to the sensory inputs of its first real environment. It lurched unsteadily towards the railing and looked down into the conversion chamber's base.

The pathetic face of a crippled human looked back.

'I am Madrox, Master. I was your Chief Overseer on this colony. I hope to be again.' The organic was frightened. The Cyberman was programmed to recognize such emotions in others, although it couldn't understand them itself. Such weaknesses would only facilitate the proliferation of its own logical kind. 'I am prepared to serve you totally,' said Madrox, voice shaking, eyes imploring. 'I have helped you. I reactivated the conversion machinery without the knowledge of the rebels. I have ensured your victory.'

Once again, the computer found insight in the memories of the entity called Hegelia. She had known of Madrox. She knew that he had taken arms against the Cybermen, even killed one. He was a traitor, his crime unforgivable. There could be only one punishment. It wasn't a question of revenge, of course. It was simply that animals had to learn, through aversion therapy, not to defy their betters.

The Cyberman brought Madrox into its sights. He must have seen it reaching for its chest controls, or the glimmer of fire which sparked in the quadruple barrels of its weapon. His fear gave way to abject panic and his good leg betrayed him, dropping him to the floor where he cried and begged for mercy, knowing that there could be none. He was near enough for a fatal blast.

The treacherous human died slowly, screaming and writhing as smoke poured from his loathsome form. The Cyberman cared not for his plight, only for the fact that its own systems had worked with just 86 per cent efficiency. Its premature arousal had precluded its optimum functioning. Still, the job was done. Madrox was dead. Now the Cyberman had but to enter the scout ship's cockpit, from where it could send its signal.

As it turned towards the downward-leading ladder, it became aware of a mechanical object at its foot. It stooped and lifted it, discerning that its purpose was to store sound waves on magnetic strips. Once again, the Cyberman accessed memories and learned that the woman Hegelia had used the device to record details of her conversion. Such actions weren't logical. The information was irrelevant and, if it improved human understanding of the Cyber race, might even be used to their eventual detriment.

Without another thought, the Cyberman crushed the machine in its powerful hand and let the mangled, inoperable remains drop. Then it resumed its journey towards the central ladder and the equipment in the cockpit.

Grant emerged onto the roof of Population Control once more, steadying his nerves with deep breaths as he made for the rearing dome of the Cybermen's scout ship. He reached for the door's opening mechanism but snatched his hand away instinctively. Stupid, he berated himself; still giving in to pointless fears. Use logic. The cockpit was empty. It was safe. He reached again – and almost yelped in terror at a sudden noise from behind.

'Can I help?' called Jolarr, hurrying over. The alien boy had evidently followed Grant up here.

'Maybe,' he said, composing himself with effort. 'Have you had much experience of computers?' It occurred to him that, through all the time they had spent together and the dangers they had shared, he and Jolarr had hardly spoken. He didn't even know his planet of origin.

'I've used them,' said Jolarr, 'but I've not done much programming. What are you trying to do?'

Grant explained. Jolarr knew most of the details anyway. He had been in the laboratory which now served as a makeshift control centre when Grant had arrived and asked Henneker to deliver his surrender. The Bronze Knight hadn't been pleased about the Doctor's rescue, but there wasn't much he could do about it – and, as the Time Lord had predicted, the prospect of sending a ship full of cyborgs to the warcraft had mollified him. Grant tried not to worry about how he might explain himself if the Doctor's mission failed and Henneker insisted on going through with the suicidal back-up plan.

'Right,' said Jolarr when the explanation was over.

'Let's see what we can do.'

Grant was intrigued. 'I thought you wanted to stay out of this. You told Henneker there were "good reasons" for not getting involved.'

'I know,' said Jolarr, a little shamefaced, 'but after seeing what the Cybermen did . . . well, none of those reasons were good enough.' Grant remembered his own reluctance to come back to Agora and he gave his friend an understanding smile.

They clambered into the Cyber ship, Grant leading the way. The cockpit was undisturbed since his last visit. The hatchway to the conversion chamber stood open and Grant felt a cold tingle of sadness at the thought of Ben Taggart, rotting away in that godforsaken pit. Dismissing the sensation, he turned to the one accessible terminal and prepared to start work. It all seemed simple enough. He had got to grips with the medical computer downstairs and this one seemed almost exactly similar in operating system and hardware design. Standardization, he thought. Very efficient – and very useful for saboteurs.

'I don't think I'm going to need help after all,' he called over his shoulder. He had already accessed the menu and was hacking his way into the sensor arrays. 'This is going to be easy. I just hope the Doctor can do his bit, whatever he's planning.'

'He's handled worse situations,' said Jolarr. 'The Hives are full of his exploits.'

Even as that unexpected knowledge was revealed, Grant found himself staring at a string of numbers which shouldn't have been there. He tried to divide his attention between the two puzzles. 'What "Hives"?' he asked absently. But Jolarr's explanation was lost to him as he suddenly realized what the on-screen anomaly represented.

'The conversion chamber,' Grant whispered. 'I'm trying to make the computer say that it's operating – *but it's already saying that!*'

Only then did he register that Jolarr's answer to his

209

question had halted mid-sentence. The prickly feeling on Grant's neck told him what was behind him, but he turned anyway and muttered a hopeless, meaningless prayer beneath his breath.

Jolarr was frozen, eyes wide, jaw open, as a monstrous silver creature stepped off the ladder to the rear chamber and confronted them. Grant's attention was riveted to the prominent gun barrels in its cranial bulge, which turned to cover both intruders in turn.

'You are trespassing on this ship,' said the Cyberman. 'You have two seconds to explain your presence, then I will kill you.'

13

Half-Life

The Doctor remained in the TARDIS for several minutes after landing, inspecting his environment on the scanner screen. He remembered all too well the speedy reception which had greeted him on Agora. He still wasn't sure how the Cybermen's instruments had detected his arrival but, on the assumption that they were sensitive to ripples in the timestream, he had disengaged his ship's temporal circuits for this short hop. He couldn't afford to be captured. It occurred to him that Grant may have been right. He was risking the safety of a world on a point of principle. Not the sort of thing which looked good when history books were written.

He stepped out into a sumptuous bedroom suite, deep carpeted and decorated to human tastes in pastel colours. The original owners of the vessel were shrewd businessmen; they knew how to entertain guests. The Cybermen, however, would have no use for this upper hospitality level, hence the Doctor's arrival here.

He eased open the door and peered into a huge, colonnaded hallway of marble and gold, relieved by the absence of an ambush – an obvious one, at least. The grand surroundings were dusty and smelt of dank neglect. The Doctor hurried across to a large, rectangular hole in the floor which, under normal use, would have resembled a swimming pool. With the water drained, its true function was revealed. It was an access hatch to the floor below, from which the Selachians could surface, water tanks in place, to greet air-breathing visitors. Immediately below, another hole led to the maintenance level – and this, the Doctor saw to his chagrin, was still waterlogged.

211

The Cybermen had dried out the operations deck to facilitate their own functioning, but Selachian engines and machinery of the sort contained beneath were designed to work best in aquatic conditions.

The Doctor had brought a length of rope from the TARDIS. He would need it, not to reach the lower deck, but for the return journey. He tied one end to a pillar and dropped the other through the hatch, praying that it wouldn't be discovered. There wasn't much chance of it, he assured himself. Cybermen didn't exactly stroll about without reason. Those which weren't conserving power in suspended animation would be in work areas, refining fuel, repairing battle-damaged comrades and planning future campaigns. He hoped.

The Doctor stripped off his beloved multicoloured jacket (he wasn't prepared to let that get water-damaged), rolled up his shirt sleeves and kicked off his shoes. Then he took a deep breath, clamped his fingers over his nose and jumped. He fell ten feet through the operations deck and hit the water feet-first.

In the space of a second, with blank, almost melancholy, teared eyes keeping him paralysed, a dozen plans jostled for attention in Grant's mind. Split up; rush the creature; try to bluff it; confuse its logical thought processes. Each required a degree of physical control which he didn't possess. Each would have resulted in his death, and Jolarr's. He chose the final option: to stare at the Cyberman and wait for it to kill him. It wasn't the most effective, but it was the only one for which he had his nervous system's support.

And then the new arrival hesitated and put a hand to its forehead in an almost human gesture. 'Jolarr?' It was looking at the alien boy, seemingly confused. 'What are you doing here, Graduand?'

'Hegelia?' Jolarr sounded astonished and repelled at the same time.

'Get out before I kill you!' This time, it was more of a

warning than a threat. The Cyberman clenched its fists as if fighting for control and Grant's body agreed that flight had become a viable proposition. He grabbed his friend's arm and propelled him towards the exit. The Cyberman's head snapped up and it fired.

The two young men leapt back as the door exploded in a Catherine wheel of sparks. Their attacker moved to block the way to salvation – then faltered again. 'The hatch!' yelled Grant, without pause for thought, fired by adrenalin. He pushed the still-dazed Jolarr first and the alien boy practically dropped into the pit. As Grant followed, the Cyberman took an unsteady swipe at him. He ducked, but was hindered by the claustrophobic surroundings. He clipped a wall and lost his balance. The Cyberman fired again, but missed (deliberately?) and Grant scrambled onto the ladder. The last thing he saw before the cockpit shot above his eye-level was the monster which might have been Hegelia, slapping both hands onto its face and emitting a keening, hopeless wail.

'The Doctor sealed this place up,' protested Jolarr from the base of the conversion chamber below. 'How do we get out?'

'We'll have to break into the complex,' Grant called. He cleared the last few rungs with a jump and glanced upwards. The Cyberman was on the ladder and descending. 'Come on,' he said, 'we can't count on it showing compassion again.' He sprinted across the chamber but came up short, realizing that Jolarr wasn't behind him. For a startling second, he thought his friend might be waiting for the Cyberman, hoping to get through to the colleague whose mind was buried in there. He was only partially relieved to see that, in fact, he had made a diversion to pluck a Cyber gun from the tangled and mangled remains of two dead monsters beneath the balconies. His attention distracted, Grant felt his heel kick something soft. He recoiled when he saw that it was Madrox's charred corpse.

Their pursuer was in the room now and striding closer

213

without a trace of indecision. Grant hauled himself to the first balcony and mentally urged his friend on as his path and that of the Cyberman converged. Jolarr, running frantically, got to the ladder first and followed Grant up. They had almost reached the top when the Cyberman appeared beneath them and tipped its head back, gun barrels flashing. Grant leapt onto the penultimate level, Jolarr close behind, as it fired and molten metal trickled from the tier above. They raced along the balcony, Grant thankful that the insides of the compartments were obscured by ice. They were almost halfway around the chamber when he saw that the Cyberman wasn't following. It had stopped by the ladder and was standing impossibly still. They halted, and neither of them could speak for a moment. Grant was acutely aware of his own quickened heartbeat, recalling its recent short cessation. A wave of giddiness washed over him and he felt a sense of sick despair at this latest unwitting descent into danger. How had he, a quiet, unassuming New Earth boy, become a magnet for situations of this type? And how many more of them could he survive?

'What's it doing?'

'Waiting,' Grant deduced. 'If it followed us, we could keep ahead of it until we got back to the ladder. By staying where it is, it's trapped us here.'

'Unless we can climb down over the balcony rail?'

'You must be joking!' Even at the peak of his health, Grant wouldn't have fancied that. It would have been a suicidal action.

'It's stalemate, then.'

'For now. But we'll have to sleep before it does.' Grant looked at Jolarr's appropriated weapon. 'We'll have to use that.' He tried to gauge the distance across the chamber and estimated it to be about a hundred metres. 'Do you think it'll be effective at this range?'

'I've no idea, but there's one way to find out.' Jolarr hefted the gun to his shoulder. Agonizing seconds passed as he carefully aimed it across the divide. To Grant's perturbation, the Cyberman didn't move. It obviously wasn't expecting to be damaged.

Jolarr lowered the gun. 'What if it's really Hegelia in there?'

And suddenly, something exploded behind them and showered them with glass fragments. The occupant of the nearest compartment had stepped straight through its door, and it now lashed out blindly. Jolarr dropped his weapon and, stooping to collect it, took a glancing blow to the forehead. Grant backed away, shouting for his friend to do the same. Jolarr, hurt but not wounded, took advantage of the newly born Cyberman's confusion and slipped through its flailing arms. Reaching Grant's side, he brought up the Cyber gun and pulled the trigger.

'It's useless!' he cried. Grant had almost expected it to be, from Hegelia's reaction. As well as summoning its kin, the dying Leader had broadcast a disabling signal to all Cyber technology within range.

The emergent monster rounded on its prey, who turned automatically and began to flee. They halted as they realized that the former Hegelia had left its post at the ladder and was marching towards them, confident now that escape was impossible.

'We're surrounded!' Jolarr dropped the useless gun and it fell through the balcony rail, to clatter to the floor below.

They cowered together as death closed in from each side.

The Doctor was trapped in a service duct, still struggling with the slippery, seaweed-like wiring of the warcraft's offensive systems, when the Cybermen found him. He became aware of a disturbance in the murky green water, seconds before he saw them swimming in from above with powerful, sure hydraulic strokes. Abandoning his task, he flipped over and struck out downwards, pushing off the glistening rocky instrument face and cursing himself for having clearly tripped an alarm. His continued survival confirmed his hypothesis that the Cybermen's guns wouldn't work down here – but if the duct wasn't open at both ends, that only meant he would be killed more slowly when they caught him.

Thankfully, it was. The Doctor emerged into an open area and tried to get his bearings. He seemed to be in an engine bay; great chunky appliances surrounded him, looking like dormant sea monsters thanks to the Selachians' organic technology. His lungs were beginning to ache and it worried him that he no longer knew where his next breath was coming from. He chose a random direction and lost almost half his air in shock as mechanical arms clamped about his neck. Another Cyberman had concealed itself and waited in ambush. The Doctor lashed out, squirmed and managed to roll so that he and his captor were upside down. A well-placed elbow dislodged the hold and allowed him to kick free. Fortunately, without balance or leverage to use their strength, the Cybermen were more disadvantaged underwater than he was – except that they didn't need oxygen. The Doctor could hold his breath for several minutes, but he had been down here for over three already.

He reached the bay's ceiling, dismayed to find that no air was trapped above the water. He swam on, praying for a hatch, and was forced to dive again as the shadows of two Cybermen loomed. This time, he wasn't followed. They knew his weakness and were guarding the route to the surface instead. He had a choice. He could either surrender in the hope that their orders were not to kill him. Or . . . the alternative was only slightly more desirable.

In the seconds remaining to him, the Doctor found the best hiding place he could, concealed by one of the hulking engine stations. He slipped partway beneath its slimy bulk and closed his eyes, forgetting his peril and turning his mind inwards until he was aware of every component of his own body and was able to switch each one to a metaphorical standby status. This Time Lord trance was deeper and more dangerous than the one in which he'd passed time in custody – but, in such a state, he could suspend his breathing for an indefinite period. He told his biological clock to wake him in twenty minutes' time, at which point he would have one last chance to slip through the Cybermen's cordon unexpectedly . . . or die.

That was if his comatose and helpless body wasn't discovered before then, he thought as darkness overwhelmed him.

'Rush Hegelia! She might let us through.'

Grant stopped Jolarr with a firm hand on the shoulder. 'I don't think she's in there any more.' The Cyberman marched on with no sign of its earlier reticence. It would soon be close enough to slay them. Grant looked to the other monster and saw that it was swaying, uncertain of its untested limbs. 'This way!' He grabbed Jolarr and pulled him along until the alien boy took control of his own flight. They dived for each side of the living obstacle and it occurred to Grant, in that cold stop-motion instant, that he would never have time to apologize if he had made the wrong decision.

He ducked and threw himself forward, the armour of the Cyberman's leg brushing his left arm. He thought he had made it, but his jubilation ceased as he felt a sharp, penetrating pressure on his shoulder and hit the floor, knees first, with a cry. The Cyberman had pivoted to follow his passage and had caught him in its unyielding grip. It squeezed and blood rushed to Grant's head. His vision blurred, but he saw that Jolarr had managed to get through. The alien boy hesitated, staring at Grant in indecision, then flung himself at the Cyberman only to be greeted by the barrier of a steadfast arm. It caught him and wound him in towards its chest, where he was held. He had sacrificed himself for nothing.

Almost blind with agony, Grant looked up and tried to meet his captor's hollow gaze. He saw a flicker of orange

217

in the barrels of its cranial weapon and inwardly railed against the unfairness of his inevitable fate.

Then the Cyberman's head blew apart in a ferocious cloud of orange fire. It released its prisoners to fling its hands up to where a sheath of spluttering wires protruded from a neckpiece to which it had nothing left to connect. Grant was on his hands and knees, trying to cope with the pain in his shoulder and to calm his stomach as his back was spattered by a hot metal rain, and blood and oil flowed over his neck and dripped off him.

Jolarr was shouting something and although Grant's blast-deadened ears couldn't hear the words, his body language was descriptive enough. The other Cyberman was upon them. With Jolarr's help, he forced himself to stand and they ran. Beside and before them, more Cybermen were waking from their hibernation, flinging open glass doors or simply punching through the ineffectual barriers. Silver hands reached blindly for the fugitives and Grant and Jolarr were forced to run a deadly gauntlet, ever mindful of the monster which had been Hegelia, relentless in its pursuit. At one point, Jolarr was caught and Grant had to prise steely fingers from his arm. He was grateful that the newborns hadn't yet attained full strength and awareness – but, with more and more of them breaking out, he couldn't help but wonder how long it would be before they started to fire. Prematurely activated or not, he couldn't expect more Cybermen to share their colleague's misfortune.

They reached the ladder and Grant began to climb down, intending to run for the cockpit. 'Go up!' Jolarr urged. 'There's an opening.' Grant followed the advice and was grateful to confirm what Jolarr had seen from the balcony's far side. This level's door to Population Control had been forced open, presumably to bring the late Chief Overseer Madrox into the chamber from his place of incarceration. Only as they hurtled along the corridor did Grant realize the implication of that deduction. The only exits from this passage led into the complex's cells

. . . locked cells! Indeed, they passed the open hatch through which Madrox must have been freed and saw only a closed door beyond. They kept on and hoped for a miracle, but as they rounded the next corner, they came up short at the sight of four approaching Cybermen. They had split up to surround their prey.

'Back!' Jolarr squeaked, sounding close to tears. They retraced their steps and hurtled into Madrox's former cell; the nearest to salvation they could get.

'The locking panel's on the outside,' Jolarr reported miserably. 'We can't shut them out.' Grant was already hammering on the far door and yelling for help. His fists were aching and the whole building seemed to shake around him, but no one responded.

'They're in sight.' Jolarr ducked back into the cell. 'Both ends of the corridor. They're coming!' He joined Grant in shouting and knocking, but both were aware that time was running out.

Then the viewing hatch was pulled open to reveal the welcome visage of a Bronze Knight. Grant almost exploded with relief. 'The Cybermen, they're after us. Get us out of here!' It hesitated for a second and then the door clicked open and Grant and Jolarr tumbled through gratefully. Barely had they done so when the first two Cybermen appeared behind them and fired. The Knight took the brunt of both shots, fell back and hit the wall, its armoured body denting the metal. Grant grabbed the keycard from its hand and swiped it through the reader. The cell door closed and locked, but he knew that its flimsy material wouldn't hold up for long against a Cyber onslaught.

The Knight knew it too. 'Tell Henneker,' it said. Then it positioned itself to await its enemies' attack. Despite their exhaustion, Grant and Jolarr found the strength to do as it had bade them. But, as they took the first corner at a run, Grant felt compelled to look back.

A Cyberman's fist had just punched through the cell door.

* * *

The Doctor woke to find himself soaked and lying on his stomach on what was clearly the bridge of the Selachian warcraft. The room was semi-circular and elegantly furnished, although a second look revealed that the comfortable chairs and pleasingly contoured instrument banks were grown from the same organic material as the machinery on the lower deck. A panorama of space took up most of the curved wall, the view dominated by the dirty brown ball of Agora at its centre. The Doctor's nose wrinkled at a musty smell, no doubt caused by the evacuation of water from this area. Despite his efforts to resist, he was doubled up by a coughing fit as his lungs strained to fill themselves. That attracted the attention of the room's six other occupants, and the Doctor was quickly surrounded by Cybermen. He made the best of it and lifted himself to his knees, forcing a smile as he faced another black-highlighted Leader, identical to the one which had perished on the world below.

'Hello,' he said pleasantly. Then, feigning recognition: 'Didn't I kill your brother?'

The Cyberleader wasn't amused. 'You were foolish to come here, Doctor. You had no hope of defeating us.'

'I did get a little out of my depth, didn't I?'

'You were first detected in a service duct. You will tell us your purpose in being there or you will be destroyed.'

The Doctor scowled at hearing yet another threat. 'You're going to kill me anyway, aren't you?' He had recovered enough to begin to feel thoroughly resentful towards his predicament.

'Perhaps not – if you give me your TARDIS.'

'Oh yes,' the Doctor retorted, 'so you can whip back in time and alter your past defeats. You'd kill me before I even met you! What sort of a deal is that?'

'You were clearly attempting to sabotage our vessel,' said the Cyberleader, refusing to follow the Doctor's conversational route.

'Oh, well done! "A logical assumption, Captain"!'

It cocked his head as if puzzled. 'My rank is that of Leader.'

'You just don't get it, do you? You never do – that's your problem!' The Doctor leapt to his feet. Two Cybermen raised their guns in threat, but he ignored them. A torrent of rage surged out of his hearts, fed by the frustration of the past weeks: his time in prison; his false escape and recapture; his brutal treatment by the Bronze Knights; his return to captivity; his release, only to blunder into enemy hands once more. Since his trial by the Time Lords, the Doctor had fought to keep the naturally aggressive nature of his present incarnation in check – but right now, he was sick of being caged, bullied and beaten, and he wasn't prepared to take any more.

He thrust a scolding finger at the Cyberleader's chest unit. 'Why do you keep coming back? Why don't you just accept defeat? You always tell me how you need to survive and propagate. Well, why do you?' He turned and flung his arms wide to include his whole audience in the tirade. 'You don't have feelings, you don't have hearts, you don't appreciate anything. Your condition is utterly meaningless! Who would care if the Cyber race disappeared from the galaxy tonight? Nobody, that's who! Not even the oh-so-cold-and-calculating Cybermen themselves! And why should you? You have no quality of life, no pleasures, no culture. The only purpose of your existence is to prolong that existence. Use your logic on that one. Tell me how you justify such a circular, pointless argument!'

'Your outburst is pointless.'

The Doctor rounded furiously on the Cyberleader. 'You're supposed to be dominated by logic. Well, prove it. Switch yourselves off. Leave life to those who have a good excuse for living it!'

'Surrender is not logical. We must endure.' The Leader turned its back on the seething Doctor and strode towards the fungal outcrop of a control panel. 'Our logic will triumph over your emotions. You will be unable to stand

and watch whilst I destroy more of the humans below.'

'You wouldn't,' the Doctor whispered. Then, more fiercely: 'What do you hope to gain from this?'

'Your compassion will force you to prevent my use of the plasma beam by surrendering your TARDIS.'

'No!' The Doctor sprang across the bridge, making to tackle the Leader. It anticipated his attack, swung about and knocked him from the air with a sweep of its arm. He hit the floor by its feet, with a new graze on his temple. His foe looked down at him, managing to seem insufferably smug despite the inflexibility of its expression.

'I will now activate the beam,' it said – but paused, to await the Doctor's reaction. 'You will surrender,' it prompted, when none was offered.

'Will I?' the Doctor said sadly. 'But that wouldn't be logical, would it? To prevent the deaths of those people by giving you a weapon with which you'd destroy them – and many more – anyway?'

'You are learning, Doctor,' said the Leader, actually giving him an approving nod as if he were a favoured pupil. 'Your application of logic has delayed your defeat. However, you are an instrinsically emotional creature. You will break eventually.' It turned back to the console and announced, for his benefit: 'Weapon systems are on line. Sensors are targeted upon Sector Two of the breeding colony Agora.'

Then it activated the plasma beam.

The Bronze Knights filed out into the corridor, led by Henneker. Grant remained behind in the laboratory with Jolarr, watching them go with cold foreboding. There were roughly thirty of the creatures now, compared to . . . how many Cybermen? Some wouldn't have come through the conversion intact, but many more would. Their newborn weakness could hardly begin to outweigh their massive advantage of numbers. The Bronze Knights were heading towards their deaths.

They made an impressive sight none the less, these

living weapons of war – though no one was there to see them as they strode with pride, in formation, along the corridors of Population Control. One floor below, Maxine Carter's head tilted upwards as their footsteps reverberated through her surgery. She ached to know the purpose of their march, but knew that it could not be good news. She would best aid the cause by continuing her work. Six more Bronze Knights were almost complete and they might serve to tip the balance in whatever war was being fought now.

The reddish-brown army moved into single file to mount the stairs. They climbed two levels in silence and dismounted on the top floor of the complex, their sure course taking them towards the cell block. Elsewhere in the building, one alien from the future and one Agoran expatriate watched their progress on a hastily established internal video link. Ahead of the army, Cybermen were swarming from Madrox's former cell. The single Knight which stood sentry was being overwhelmed and ripped apart.

'We've got to help,' said Jolarr. 'What if we got an Overseer gun each? I saw where Henneker put them.'

Grant shook his head. The thought of joining the battle terrified him – but more than that, he could see how little good it would do. 'We've got control of the computer system here. We must be able to do something with it!' But nothing came to mind.

The Bronze Knights and the Cybermen had closed in battle now; the metal walls of Population Control vibrated with the sheer kinetic force of their clash. The narrow confines of the corridor worked against both sides, but the Cybermen were especially hampered. They queued to climb through the jagged hole in the cell door, whilst their comrades fought alone and in vain.

For a moment, the situation looked hopeful for the defenders of the colony – but only for a moment. The Cybermen were quick to adapt to their disadvantage, and as their troops continued to march up from the

223

conversion chamber, they gained access to other cells and began to tear paths through them. They attacked their foes from ahead, behind and between. The fight would be long and brutal, but the ending was already inevitable. And once the Bronze Knights had fallen in martyrdom, could those who were known to be their allies long endure?

'The beam has not functioned, Leader.'

The Doctor picked himself up as the Cyberleader swung to face him. 'What have you done?' it demanded.

'Disabled your gun, of course.' He grinned with pride. 'Actually, I've been quite clever.'

'Alert!' squawked a Cyberman suddenly, its tone a step away from panic. 'Radiation is seeping into this area.'

The Doctor paced the bridge, his hands behind his back, with the air of an indulgent tutor. 'You see, I had my suspicions when I saw your conversion machinery. Then I learned that one of your kind had been killed by an Overseer gun emitting microwave energy which should have been harmless to you. You're cutting corners, Leader. The war with Voga has taken its toll. Your Cybermen have more organic components than any model since the original Mondans – hence the resurgence of an old weakness.' He halted, deliberately not looking at the nearby exit, and skewered the Leader with a hateful glare. 'Your weapon of choice wouldn't have used hard radiation – but then, this isn't your ship, is it? It's not your choice. Before you caught me, I fixed the plasma beam to discharge a lethal radioactive backblast. Lethal, that is, to you!'

'And to you also, Doctor.'

'I know.' He turned and sprinted for the door, but the Cybermen were too fast and his way was blocked by two unbending arms. He was seized and hurled back across the bridge, to where the Leader fastened a hand onto each of his shoulders.

'You will reverse what you have done.'

'Impossible, I'm afraid. Even by the time I reached the maintenance level, this ship would be irrevocably contaminated. You're dead, Cyberleader!' He took great pleasure in sneering the words. 'You're being killed by a weapon you stole – and you can't even evacuate because your scout ships are all out searching for more helpless civilizations to plunder. Poetic justice, really. Not that you'd appreciate the concept!'

'One means of egress is still available: your TARDIS.' The Cyberleader increased its grip. 'You will be unable to save yourself without allowing me into your vehicle. Your animal sense of self-preservation will require you to do so.'

'Then I'll have to override that sense. Logic, Cyberleader!' The Doctor spoke through gritted teeth. He was short of breath, beginning to perspire and he could feel a dull ache in his stomach. He had taken an anti-radiation pill in the TARDIS, but that would only have been effective against an accidental mild exposure. He hadn't counted on being trapped like this, nor could he have guarded against the eventuality if he had.

A crash behind him told the Doctor that one of the Cybermen had fallen. Its body was splayed out on the floor and a viscous fluid oozed from its joints. 'And then there were five,' he taunted, but his throat burnt and his voice sounded hoarse. 'Not to mention the dozens who are dying around this ship; the hundreds in suspended animation who will never wake now. What about you, Leader? How long before you succumb? Think you can outlast me?' He clung on to his enemy's arms and tried to break its hold, to no avail.

'I will not have to. This craft's weaponry may be inactive, but I can crash-dive it into the colony if you do not co-operate. Its fusion drive would create quite a magnificent explosion. You will not want to see so many humans eradicated, so you will surrender.'

'Illogical again,' the Doctor panted. Stars danced in his vision, but he cleared it to see that a Cyberman had stalked over to the navigational controls.

'Your choice,' said the Cyberleader implacably.

'Wait! Before you do that, check your instruments. The colonists have restarted the conversion process. Hundreds of your own kind are already doomed. Do you want to wipe out five hundred more in a petty act of revenge?'

'He is correct, Leader,' said the Cyberman. 'Three hundred and twelve conversions have been completed on the planet. The neo-units have left their chamber to retake . . . to retake . . .' It tottered and extended a hand to steady itself. The Doctor was relieved that Grant had evidently fooled the Cyber computer – although such detail had not been strictly necessary. He could feel the Leader's grip weakening, but only as his own strength drained too. The skin on his face was beginning to peel and every pore in his body leaked sweat. Two Cybermen sagged and hit the floor, but the Leader remained steadfast and the Doctor couldn't prise it loose. They lurched across the bridge in a macabre dance, each straining to prove their own strength the greatest; each hoping not to be the first to die.

'You have defeated this contingent,' admitted the Cyberleader, its voice slurred and indistinct, 'but our race will proliferate. Even should I expire before you, you will be unable to break the hold of my hydraulic muscles. I have destroyed the Cybermen's greatest enemy. Now nothing can prevent our rise to power!'

'Look on the bright side,' said the Doctor, eyes closed, a hammer pounding in his head. 'I can't think of anyone I'd rather share a suicide pact with.'

Their dance turned into a close-contact waltz, two bitter foes keeping each other supported although they had become barely aware of each other's presence.

Locked into a fatal embrace, they waited for the deadly radiation to ravage their bodies and steal both their lives.

14

Endurance

Jolarr was feeling useless. It had been several minutes since Grant had announced that he wanted to try something, whereupon he had set to work at a terminal which ostensibly controlled the lab's genetic scanners, but which Henneker had earlier hooked up to Population Control's main computer. Jolarr had been left to monitor the uneven struggle upstairs and to fret about its probable outcome. He was feeling extraordinarily cold and he wished for something to keep him occupied, to take his mind off the massacre. The sight of yet another Bronze Knight crumpling into a pool of oil and blood was not conducive to calming his nervous state.

He wondered which of the attacking creatures was Hegelia.

'That's it!' said Grant at last.

Jolarr gazed eagerly over his friend's shoulder, but the tiny screen before him showed only a string of letters and numbers, which he found incomprehensible. 'That's what?'

'I've hacked into the scout ship's systems. I've got control from here.' Grant's excitement melted into a frown as he studied the hard-won data on the screen. 'There are two hundred and eighty-six Cybermen active in the complex.'

'Oh.' Jolarr thought miserably of all the Knights he had seen killed and decided that half as many foes would have been too many. 'They outnumber us ten to one, then.'

Grant nodded distantly, his concentration reserved for his resumed work at the terminal. 'I'm trying to even the odds a bit. I've lowered the temperature as far as it'll go throughout the building.'

'I thought it was getting frosty! How's that going to help?'

'These Cybermen should have been frozen after conversion. They must have some sort of a hibernation protocol, triggered by intense cold. Since they were woken early, I'm guessing that protocol's still current. The colder it gets, the more likely they are to shut down.'

Jolarr looked doubtfully at the video picture. Obscured though his view of the battle may be, it did seem that Cybermen were falling more quickly than the Bronze Knights were disposing of them. 'I think it might be working,' he hazarded. 'Well, a little.'

'Good. The next stage is to put the conversion chamber's air-conditioning on full blast.'

Jolarr marvelled at his friend's confidence, remembering how frightened he had seemed before. With a logic problem to solve, a computer to aid him and no immediate threat to his well-being, Grant was in his element.

But could he out-think the Cybermen, all the same?

The Doctor was hardly aware that he had fallen, except in blurred snatches of recollection as if of dreams. He forced his eyes open to see that the roof was spinning. It took him a moment to recognize the motion as illusory. He focused his vision to bring together two images of the Cyberleader. He didn't know why the creature had released him, but as he watched its thrashing and screaming, it occurred to him that even its semi-organic brain had been addled by the all-pervading radiation. He too was near death and it was difficult to concentrate, but his thoughts were sharpened by hope. He had a chance to survive.

The Doctor tried to stand, but his arms wouldn't lift him. He crawled, instead, across painful inches of dirty floor. The exit was tantalizingly close, yet it seemed to be moving from him faster than he could approach. He heard a rattling, gargling sound from behind and turned his head. The movement hurt, like he was rubbing his raw neck against sandpaper. The Cyberleader had noticed his escape attempt. It had meant to utter a threat, but its voice had failed it. Conversely, the Doctor realized, its handheld gun was fully mechanical and had no reason not to function. A section of floor exploded by his arm and, temporarily reprieved by the Leader's disorientation, he took cover behind a pulsating brown console.

It fired again and the Doctor leaned against the soft, warm surface, gasping for breath and feeling as if his face was on fire. There was no way to reach the door without making himself a target. His eyes closed and his mind drifted, but an inner sense scolded him into alertness and he saw the body of a dead Cyberman before him. Hardly daring to hope, he tipped it over. Its gun lay beneath it. Feverishly, he prised it loose from clinging fingers.

As he raised his head above the console, the Cyberleader fired again, its shot going wild and ricocheting off the wall. The Doctor's aim was almost as bad and the kick from the powerful gun both surprised and floored him. By the time he had recovered his senses, the Leader had brought the fight closer. It stood astride its foe and aimed for his head. The Doctor didn't have time to retrieve his own weapon. Pitiful though the battle had been, he had lost. The price was to die a little earlier than the victor.

Then the Cyberleader swayed and fell against the console. The Doctor seized his advantage, went for the gun and blasted the monster four times in the back. It sank in three jerky stages and the Doctor, overcome by dizziness, was forced onto his hands and knees as he gritted his teeth and made himself keep going.

He reached the door and paused on the threshold, three corridors looking like six. He tried to remember what he knew about the layout of Selachian craft, to work out which direction would take him to the TARDIS. The effort was too much.

With a sickly groan, the Doctor passed out.

'It's working,' breathed Grant. 'They're falling.'

'How many left?' asked Jolarr.

'Two hundred and twelve.'

'Not fast enough.' He wondered how this would work in HyperReality. He had played through numerous adventure scenarios — all chosen for their improving effects upon the mind, of course. If a software laboratory had manufactured this problem, Jolarr would have solved it thus: cold demonstrably weakens the enemy. It isn't yet cold enough to make them all dysfunctional. Ergo, within the parameters of the game, there must be a way of making it colder still. He told Grant of his thoughts, but then his attention was drawn towards the monitor, which reminded him that this adventure was far more than words on a screen or false images projected into his brain's frontal lobes. This was real life. People were dying and he might well be next.

'You're right,' said Grant unexpectedly. 'Of course, it's the logical answer!' He was working at the computer again with feverish haste and Jolarr watched him with a frown. Make it colder, he had said. How was that possible?

Logic, he reminded himself. Look for a cooling agent.

Then, with a sudden, involuntary grin, he realized where a good one had to be.

Max hadn't screamed for a long time, but she did so now as the door to her surgery was blown open and a quartet of Cybermen strode in through the smoke of their own blasts. The first of them tilted its head in her direction and tapped its chest unit, unleashing a bolt of fire which crippled the apparatus behind her. Max fell and tried to hide behind the pallets on which her latest Bronze Knights lay. To her relief, four of the six were alert enough to clamber to their feet, to stand in her defence. She heard the Cybermen firing again and watched as

230

her creations braced themselves against the onslaught and moved to retaliate. But the Knights were at a disadvantage. Two of their number lay unconscious like useless metal sculptures – and the weapons with which they should have been fitted were still piled in the corner. Max regretted her part in designing the guns so that only a direct nerve stimulus could operate them. They were no good to her.

As in the skirmish at the bunker, all Max could do was watch and hope. This time, it was infinitely worse, as the prospect of victory seemed more remote. The Cybermen's guns were activated over and over again, and even with her face at floor level, Max felt her throat catch and her nostrils trying to close, assaulted by their burning odour. Her eyes were beginning to water, but she continued to stare, spellbound, from beneath the pallets – until her view of the participants' legs was suddenly, shockingly, blocked by the head of a Bronze Knight which hit the ground and rolled towards her. Max covered her face and ears and tried to blot out the sounds of rending metal and electronic screams.

When the surgery finally ceased its upheaval about her, Max didn't move. She was praying that the Bronze Knights might have triumphed – but, weaponless, newly activated and surprised as they had been, she knew that was unlikely. She didn't dare to look. She didn't have to. She would be killed or not; she could do nothing either way. But that wasn't how she wanted to go, she scolded herself. She would confront the Reaper with all the defiance she could muster, kicking and screaming although her cause may be lost. Max Carter had never been a coward. It was too late to become one now.

The baby inside her shifted and she remembered that she had two lives to fight for.

Max opened her eyes and gingerly raised her head above the pallets, fighting the urge to sneeze as she breathed in dust and smoke. She saw the bulky, haze-shrouded form of the combat's sole survivor and squinted to make out what it was. With a dull clank of metal on metal, it took four steps towards her and she saw.

It was a Cyberman.

For a moment, the Doctor believed himself free. With a supreme effort, he had made his way across the main operations deck and climbed up to where he had left the TARDIS; a long time ago, it seemed. Then he opened his eyes and felt a rush of misery as he saw that it had all been dreams. He was lying on the floor, half on and half off the bridge. His face was flushed and blistered and his head was hurting enough to rupture the coherence of his thoughts. He lurched to his feet and rocked on his heels, not sure if the movement had been real this time or just another cruel deception. He used the wall for support in an environment which, it seemed, was bucking deliberately to steal his balance and to pitch him to the ground for the final time. He was blind, but he fumbled his way across the smooth and comfortingly upright surface. The radiation would be strongest on the bridge, he reasoned, where the leak originated. It would help him to get clear of it. But not much. Not at this stage.

The journey seemed to take hours, the distance between him and the TARDIS growing steadily more vast until it felt insurmountable. Still, the Doctor staggered on, the muted inner voice of his own strong instinct for self-preservation driving him to greater efforts of will to keep the ransacked shell of his body going. As he passed along the corridors of the Selachian vessel, he encountered isolated groups of Cybermen. Exposed to less radiation than those on the bridge, they still stood, albeit without prospect of continuing to do so for long. He ignored them, knowing that he was in no condition to fight; that he had to take his chances with what perils they could pose. Fortunately, they could do little. A spattering of blaster fire sizzled by, but nothing came close — at least, not that he was aware of. The Doctor's concentration was reserved for one thing only.

He remembered lying on the TARDIS floor, paralysed by the extensive damage done to his third form in the Great One's radioactive caves on Metebelis. The regeneration had been long in coming, quite agonizing and made possible only by the healing, timeless cocoon of his craft. Without it, there would be no such options. He might well be granted a new body, but the cellular degradation of this one could not be totally undone. The seventh Doctor would perish minutes after his birth, in the same excruciating pain as the sixth. The eighth would follow. And so on, until final darkness.

At last, he reached the access point to the hospitality level and saw, with dull gratitude, that his rope had not been removed. He knew that, if he hesitated, his muscles would betray him. He summoned what strength he had and leapt for it, almost crying out with the pain of clinging to the slender lifeline with sore, peeling hands and knees. His arms screamed and locked, refusing to allow him to climb. The rope swung and circled and he felt liquids sloshing in his stomach and head. When he dared to look, he saw only the glittering surface of the water, lapping gently at the rim of the downward-leading hatch below. If he lost his grip and plunged into that aqueous grave, there would be no leaving it. He strained to look up instead, but the dizzying height of the topmost level only fuelled his sense of futility. The TARDIS was two metres above, but it might as well have been on the second moon of Thoros Beta.

Perhaps it would be best to surrender; just let go of the rope and allow cold water to soothe him, to take his troubled consciousness away. He had discharged his responsibilities, after all. Peri was gone, Grant was back on his homeworld – and both had justification for wishing that they'd never met him. The Doctor's death could work to the good of so many. He wouldn't be able to hurt anyone else. Like Angela . . .

He had only ever wanted to do right, to help people. But such simple days were long gone. He had allowed so

233

many deaths on the Network. He had been outwitted by the Cybermen here, so that all he had been able to do was to throw his life away or watch a planet die. What use had he been to the five hundred Agorans in the conversion chamber? To the boy who had begged him for a release that he had been too late to provide? He had been right to cease his interference, to settle on Torrok. His sin had been in not making that retirement a permanent one. There was one way left to do so. A way to ensure that the Valeyard, his premonition of an evil future self, never came to pass. One way to end it for good; quite possibly for everybody's good.

Just let go of the rope.

The Cybermen were gaining the upper hand. They were making the most of their biggest advantage – numbers – by dragging their foes away from each other and surrounding them in groups of nine or ten. Unable, for the most part, to aid their fellows, the Bronze Knights were forced to fight defensively to keep their own lives.

'They've got two of ours in the ship!' cried Jolarr, startled by the new picture on the screen in the laboratory. 'They're tearing them apart! I think one of them's Henneker. Can't you do something?'

Grant moved to his side, his work apparently finished, and they stared together. The scene was relayed to them by a camera near the conversion chamber's ceiling, which offered a rigid and rather forced perspective. 'I've done all I can. It's up to the pipes now; how much they can take. They might not blow.'

'They've got to!'

'Let's hope so. There was more freon than I expected, that's something. The Cybermen used it as an engine coolant, as well for the hibernation stuff.' Grant frowned. 'Wait a minute, what's going on down there?'

Jolarr saw it. The cluster of Cybermen which had gathered around Henneker was dissipating, abandoning him (alive, it appeared) to head for the exits. Their comrades joined them in short order, though they left behind what looked like a red metal-plated corpse. 'They're evacuating!'

'They won't get far,' said Grant with grim satisfaction. 'There's only room for one at a time on each ladder.'

'But they know what you've done!'

'And they're expecting it to harm them. That's good!' Grant clenched his fists and quietly urged the laws of physics to take their toll. 'I've backed up so much freon in that cubicle . . . it can't hold out. It can't!'

And then the nearest conversion compartment to the ladder on the topmost balcony exploded. A torrent of white liquid, so cold as to trail vapour, cascaded over the railing and scattered the hapless Cybermen with the force of its deluge. The last thing Jolarr and Grant saw, before the camera itself was knocked out of alignment, was a sea of thrashing, useless silver hands. Then Jolarr gave a whoop of victory as Grant, more practically, hurried to his terminal and checked its display. 'They're shutting down like storage comps in a magnetic storm!' he crowed.

'Like what?'

'I mean, the Cybermen are switching to hibernation mode. A hundred, at least.'

'And Henneker? Will he be all right?'

'He was built to withstand more than a bit of cold. So were the Cybermen – it's just that we've convinced them it's bedtime.'

'How many are left outside the chamber?' Jolarr was already scanning the various scenes available, to see how the battle had progressed elsewhere. He frowned as the monitor alighted upon a patrol of eight Cybermen, marching swiftly along a plain corridor. Where was that? he wondered.

'Seventy-eight,' reported Grant.

Then Jolarr heard footsteps and, with a horrible realization, he pushed Grant aside and lunged across to the door control panel. He stabbed at the 'close' button even as the

first Cyberman appeared on the threshold. An unnerv-
ingly thin metal sheet slid across to conceal it and to take a
fatal blast meant for him. 'They've traced your terminal!'
he exclaimed unnecessarily. Grant was trembling, almost
pale enough to be Jolarr's reflection. They looked to each
other helplessly, then fright catapulted Jolarr across the
room as a loud bang sounded from behind him. The door
now sported an inwardly protruding, fist-shaped dent. A
second punch and it began to buckle. It clung to its frame,
but couldn't do so for much longer.

Jolarr began to gather chairs and to hurl them towards
the besieged portal. Seeing that they would do little good,
he tried to manhandle a table across to bolster the flimsy
barricade. He shouted for Grant's help, but his friend was
back at the computer. 'Never mind that,' he called, 'I
need you here. Get me one of those things off the wall.'
He gestured towards a pair of thin, cylindrical pipes
which spanned the width of the room just above floor
level. Jolarr had assumed them to be part of the complex's
heating system. He couldn't imagine what Grant was
hoping to achieve, but a quick glance at his own collec-
tion of furniture persuaded him that this new plan could
be no less effective than his current one.

He knelt by the pipes and pulled at the top one where a
bracket fixed it to the wall. It didn't give, and Jolarr was
terrified to hear a crunch of tearing metal as the door was
ripped from its hinges and the Cybermen gained access to
the laboratory. Had he been alone, he would have surrendered – but Grant was still typing away, despite being
more directly in the line of fire. His courage gave Jolarr
the strength to ignore the approaching army and to make
one last attempt to complete his task.

'You will step away from the computer,' the lead
Cyberman ordered. Grant made no attempt to acknow-
ledge the instruction.

Jolarr planted a foot against the wall and pulled with all
his strength. The pipe snapped along a vertical stress
fracture and came free, turning out to be quite flexible.

236

But the act of vandalism resulted in none of the destructive consequences he had hoped for. He had merely drawn the Cybermen's attention. He faced them, his expression almost apologetic, a useless metal tube in his hand. He couldn't even hurl it at them; more brackets pinned it to the wall further along its length.

The Cybermen closed in and Grant leapt back from the terminal at the last possible second as a silver fist swiped down and crushed it. The eight monsters had arranged themselves into a row now, blocking off all hope of retreat. Jolarr felt tears in the corners of his eyes. After so many close calls, so many dangerous escapes, he had almost begun to consider himself invulnerable. But there was no way out of this one. He saw an orange flame igniting in the head-mounted weapon of the nearest of his captors as it reached for its chest unit, preparing to deliver a fatal blast.

And then the pipe bucked of its own accord and Jolarr realized that something was surging through it. Instinctively, he aimed for the head of his would-be executioner. He felt a cold sensation in both palms and, suddenly, a liquid which could only have been freon from the Cyber scout ship shot from the makeshift hose to extinguish the fire of his impending death. Grant had come through after all.

The Cyberman staggered, not with the force of the attack, but with the realization that the freezing substance posed a hazard to it. Uselessly, it attempted to deflect the onslaught with its hands. Then its arms fell to its side, its head drooped and it became immobile. Its hibernation protocol had been activated. Still, seven of its fellows remained.

The Cybermen on each end of the line moved in to seize Jolarr and he was forced back, shaking the pipe so that its contents sprayed in a random arc. That did no good. Instead, he concentrated his fire on the nearest monster. It walked on, despite the white liquid jet which beat against its chest. Its hands reached out to inflict deadly punishment and Jolarr cringed against the wall, with no avenue of escape left open. The Cyberman, finally, was shut down – but its comrade was already too close. Jolarr tried to turn, but a hand gripped his shoulder and twisted so that his arm felt as though dislocated and the pipe fell from pain-spasming fingers. His hands were raw from clutching freezing metal and his toes felt like ice cubes as freon lapped about his shoes.

Six Cybermen gathered before him and even if Jolarr could have guessed which one was to deliver the killing blow, he was helpless to avert it.

Max backed away from the approaching Cyberman. She passed the two remaining Knights-in-progress (resolutely inert on their slabs) and the steaming vat of armour compound; the trappings of her greatest work, so useless to her now. She couldn't comprehend that it was going to end like this. She wouldn't accept it.

'How did you get in here? Where did you come from?'

To her surprise, the Cyberman answered her desperate questions. 'I am from the conversion chamber.'

'But how? We shut it down!'

It seemed to consider that. 'The details are available in our history computer. The chamber was reactivated by the late Vincent Madrox.'

Max seethed at the mention of the name. Madrox was ruining her life even now, from beyond the grave. She wasn't going to let him win again. She had engaged her attacker in conversation; she was beginning to pierce its artificial hide. She could work with that. 'Who are you?' she asked. 'Does your computer have a record of that too? You must have a name, buried somewhere.'

This time, there was no pause. 'The information is recorded, but it is of no value.'

'Oh no? Listen to me. I've carried out operations similar to your own conversions. I've altered people's brains and I know how it affects them. The man you used

to be would be appalled if he could see himself committing murder. He wouldn't want you to do this. So stop.
Think about it. You owe it to the person you were; the
person you still are!'

'I am a member of the Cyber race,' it said. But Max
had piqued what curiosity it had. It didn't make to attack
her, and she couldn't believe that it would now. The
still-newborn Cyberman had to have some sense of
compassion, of humanity, no matter how deeply hidden it
was.

'They haven't taken your brain, they've simply grafted
spare parts on top of it. They're telling you how to think,
what to do. It's little more than advanced hypnosis. You
can resist. Be true to yourself!'

The Cyberman seemed to think for a long time.
Max watched it and ached with anticipation. She hadn't
realized before just how much she needed to live through
this; how much she wanted to see her baby born. The
news of Madrox's death had made clear the long-denied
conviction that she wanted this child. For herself, not for
him.

Then the monster which held her future – and her
offspring's – in its grasp announced: 'My duty is clear. We
will proliferate.' And it fired at her.

Max ducked instinctively, a half-second before the
blast came. She flung herself behind the nearest, largest
obstacle, but knew that it could not protect her.

The Cyberman fired again, but its shot hit the vat
which concealed its true target and unleashed a deluge of
lava-like red sludge. Taken unawares, the Cyberman
toppled and put out a hand to save itself. But the compound, kept in a liquid state only by a complex heating
system, was solidifying. Its feet and one hand were held in
an amalgam of plastic and metal almost as durable as its
own shell. It was trapped, its face to the wall, and despite
its struggles and its whining, mechanical pleas, it couldn't
tear itself loose.

Max scrambled across the room before she too could

be caught by the fortuitous leak. She leant against the wall and breathed heavily, regarding the captive creature with grateful incredulity. She felt a fierce, brief twinge in her stomach and, for a horrific moment, she thought she had been injured.

Then she realized that her baby girl was kicking and she laughed until she started to cry.

Which didn't take long.

The sound of a Cyber weapon rang out and Jolarr flinched as something hot and sticky hit his face. He recovered his senses to see that one Cyberman was missing its head. It fell and the other five turned as one to where Grant crouched behind a work bench, re-aiming the gun which he had clearly snatched from one of the dormant monsters. Jolarr took his chance to dive for cover and the Cybermen hesitated as if unsure who to destroy first. They decided on Grant, who let loose three more shots before they drew uncomfortably close and he was forced to retreat. A row of blaster burns scarred the far wall in his wake. He should have been killed, but Jolarr realized that his attackers were moving sluggishly, affected by the temperature.

He crawled beneath a table and reached behind him for the heating pipes on the wall. His erstwhile weapon still spurted freon at the Cybermen's feet. By yanking his end of the pipe, he managed to send it springing back into action. It reared like a snake, discharging its payload in all directions. The Cybermen were distracted from Grant and two more shut down, overcome by the twin perils of cold and fire.

Grant was strafing them from cover again and the three remaining creatures reeled. One fell, its chest unit exploding with a billow of black smoke; another found its hibernation protocol engaging. Emboldened by success, Jolarr ran towards the last one, scooped up the end of the pipe and blasted freezing liquid into its face. It squealed and toppled, landing atop its fellows with a painful-sounding crash. Jolarr couldn't tell if it was dead or simply inert.

In the aftermath of the short but frantic battle, he stood and listened to the gasping of his lungs as the liquid in the pipe ran dry. Grant raised his head and cautiously stepped out into the open, still holding his weapon and eyeing the ranks of the fallen suspiciously.

'We've done it,' said Jolarr, hollow-voiced. 'We won.'

'I thought we were dead,' said Grant in the same disbelieving tone.

'If you hadn't diverted the freon to those pipes – or grabbed that gun . . .'

Grant tried to shrug, but his muscles didn't seem to know quite what to do. 'I'm not sure what happened. If I'd had time to think, I'd probably have seized up at the sight of those things. I guess I was just more frightened of dying, in the end.'

They stood together in silence, surrounded by the bodies of the Cybermen, still managing to seem somehow frightening in death. A minute or more passed before it occurred to Jolarr that something was different. It was too quiet.

'The fighting,' he whispered. 'It's stopped!' He could see that Grant had noticed it too. The previously overwhelming clangs of metal against metal; the vibrations of the walls as ferocious combat shook Population Control . . . all had ceased. It was over.

One way or another.

Grant was the first to move. He picked his way across the room until he reached the destroyed computer terminal. Despite the damage, the screen was active. Grant looked at it. He blinked and looked again. Then he fell back against a table, breathing deeply and too overcome to speak.

'What does it say?' asked Jolarr hoarsely, feeling as if his heart had stopped in anticipation of the news. 'Who won?'

* * *

This time, the Doctor knew for sure that he had come home. The healing embrace of the TARDIS was unmistakably real. The white walls seemed to wrap themselves about him and he felt as if he had slipped into a tank of soothing salve. He had even managed to retrieve his colourful jacket . . . well, he couldn't have left that behind! He clung to it, comforted by the familiarity of its patchwork design.

The events of the past few . . . minutes? hours? days? . . . were an indistinguishable blur of corridor walls and vivid imaginings. He wasn't quite sure how he had managed to climb the rope and make his way across the hospitality deck, but he felt pride at his own resolve and stamina. Give up? Not this Doctor! Once again he had triumphed, saving thousands of lives. What's more, he had done it his way. The right way. He had not given in to Henneker or to anyone. He had not compromised his lofty principles.

He would sleep now, letting his ship and his Time Lord constitution work together to rebuild his shattered cells. The damage wasn't as extensive as it had been on Metebelis. He might survive, this time, without having to regenerate. No, he corrected himself. He *would* survive. There was too much left for the sixth Doctor to do – and he was ready to do it, despite the spectre which hung over his future. That too could be overcome.

'I'm still the Doctor,' he muttered to himself through cracked and parched lips, 'whether I like it or not!'

Epilogue

The TARDIS arrived on Agora once more, inside Population Control. The Doctor emerged, feeling a momentary weakness as he left the protective environment of his ship. He walked through the building, alarmed by the number of part-mechanical corpses, of both persuasions, littering the corridors. Their distribution became more dense as he drew nearer to the cell block and the Cyber conversion chamber beyond. For the first time, he realized that Grant and the colonists had had more to occupy them during his absence than simply a waiting game. For a second, he wondered what the outcome of the struggle had been – but only for so long. Although he had encountered nobody, the Doctor could sense an atmosphere of strained anticipation which could not have emanated from machine creatures.

'Where have you been?' Maxine Carter remonstrated with him, when they finally met. 'You disappeared hours ago!' He told her that, in fact, it had been weeks. The evidence of his healed face supported the unlikely claim. Max didn't waste time worrying about it. The Doctor had brought the news for which a world had been praying. The Cybermen had fallen.

Celebrations began almost immediately. The parties would continue through the day and well into the formerly forbidden night. But there was sadness, too. Long years of occupation had left deep scars across the planet and its people. The civilization which had once been committed to the ideals of an agricultural paradise would always be dependent upon second-hand alien machines now. Furthermore, the fates of the most recent victims – the villagers of Redemption and the five hundred final sacrifices – hung like an invisible weight over the proceedings. The survivors wept, with tears almost equally of misery and of relief. The war was over, but the difficult task of rebuilding was yet to start.

In the aftermath, five Bronze Knights stood triumphant, still led by the seemingly invulnerable Ted Henneker – except that he would no longer answer to that name. The cyborgs had given themselves identifying numbers instead. He was One.

The Doctor found Grant, shell-shocked and only beginning to adjust to the events of the past weeks. There was nothing left to keep him on his homeworld. The boy was relieved when the Doctor made it clear that he was still welcome aboard his ship. He meant it too. He had originally invited Grant to accompany him out of some perverse desire to avoid his future by eschewing the brave and capable mould of his usual companions. He had proved himself beyond the Doctor's expectations.

Grant's friend, Jolarr, wanted to travel in the TARDIS too. However, he required passage only to his own place and time. He explained about the disappearance of the Arc Hives' vessel and Hegelia's guess that it had suffered 'temporal drift' – and Grant recalled his father's story of a ship which had once appeared from nowhere. Jolarr found it ironic that, after all his efforts not to change history, he had done so simply by landing here. In a roundabout way, he had brought the Doctor to Agora by facilitating his first meeting with Grant. He had been a key figure in the Cybermen's defeat. But Jolarr had had enough of 'real life' and its dangers. He wanted to return to his studies. In any case, he had made a promise to a most remarkable woman, to carry on her work.

Only the Doctor had doubts about the outcome of the struggle, and he kept those to himself. Even so, he was spotted several times regarding the Bronze Knights through hooded eyes as they discussed what future they could have. It was left to Max to announce their decision, once it was made, to the revellers outside Population Control. 'You can see how it would be difficult for them to reintegrate into society,' she said. 'They appreciate that. They also appreciate the fears which have been expressed to them; that, some day, the Cybermen may return and take revenge. We have found a solution to both problems.'

The Doctor watched Grant, later, as he tried to talk Max out of it. His cause was a lost one. She was determined to see her choice through. She could not, she said, settle into an ordinary life after her most extraordinary one. Their parting was a tearful affair and Grant returned to the TARDIS in a subdued mood. For several days thereafter, he slept or skulked in corners, lost in morbid thoughts. He had been through a lot, both physically and emotionally. The Doctor empathized with him. He had suffered too.

It ended more or less as it began. The Doctor and Grant stood in the TARDIS, watching on the scanner screen as the Cybermen's former scout ship struggled free of Agora's gravity. It passed the Selachian warcraft, abandoned to its orbit and destined to remain uninhabitable for decades, and set out into the unknown.

'So where now?' the Doctor asked. 'You wanted to go to mid twenty-first century Earth, I believe? The zenith of the Technological Age?'

Grant looked at him uncertainly. 'Eventually, yes. Maybe not just yet.' The Doctor smiled and nodded understandingly. Perhaps a vacation, he thought. Somewhere without machines.

'Do you know what will happen to them?'

He couldn't answer Grant's question. 'If we're lucky, they'll do just what they said. With their main base knocked out, the remaining Cybermen are scattered across the galaxy in ships like that one. Henneker and company could do a lot of good by stopping them before they cause more harm.'

'And if we're unlucky?'

He frowned. 'The Bronze Knights could become as big a threat to humanity as the Cybermen.'

'Isn't that partly why Max went with them?'

'Maintenance, technical support and moral yardstick, rolled into one,' the Doctor mused. 'I hope she's up to the task. The Agorans have already travelled too far down the same road as the Mondans.'

'She can do it,' said Grant. 'I know she can.'

'I'll give her one thing,' the Doctor conceded with a hopeful grin. 'It's a logical idea.'

He turned to the console and began to set new co-ordinates.

Available in the *Doctor Who – New Adventures* series:

The next Missing Adventure is *The Scales of Injustice* by Gary Russell, featuring the third Doctor, Liz Shaw and UNIT.